MW00478189

THE CRIMES OF GALAHAD.

THE CRIMES OF GALAHAD;

OR,

PRIVATE MEMOIRS OF A DESPICABLE CAD:

A Novel.

BY

H. ALBERTUS BOLI, LL.D.

Author of "Encyclopedia of Misinformation,"
"Admiral Hornswoggle's Nautical Adventures,"
"Case of the Missing Case," &c., &c.

FIVE VOLUMES IN ONE.

*Ye shall know them by their fruits. Do men gather grapes of
thorns, or figs of thistles? Even so every good tree bringeth forth
good fruit; but a corrupt tree bringeth forth evil fruit.*

——Matthew 7:16.

Pittsburgh:
DR. BOLI'S CELEBRATED PUBLISHING EMPIRE.
MMXII.

Copyright 2012 by Dr. Boli.
Copyright infringement is somewhat impolite.

Uniform with this edition:
Dr. Boli's Encyclopedia of Misinfor nation.

TO

DAVID LEWIS BAILEY

THIS STORY IS RESPECTFULLY DEDICATED.

THE CRIMES OF GALAHAD.

CHAPTER I.

*I am born, and grow to manhood, in such circum-
stances as would hardly seem conducive to evil.*

EVIL HAS BEEN very good to me. I have wealth
and social position, and moreover the nearly
universal esteem of all men, who seem to regard
me as a prodigy of virtue. All this has come to
me through relentless devotion to the principles
of evil. Indeed, I believe that the benefits of a
course of evil, conscientiously pursued with
unflagging vigor, have not been adequately impressed upon the minds of our young people.

I write, however, not to effect any improvement in our scheme of education, nor indeed
necessarily to be read at all. If you, dear reader,

have these words before you, then I must be dead and buried; for until the melancholy but inevitable event of my death, I shall take great care to keep this manuscript concealed. I write, therefore, mostly to amuse myself, and to have the satisfaction of living over in memory that brief period of my youth when I first understood and adopted the principles of evil. Nevertheless, the idea of future readers is not entirely absent from my mind as I write. If I occasionally address you, dear reader of the distant and unknown future, in a manner that seems quaint or antiquated to you, I trust you will be indulgent. I have every reason to believe that a great many years will pass between my writing and your reading. I have as yet reached only what I may reasonably expect to be the middle point of my life; I am in excellent health; I have no remaining enemies. That demise which is a necessary precondition of your reading these words seems a long way off.

It occurs to me that you, my distant reader, may wish to ask whether I recommend my own example, as you see it portrayed in these pages. It is not an easy question to answer. To persist in evil requires dedication and perseverance. At every step, the temptations to do good are numerous, and at times nearly overwhelming. Nevertheless, if you, dear reader, have the strength of character to resist such temptations, you may well profit by my example. The rewards of evil are many; it is a plant worth cultivating assiduously.

Now, I suppose, I must begin. I was born in the year 18— in the city of Allegheny, Pennsylvania. My mother did not survive my birth, which doubtless spared us both a great deal of trouble in the long run. My father, in a fit of fashionable medievalism, named me Galahad; but I have always hated that ridiculous name. Since I reached my majority I have gone by my middle name, Newman, which was my mother's maiden name, and so I sign my name G. Newman Bousted—"Bousted" being pronounced as if it were spelt "Boasted."

Shortly after my birth, my father removed the family—my older sisters Viola and Camellia and myself—across the river to Pittsburgh, where he opened a small stationery shop on Wood-street. Having thus reached the summit of his ambition, he was content to spend the rest of his life as an oafish tradesman, providing ink-pots and blank books to schoolmarms and junior clerks. That there was a world above this exalted station seemed to have escaped his notice; or, if he did take notice of it, it was only as one might take notice of the moon or the stars, without ever supposing that one might eventually inhabit those aethereal regions.

For the first few years, it was all my father

could do to keep the store going and my sisters and me fed; but by the time I was eight years old, business had picked up to the extent that my father felt himself able to send me off to a cheap boarding-school, which he seemed to think would provide me with a "first-rate" education, —"first-rate" being his favorite term for anything that met with his approval. I suppose I was successfully educated, in that I can read, write, and cipher well enough. Whether the other stated objective of the school—viz., to inculcate in me a lively sense of Christian virtue—was duly accomplished, I leave for any future readers to determine. Certainly it would be difficult to find any evidence of Christian principles in the running of the place. Aside from the daily Bible readings, I saw little that would indicate any acquaintance with Christian doctrine either among the instructors, who administered the severest beatings for the most trivial offenses, or among the older boys, who administered even more severe beatings for no offense whatsoever: so that I sometimes thought the founders of the place had intended to make boys virtuous by giving them a foretaste of the torments prepared for the damned. I am sure that I never did anything to deserve such treatment, except on a few occasions when another boy had dared me to do something that was perhaps not in strict conformity with the rules; for if I had a single failing, it was that I could never refuse a dare. In the eyes of the other boys, of course, I had every other failing as well; but the chief among them was that I was two years older than anyone else in my class, owing to my father's insistence that I must start my schooling at the beginning, and his inability to pay for it any sooner than he did. For some reason, this difference of age was enough to make me a universal object of scorn and contempt. Though I was always conscious of my own superior ability, I could not succeed in conveying a proper sense of that superiority to the boys around me.

In those months when school was not in session, I was given certain duties in the store, in preparation, as my father often told me, for my taking his place one day as proprietor. He was so certain that this prospect must be as pleasing to me as it was to him, that it never once registered on his mind how my shoulders slumped and my brow clouded over every time he mentioned it. For from the very earliest age, I could not view with equanimity, or indeed with any other feeling than horror, the prospect of a life like my father's. It was apparent to me that my father had dedicated himself to the pursuit of oafish mediocrity with an almost religious zeal. The contempt with which he was regarded even by the junior clerks who stopped in to buy a gross of pens was never visible to him, but it was quite

obvious to me. Was it my destiny to be lower
than secretaries and schoolmarms, bowing obse-
quiously to men who lived in terror of assistant
directors? The very children sent in to buy
themselves exercise-books—children of other
shopkeepers, equally oafish—felt no obligation to
treat my father with even rudimentary politeness. Why was I suffering all the indignities of
education, so called, if my lot was to perform
such duties as an organ-grinder's monkey might
well consider beneath him? If this was my station
in life, far better to have remained ignorant. Far
better never to have learned to read.

For it was through reading that I learned of
another world:—a world in which men thought
thoughts beyond foolscap and writing-fluid—a
world in which a conversation might touch on
more than blank books and ruling-pens—a world
in which men *lived*, and did not merely exist.
This reading, I acknowledge freely, was not always in the best literature; but even the worst
novels—and I have read, if not the worst novels,
then at least some very indifferent ones—depict
a world in which things are done, and men and
women do them. I do not recall a single novel in
which the action was confined to repeated sales
of identical commercial goods.

As for my schooling, my only joy was in reading the great literature of the past. I could, when
reading a play by Shakespeare, forget for a mo-

ment that I was immured in a dreadful prison,
surrounded by boys who hated me and instructors who held me in contempt; when I closed the
book, the walls closed in on me once more, and
all my misery returned. This habit of reading has
remained with me to the present, though it is
now a delight for its own sake, my surroundings
being such as I have chosen for myself according
to my own taste, so that I no longer dread the
end of the book as I did at school.

If I say little of my childhood, it is because I
did not enjoy it, and it does not amuse me to
dwell on it. I recall, therefore, only so much as is
necessary to establish a proper foundation for the
narrative that follows. I will say this much of my
childhood in general: that, in spite of all that was
vexing and unpleasant in my early years, I tried
very hard to be good. How hard I tried! I was
certain that virtue was its own reward: it must
be so, since neither at home nor at school did I
see any other reward for virtue. On the contrary,
at school I saw clearly that cheating, pre-
varication, theft, violence, and every kind of
wickedness were the certain roads to success and
happiness. And yet I tried to be good! By what
defective reasoning was I induced to love virtue,
when vice carried off every prize? I have but one
defense, which is that the misconception that
virtue is of all things most desirable is inculcated
in us from our earliest years. Nor would I make

any alteration in that education, for now I see clearly the utility of it. For one who has given his life over to wickedness, nothing is more necessary than that the great mass of mankind should believe in virtue. In any jungle there must always be many more prey than predators. Therefore I applaud virtue; I give it my highest commendation whenever I meet with it; I lend it all possible aid and encouragement; I fatten it up, so that it shall in time fatten me up.

In my pursuit of virtue it seemed that all the world was against me. My fellow pupils at school made certain to take full advantage of the one boy who would not lie; and, of course, they were happy to find ways to cause trouble for me by daring me to do this or that. My instructors, though they were compelled to acknowledge my honesty, found as many reasons for punishing me as they found for punishing any other boy.

Of all my enemies, however, I had none more dedicated or implacable than my sisters Viola and Camellia. Never showing overt hostility (which my father, who doted on me, would not have tolerated), they contrived nevertheless to make every day just a little worse for me than it would have been without them. Viola, the elder, was old enough to remember our mother, and to hold me accountable for her loss; Camellia did not remember our mother, but was guided in everything by Viola.

My sisters are paragons of virtue, as I know
from their having told me so on innumerable occasions. If, however, there is one virtue in particular that they possess to a pre-eminent degree,
it is the gift of discerning the faults of others, and
the ability to make those faults known to the
possessors of them, for the sake of salutary re-
proof and correction.

This particular virtue they so often exercised
with me, that I question whether I was more often reproved at school or at home: for whatever
my father (who was foolishly indulgent of all his
children) lacked in discipline was more than
made up by my sisters. As they had already become paragons of virtue at a very young age,
they keenly felt the magnitude of their responsibility toward me; and I lived with contempt for
my father, but in dread of Viola and Camellia.

So much for my early youth.—Now my
childhood is ended: behold me a young man of
twenty, returned from school for the last time,
and immediately put to the most degrading work
I could think of: which is to say that I stood
behind the counter in the store, waiting for the
next patron to come in and insult me.

Imagine me having done this for a week now;
imagine the cloud of gloom darkening every day
as my hope dwindles and dies, and I face the
prospect of living this way for the rest of my
days. Now imagine one day that is slightly

different from the rest: my father (who, mistaking my despair for diligence, is certain that I must be happy in the store, because, oaf that he is, he cannot conceive of any reason *not* to be happy in the store) sends me out on errands that will consume the whole day; sends me, moreover, with ready money for my luncheon, an extravagance he would not ordinarily have countenanced when, as he had told me more than once, Viola or Camellia could prepare a better meal than could be had at any cafe or restaurant (and that I never dared dispute this assertion must be an indication of how much my sisters terrified me).

This was at least an outing. I would still be required to be obsequious to clients on my itinerary, but I could be politely demanding of suppliers, and my luncheon money would buy me an hour of being served rather than serving.

"Take your time," my father told me cheerfully. "We'll manage without you for a day. No need for you to be back before dinner." All this was, of course, in complete contradiction to his usual assertion that the store couldn't do without me. Yet I thought nothing of it, except that my father seemed unusually cheerful. I have since learned to be more observant. Human nature is, of all studies, the one most essential for a successful life of wickedness.

But on this day I was far too eager to begin my

adventure in the great world to question my father's reasons for sending me out into it. I
stepped out the front door of the store without a
backward glance—quite unlike my father, whose
usual practice on leaving the shop was to stare in
oafish admiration at his own name spelled out in
black paint over the display window. It was apparently as great a wonder to him to-day as it
had been yesterday, and would doubtless be an
even greater wonder to-morrow, to know that
his own name, in large and ornate blackletter
(which had been very fashionable nineteen years
before, when it was first painted), was visible to
all who passed in the street.

What I always saw on leaving the store, however, was not the name of Samuel Bousted behind me, but the enormous and inescapable
name of Rohrbaugh in front of me. Rohrbaugh's
Department Store, at the corner of Diamond-
street, towered over the other stores as a medieval castle towered over its client village. It
occupied the better part of the next block, with
five sales floors and a sixth for offices. I was certain that Mr. Rohrbaugh did not stare at his own
name in oafish pride every time he passed
through the door of his department store. Mr.
Rohrbaugh was (to my mind) a great man; his
brain must be filled with great thoughts. Every
time I saw that name on his enormous building, I
vowed that, some day, I should be as great a

man as Mr. Rohrbaugh. In the interval before
that happy destiny, I could at least refrain from
such ostentatious oafishness as my father practiced daily.

My first visit was to a law office around the
corner from my father's store, where I was to
deliver five gross of the No. 910 Cashier's Pen
and inquire discreetly about settling the bill.

As soon as I walked in the door, I was met by
a middle-aged woman who apparently handled
some of the clerical duties in the office.

"What can we do for you, young man?" she
asked with a cheerful and motherly contempt. At
once I felt my dignity compromised, and the
thing I had known I was going to say when I
walked in vanished from my mind.

"I've—brought—the pens, from Bousted's," I
hesitantly told her.

"Oh, yes. Are you the new clerk? I don't
believe you've come around before."

"I'm—the son." What else could I tell her?

"You mean little Galahad? My word, how
you've grown! Why, I didn't recognize you at all!
The last time I saw you, you were *this* high. Your
father must be very proud of you!"

I think she babbled in this manner for about a
quarter-hour, and I could only stand smiling like
an imbecile while she talked, wondering whether
the ordeal would ever end, and feeling as though
I had been undressed and stuffed back into knee

pants. When she finally ran out of breath, I set the five little boxes down on her desk and was about to mumble my farewell when I recalled that there was still the matter of the bill to settle.

"I—" I began uncertainly. I had walked in knowing exactly what I planned to say, but her incessant prattle had driven it completely from my mind. "I have brought the,— the statement of your account, and— and I was—"

"Oh, yes, of course, the bill! I suppose Papa would be very disappointed if you returned without the money, wouldn't he? Well, we mustn't disappoint him. Will a bank draught be acceptable as usual?"

Thus, dear reader, I departed from that first encounter of the day having succeeded perfectly in both my tasks, but with an inescapable sense of utter failure. I had left my father's shop feeling, for the first time perhaps, an independent man; I had been reduced in half a minute to a boy.

Nor did the rest of my rounds lift my spirits at all. At every step, clients and suppliers treated me in the most insulting manner: a manner made all the more insulting by the absence of any intent to insult me. They did not intend to degrade me: it was quite obvious that they saw me only as the insignificant son of an insignificant shopkeeper. For them I had no independent existence apart from my father.

Even at the Allequippa Hotel, where I took my luncheon, I was treated with obvious condescension. There was nothing I could complain about in the service; my orders were filled with alacrity—but with a knowing, superior smile, as if the adults around me were indulging a boy in a game of make-believe. How it irked me! Today, of course, I should simply find some way to turn their impression of me to my advantage, for evil does not spurn any ready tool that presents itself. But then I still hoped to be a man pre-eminent in virtue!

In this morose state of mind I walked back toward the store in the late afternoon, my eyes cast down, my mind filled with despair. I should never be as great a man as Mr. Rohrbaugh (it astonishes me to think of it, but such at that time was my limited notion of greatness). I should not even be so much as an oafish shopkeeper like my father, at least not for twenty or thirty more years. No, I should always be the *son* of an oafish shopkeeper. I could see nothing beyond that for me: my education, which, such as it was, had taught me to look above my station in life, was of no more use than to prevent me from making gross errors in letters to junior clerks. I saw the world above me, but I could no more reach that world than I could expect to dwell in the clouds.

It was in this frame of mind, therefore, that I entered my father's store, having seen little but cobblestones and shoes along the way, to find my father brimming over with some fresh oafishness, a sickeningly cheerful smile on his face. I laid the payments I had collected, and the receipts from the suppliers, on the shop counter; my father, instead of immediately counting the money, continued to smirk in the most revolting manner, completely ignoring the fruits of my labors. At last, unable to contain himself any longer, he spoke.

"Well, then,—what do you think of it?"

"Of what?" I asked, barely repressing my impatience.

"Of the sign, of course!" he answered with an oafish laugh.

"He didn't even see it!" Viola exclaimed, taking obvious delight in my stupidity.

"The goose!" Camellia added.

My father laughed even more. "Oh, Galahad, you have been diligent today! But your mind was so much on your work that you missed what was right in front of your nose. No matter—this way I shall have the joy of showing you myself. Come outside with me. I think you'll be very pleased."

It was something to do with the store, certainly, so how could I be pleased? Nevertheless, the irrational optimism of youth was irrepressible. For a fleeting moment, because my father had said I should be pleased, because even my sisters seemed to imagine that I should be pleased, I thought that, somehow, I *would* be pleased: that perhaps, in some mysterious and altogether un-oaflike way, my father had found something, some gift to give me, that would really increase my happiness. In spite of my certain knowledge to the contrary, for one brief moment of utter folly I allowed myself to believe that things were looking up.

We stepped out the door and, when the stream of passing pedestrians cleared, took a position in the street in front of the store. "Now turn around," my father directed me.

I turned around.

"Look up," he said.

I looked up.

The unfashionably medieval blackletter that had spelled my father's name over the display window was gone. In its place were crisp modern gothic letters, very large ones, that spelled out

S. BOUSTED & SON.

"There you are, Galahad!" my father cried, gleefully slapping my back. "My son and my partner! What do you think of that?"

"It's very large," I said. I was holding back tears.

"Large enough for the whole world to see!" Clearly my father interpreted my remark as an expression of approval. "This is my proudest day, Galahad!"

Then, as I gazed in blank horror at the pitiless assassination of all my dreams and ambitions, I heard the sound of feminine laughter—surely of all sounds the most jarring and revolting. I let my gaze drop to behold my sisters standing in the doorway.

"Oh, Galahad!" cried Viola, still laughing her corrosive laugh. "If you could see the look on your face! It's simply priceless!"

CHAPTER II.

Owing to the niraculous intervention of a certain tooth-powder, I do not kill nyself.

"GALAHAD!"

My father's voice rose sufficiently to break through my own thoughts and impress itself on my mind. I looked up at him as if he were some hitherto unknown species of creature.

"You're hardly eating at all," my father continued. "Viola boiled that beef all afternoon for us."

Viola rushed to my defense in her usual way. "Now, Father, you can't expect Galahad to be paying attention to what he's doing. You know he's a noodle."

Camellia cackled in a manner that I was sure accounted for her not having found a husband yet. The girls had certain innate abilities to discern my thoughts, or at least my feelings; they knew that I was not as happy as I ought to be about the sign and my supposed new position as part-owner of the store, and they were relishing my distress, though they could form no notion of the reason for it.

My father ignored my sisters, as he always did when they attempted to insult me. That they should not share his oafish pride in me was simply beyond his comprehension; and what he could not understand, he ignored, which I believe was the very foundation of his happiness.

"Now, Galahad, you must eat." he told me, smiling outrageously. "We have a big day tomorrow, getting you situated as a real businessman."

"What Galahad wants is more mustard," Camellia said, as her arm, with a simply obscene reach, shot in front of my face, retrieved the mustard from the other end of the table, and drowned my beef in the stuff. I have always despised mustard.

"I think," I said, forcing myself to smile,—"I think I may be a little fatigued from my expedition to-day. There was a considerable distance to cover on foot."

"Although," Viola hastened to add, "with your exceptionally large feet, it must have been a great deal shorter for you than it would be for most people."

"Yes, it's no wonder you're tired, my boy," my father replied, as if Viola had not spoken at all—and indeed, according to his usual rule of ignoring what he could not understand, he probably had not even heard her. "You can eat a little more, then off to bed."

As discreetly as I could, I scraped the mustard off my beef and cut a few more bites. The flavor of Viola's boiled beef (her method has not changed in all the years since) is what I would imagine one of those penmanship exercise-books we used to stock in great numbers would taste like; mustard did not improve it, any more than mustard would improve the flavor of an exercise-book. I excused myself after a few more minutes, having spent that time assiduously maintaining a cheerful countenance; and I went up to my tiny chamber on the fourth floor, as my father called it, over the store: really an attic with a narrow dormer projecting from it. That we had one more "floor" than most other oafish shopkeepers' families was a point of intense pride for my father, who frequently remarked on the distinction without the slightest provocation.

Here at least I was alone. My father had the large front room on the third floor, and Viola and Camellia each one of the tiny rooms in the back; the attic, though I could not stand upright

in it, at least was my own domain. From my
dormer I could look out on Wood-street, a bright
hollow of gas-light in the encroaching night, and
over the three-storey shop-front of the inferior
oaf across the street I could see eastward as the
streets climbed the Hump, which had not yet
been reduced to its present more manageable dimensions. The last evening light was deserting
the sky; a few late clerks were hurrying up the
street toward whatever they called home; behind
me, in the warren of old houses and warehouses
that began a block west of us, ruffians were beginning their nightly round of debaucheries and
petty crimes—how the thought disgusted me!
And indeed it does now, but for other reasons: I
object not to the crimes, but to the pettiness.
Over all hung that pall of foul-smelling smoke
that descended upon us whenever the air was
still, wrapping the darkening city in a mystery
that familiarity could not disperse. Horses and
wheels clattered on cobblestones somewhere in
the near distance; some family well above the
humble station we occupied was off to the the-
ater, or returning from a supper with other leading families, where doubtless they all found time
to laugh at oafish tradesmen like my father.

—Or like me: once again this reflection smote
me like a slap across the face. I was a shopkeeper
myself; it was my destiny to be one—not a
philosopher, not a general, not a captain of in-

dustry, not a gentleman, not anything admirable or worthy, but a shopkeeper. Nor would I really be as much as that: for most of my negligible existence I was damned to be the son of a shopkeeper. My name on the sign was "& Son," and the sign spoke the truth of my position in the world.

But if I had already reached the summit of my existence, then what reason had I for continuing to exist? To what hope could I look as my guide? My present life was an unremitting annoyance to me, which nothing could alleviate but the hope of a brighter future. Remove that hope, and what reason remained to prolong my misery? At that moment, the obvious answer struck me with dreadful force: I had no reason to live. Suicide appeared, not as a possibility, but as a logical necessity. I was resolved: I would not live till morning.

How to accomplish the deed? Here I ran against what at the time I called cowardice, although I now see it as the very reasonable impulse to seek comfort and avoid pain, the foundation of all civilization and improvement. A pistol might do the job at once, with admirable efficiency; but there was no pistol in the house. I must therefore find an alternative, but each method I considered had its flaws.

At first I thought I might simply leap from my window. A fall from that height, however, though dangerous, might not necessarily prove fatal: I would run the serious risk of adding to my pain without ending it. The simple plummet, therefore, had to be rejected.

Hanging might be more certain, but was still open to numerous objections. First, I have always detested tight collars. Second, the deed would have to be done elsewhere, since even in the tallest part of my attic room I could barely stand straight; but attempting the deed anywhere else invited detection and interruption. Hanging must be rejected as well.

Poison, carefully chosen and properly administered, might be painless and effective; but it required a certain knowledge that I did not possess.

How I wished that I could simply sleep and never wake! But the body would not obey the mind's instructions; I could sleep, but I should wake whether I wished it or no.

As I looked here and there around the room, my eyes lit on the ivory-handled razor which my father had given me for my eighteenth birthday. For a moment I thought how completely satisfactory it would be if my father's gift could be the instrument of my demise. But it would be a more painful means of accomplishing my objective than I desired: for what, after all, could be the use of ending a life of pain if the end itself should be painful?

And then, just beside the razor, I saw the

thing that effected the first great change in my life.

To this day I cannot give an account of how such a humble object set such a long and mighty train of thought in motion. My analytical faculties must have been aroused to a heightened state by my long consideration of the various means of doing away with myself.

The object was a can of tooth-powder, bearing these words, which I still recall as accurately as you might recall a favorite poem:

DR. BRENNEMAN'S FAMOUS TOOTH-POWDER.
"The Favorite of Five Continents."
ASK FOR IT BY NAME AT YOUR DRUGGIST'S.

I had certainly seen this can dozens of times: every night when I brushed my teeth, in fact. But until this very moment I had never understood the *neaning* of it.

This was the meaning. I had bought this can of tooth-powder from a druggist on Smithfield-street, an oafish shopkeeper like my father. That druggist, however, was not the source of Dr. Brenneman's Famous Tooth-Powder. He was merely one of the thousands of oafish shopkeepers who stocked the stuff. He was a foot-soldier in an army of which Dr. Brenneman was the general. Though this Brenneman doubtless began as a shopkeeper like my father, he had risen far above that humble estate, building an empire of tooth-powder on the backs of the oafs he had left behind.

Suddenly—because of one can of tooth powder—the world was different, altogether transformed. The store was, in effect, half mine. What had been a prison sentence a quarter-hour before was now an opportunity. I had looked today and seen only a store, as one who looked at the Rome of Numa might have seen only a squalid village. But now I saw an imperial capital of the future—and myself, of course, as the emperor. In that brief moment, through that can of Dr. Brenneman's Famous Tooth Powder, I had a glimpse of a future, not as a shopkeeper, but as a merchant prince.

And so, instead of killing myself, I brushed my teeth and went to bed.

I woke early, wonderfully refreshed, with the certain knowledge that I stood at the beginning of a new era. I suppose Alexander must have felt much the same way the day it first occurred to him that Greece was too small for his ambition. I dressed quickly and—for the first time—was down in the store before my father.

Here I surveyed my domain. It was not a great empire—not yet—but it was my Macedon. I saw boxes of pencils, pens, pen-handles, bundles of paper, clips, bottles of ink, exercise-books—but I perceived infantry and cavalry, soldiers and officers, with which I might conquer the world, or at least the world of commerce. When my father came down, I had already sorted the pencils by the grade of the lead (they had, I thought, been left in an appalling state of disorganization).

"Well, Galahad," my father greeted me, "you certainly are at it early this morning! Very good —first-rate—the early bird gets the worm! Early to bed and early to rise, right, my boy?"

It is a measure of my contentment—no, my near-euphoria—that even my father's oafishness could not puncture it. "I was up early, and I thought I might use the time to advantage. The readier we are, the quicker we serve our patrons, and the more satisfactory that service is to them."

"That's thinking like a businessman, Galahad! I have every confidence in you, my boy—every confidence."

I am certain my father must have continued in that manner for some considerable length of time: it would have been entirely uncharacteristic of him to keep silent. I cannot recall anything more, however, since I had stopped listening to his oafish prattle. I was busy reorganizing the pens according to a scheme that seemed rather clever to me, so that they were arranged vertically according to manufacturer, but horizontally by type. If a patron asked for a stub point, we could show him the range offered by different makers; if a patron asked for an Esterbrook Jackson Stub, we could find it instantly. Though years have passed since then, it still gives me great satisfaction to think how logical and practical this arrangement was. Even my father, oaf though he was, found it commendable, although I suspect he was at least as much pleased by the interest I was taking in the shop as by the particular form in which that interest manifested itself.

By the time we opened the doors that morning, I had made a similar arrangement of the ink—columns by manufacturer, rows by color—and I was contemplating something like it for the draughting tools. I thought of it as something like drilling my recruits, turning a rabble of bumpkins into a disciplined army.

The moment we unlocked the doors, Mrs. Rockland stormed into the store. She was what businessmen might call a difficult customer, and even my father, whose obsequiousness ordinarily knew no bounds, had come very close to losing patience with her on more than one occasion.

"This paper," she announced in her booming baritone, "is entirely inadequate." She waved a handful of half-crumpled sheets in the air as she thundered across the floor to the counter, where she emphatically slapped them down. My father stepped behind the counter to face her and made a show of examining the sheets. I joined him as Mrs. Rockland began her complaint.

"The ink came right through the page," she declared, pointing at the sheet in front of her.

My father and I looked down at the page under her finger, and I know we both reached the same conclusion. Her penmanship was atrocious. The page was full of blots, and even holes where the pen had torn the paper. She obviously wrote the way she spoke, pressing down mercilessly upon the pen as if it must be subdued and bent to her will. Doubtless her pens gave out after a page or two, but it was the paper—a fine linen stationery that never did anyone any harm—that suffered the most from her assault.

"You can see how entirely unacceptable it is. It is utterly impossible to write on the back of a sheet. At the simply outrageous prices you charge for it, I should be able to write on the back. I'm surprised this sort of fraud is tolerated in a civilized country. If I had my way, the law would certainly not be so lax."

My father was still gazing down at the wreckage Mrs. Rockland had deposited on the counter, but he spoke clearly and distinctly.

"The paper is not at fault, Mrs. Rockland."

"I beg your pardon—!" Mrs. Rockland's eyes grew to the dimensions of soup plates: she was not accustomed to hearing anyone contradict her.

I realized at that moment that, after countless years of spineless obsequiousness, my father had finally had enough of Mrs. Rockland. He was about to tell her to her face what he thought of her writing, and probably of her manners as well. I knew at the same moment that I could not allow that to happen. My mind, still in its heightened state, quickly added up the business we might lose if Mrs. Rockland persuaded all her wretchedly pretentious friends to abandon us: it would at the very least retard my progress toward my first goal, which was to make Bousted & Son the leading stationer in the city. Just as my father was inhaling to begin Mrs. Rockland's richly deserved telling-off, I took hold of the conversation.

"Certainly the paper is not at fault," I said quickly before my father could begin. "It is we who were at fault for attempting to sell you that stationery without inquiring into your writing."

My father and Mrs. Rockland both looked puzzled beyond words, although for entirely different reasons.

"The paper, you see, must be matched to the writer," I continued, as if it were a well-known fact, and not a strange notion that had suddenly sprung up from pure desperation. "Now, this paper here is very well suited to a diffident and uncertain hand, such as we often see in younger ladies who have not yet found their place in society. Yours, however, is clearly a hand of weight and authority. You write with confidence. An insubstantial paper is clearly not suited for a person of substance, and it was our error to recommend it to you."

"I see." Mrs. Rockland was a bit mollified, although she still sounded wary. It was imperative that I carry on, even if my plan was still only half-formed.

"The irregular surface of the paper will also tend to catch your pen, which is what causes the blotting and tearing you see here. Again, for a writer who makes tentative and uncertain strokes, that texture is positively necessary to catch the ink at all; but it stands in the way of someone who is accustomed to writing with— with determination."

Here my rambling about the texture suggested something to me, and I cheerfully continued without giving Mrs. Rockland an opportunity to speak, or perhaps even (however unlikely it might be that she would do so) to think. "What you need, then, I would suggest if I may, is a paper with more weight, and with a smooth surface that will not interrupt the motion of the pen. I think we have something over here that will answer the purpose." I stepped back to the shelves behind me and found a stack of card stock, of the sort we usually cut down into visiting cards or place cards. Glancing behind me, I saw that I had succeeded in engaging Mrs. Rockland's attention completely—which was just as well, since, if she had turned to look at my father, she would have seen him gawking at me like a West Virginia bumpkin gawking at the dome of the courthouse, as if I were something wonderful and unaccountable, and more than a little frightening.

"Now this paper," I said, setting a few sheets of the card stock in front of her, "would probably suit your style of writing much better. You can feel how smooth it is, and the extra thickness prevents your writing from showing through, so that you may write on the back as easily as on the front."

Mrs. Rockland's fingers were examining the surface of the card stock, and I was beginning to think I might succeed.

"If you like," I suggested, "you can try it with the counter pen and see whether this paper suits your writing better than the other. The ink is right here. A sample of your writing will give us both a better notion of what you need from us."

Mrs. Rockland appeared to be pleased that we were taking her seriously: she took up the pen at once and scratched out the first two verses of the twenty-third Psalm. I was privately amused by her choice. If I had been asked to assign her a

place in the animal kingdom, I should have been
more likely to think of her as a wolf than as a
sheep. She used the pen as a weapon with which
to attack and conquer the paper, and it was
immediately clear that ordinary paper would
have given way with the first letter. The card
stock, however, held up under her merciless
assault. When she had finished writing and made
use of the blotter, I picked up the sheet, turned
it over, and pointed to the perfectly blank
expanse of white that greeted our eyes.

"As you can see," I said, carefully refraining
from sounding triumphant, "none of the ink has
bled through, and none of the writing from the
other side is visible at all. It is simply a matter of
matching the paper to the writer."

Mrs. Rockland picked up the sheet herself and
carefully examined it. When she did speak, her
tone was almost pleasant.

"And how much would you charge for this
grade of paper, with my monogram and
letterhead, in the same quantity as before?"

"Well, now," I said, once more thinking very
quickly, "this is, of course, a more expensive
grade of paper, since—as you can see—more
material goes into it, and the surface must be
carefully polished for the requisite smoothness.
However, we would, of course, deduct the price
you paid for your previous order. It was the
wrong paper for you, and you should not pay for

our mistakes. So—" here I picked up a bill of sale and wrote "$10.50" on it. Then I made a great show of subtracting $4.50 from it, and wrote "$6.00" in the total. "That would leave only six dollars," I told her.

"That is satisfactory," she replied. "How soon can it be ready?"

"Give us three days for the printing," I said, "which would mean Monday afternoon."

"Very well, then. I shall return Monday at precisely three." She turned to my father, who had been staring at the whole proceeding slack-jawed, but at least had the presence of mind to close his mouth when she looked his way.

"Mr. Bousted, your son is a valuable addition to your establishment. I commend you for rearing an intelligent and capable young man. I hope to see him on Monday at three."

She turned and left, thundering across the floorboards like a herd of buffalo. My father just barely contained himself until the door closed; then he burst into appallingly undignified laughter.

"You sold her card stock!" he managed to croak out between paroxysms.

"It was the only thing that would stand up under her scrawl," I said quite calmly. "You saw how she wrote. This pen is done for." I plucked the pen out of the holder, replacing it with another Turner & Harrison ball-pointed pen and tossing the mangled wreck of the old pen in the rubbish.

"Galahad," my father said, "that was a fine piece of work. I don't even mind giving her the money back if it's the price I pay for seeing a performance like that."

"She didn't get her money back." I was surprised that my father had forgotten his own business that way. "Her first order was the best linen wove. Her second order is cheap card stock. A dollar for the card stock, two dollars for the printing. She's giving us six, so we make three in profit."

My father's face went completely blank for a moment; then an enormous smile suddenly exploded across it.

"You're absolutely right!" he exclaimed with uncontrolled glee. "Dear boy, you even had me fooled!"

Here, I am ashamed to confess, I felt myself begin to blush. Today I look back on this accomplishment as my first truly wicked deed, but at that moment, I had not yet embraced evil as my calling. On the contrary, I abhorred the very name of evil.

"There was nothing dishonest about it," I insisted. "I simply took into consideration a fair profit for us, and presented it in a way Mrs. Rockland found acceptable. I expect her to be very happy with what she ordered. It may be that she will find herself able to write legibly for the first time in her life. I see nothing dishonest in serving a customer well, and at the same time assuring us of a sufficient profit."

"Exactly," my father agreed. "Nothing dishonest in that." Then, once again, the most undignified laughter burst forth from him, making me blush even deeper.

The rest of that day was for me a curious alternation between satisfaction and shame. I was aware that I had accomplished something rare and unique: Mrs. Rockland was a terror to every shopkeeper on Wood-street, and I had not merely succeeded in mollifying her, but had done so with a profit that was not negligible. It was not terribly rare for a whole day to go by without our making three dollars in clear profit. Yet, on the other hand, I could not dismiss the nagging sense that I had won that profit dishonestly. Of course it was dishonest: I revel in that declaration now. If ever there was a woman who deserved, nay demanded, to be cheated, it was Mrs. Rockland. At that time, however, I still believed that evil was to be avoided, and good cultivated.

When my sisters came down to the store later in the morning, my father of course related the story to them. If something had made him happy, no consideration could persuade him to keep silent: he must publish his joy to the

masses. My sisters expressed the appropriate
approval, and privately stored up my supposed
triumph as one more grievance for which they
must eventually exact revenge.

It was, nevertheless, a good day for me on the
whole. My business (as I called it) had been
successful to-day, and Mrs. Rockland, dreadful
though she was, would certainly prove a valuable
ally if she believed she had received good service
from Bousted's. It seemed to me that I was well
on my way to that prosperity which had always
been my fondest dream.

CHAPTER III.

Bousted's Famous Graded Stationery grows to be a "sensation," and I travel to the mythical land of Altoona.

ON MONDAY, JUST as the clock at St. Peter's was striking three, Mrs. Rockland appeared, picked up her card-stock stationery, and left us six dollars, which my father declared the most satisfactory payment he had ever earned. It had cost me some little trouble at the printer's, which I cleared up only by undertaking to absolve him of all responsibility for his complicity in the thoroughly ridiculous notion of house stationery on card stock; but Mrs. Rockland displayed every indication of complete satisfaction with her purchase. That evening I retired to my attic with a profound sense of accomplishment, and with last month's copy of the *Gentleman's Cabinet,* a magazine my father took, though I am not certain that he ever read so much as a page of it. I mention the magazine now because it will soon have a prominent role to play in my story, and it must be in place, ready to perform, when the proper moment arrives. I read the first article—I have the very magazine before me here, so I can report that it described a journey up the Ocklawaha through the jungles of Florida, illustrated with engravings of monstrous alligators that seemed ready to devour the little sternwheeler as it passed through their domain. Then I turned down the gas and went to bed.

The next morning, a small and timorous woman of about fifty entered the store and approached me cautiously, as if I might secretly harbor a strong desire to beat timorous middle-aged ladies senseless with a blotter. When I asked how I might help her, it seemed to require all her courage just to form a few words.

"Yes," she said, "I— I wonder if you might be able to help me."

That was as far as she could go without prompting, so I reiterated that I was ready to render whatever assistance she required.

"You see," she explained, "my neighbor—I believe she was here just yesterday—her name is Mrs. Rockland—and Mrs. Rockland told me that you, or someone in your shop, might be able to recommend, or to help me decide on, some kind of stationery that would fit my—my writing."

Now, this was, on the face of it, a singular victory. Not only had we satisfied the impossible Mrs. Rockland, but we had even obtained a recommendation from her.

And then, all at once, I understood what was really happening. Our timid visitor was probably unaware of it, but Mrs. Rockland had devised a test for me. If I succeeded, I might look forward to more recommendations from her; if I failed, not only would I lose her custom, but she might very well decide that she was dissatisfied with her own purchase. The task at hand, therefore, was not so much to satisfy Mrs. Rockland's neighbor as to satisfy Mrs. Rockland's expectation of what would satisfy her neighbor.

"Certainly, madam," I responded with a great show of easy confidence. Then I began to repeat, in an abbreviated form, the patter I had given Mrs. Rockland, all about the marvelous science (apparently my own discovery) of matching the paper to the writer. We came soon enough to the practical demonstration, in which I discovered that she wrote timidly, as if she were afraid of offending the paper by too much pressing. The inevitable result was a good deal of skipping, which at times made her writing nearly illegible.

I shall not weary myself, or any indulgent reader who might happen upon this manuscript in the distant future, with a complete transcription of my dealings, whatever interest they might have held at the time, with the timorous neighbor of Mrs. Rockland, whose name I have entirely forgotten. I selected a good rag paper for her, reasoning that the texture of it might be more likely to keep the ink flowing, and she was greatly pleased to discover that her writing was indeed much more visible on the paper I had selected. Perhaps I had stumbled on something really useful. Perhaps there was in fact a science to matching the paper to the writer, and I was the Newton who would give laws to that science. She placed a large order; and since the paper was exceptionally expensive, my father was ecstatic. He could not contain himself for the rest of the day, much to the annoyance of my sisters, whose displeasure with me was always proportional to my father's pleasure. Viola could not even spare a smile for the timid clerk across the street, who was far too diffident to speak to her, but who was nevertheless the closest thing she had to an admirer.

The day following was a slow one for the store: I spent most of the day cleaning up a bottle of Carey's Indelible Writing Fluid that Camellia had broken on the floor but was somehow too busy to attend to herself. The day after that, however, no fewer than three women came to have me examine their writing and select their stationery for them. On Friday two more came in; on Saturday, five. My father was simply astonished. The ledger showed that fully three-quarters of our sales for the week, in terms of profit, had been in stationery.

I find it difficult now to imagine that I was ever such a fool, but I allowed this success to disturb my tranquility to a great extent. I could not divest myself of the notion that I had obtained my success by means of some fraud or deception. Saturday evening I had more than a little trouble getting to sleep. Sunday morning—it fills me with shame to admit it even to myself, but the light of my future triumphs will shine all the brighter against the darkness here at the beginning—I recall praying for guidance in church, and being absurdly disappointed when none came to me; as if the Supreme Power of the Universe, whom I imagined as a being of awful and unlimited might, had useful advice to give a shopkeeper on matters of stationery, and ought to make himself available to me personally whenever I found myself harboring doubts about some transaction with an inconsequential middle-aged woman from the merchant classes.

I did, however, come to a conclusion on my own, with no obvious help from any omnipotent and omniscient beings. It would not be deception, I reasoned, if there were some science to my method. After Sunday dinner, I spent the rest

of the afternoon down in the store with various
pens and inks and every sort of paper commonly
used for stationery, as well as a few not commonly used. Each paper I rated by its surface
and its opacity, making notes on several other
properties as well. By the end of the afternoon, I
had a system worked out that seemed logical,
and I felt confident that I might be able to find
something to suit even the most difficult middle-
class matron;—or at least the second-most-diffi-
cult, since in Mrs. Rockland I had undoubtedly
faced a superlative whose difficulty no other
woman would ever match. I made some attempt
to explain what I had done to my father, but it
was not immediately clear that he had understood any of it: he only repeated, over and over,
how clever I was; and, as much as I might be inclined to agree, I gained little from that information. I had hoped that I might show it to him, see
that he understood it at once, and then be able
to trust that he could perform the diagnosis and
select the paper if I happened not to be in the
shop. Now I feared it might be forever beyond
his comprehension.

Monday four more women, and for the first
time one man, came in to have their writing
rated. Tuesday we had three; Wednesday we had
eight. We were beginning to run seriously short
on paper: we had sold three months' worth in a
week and a half. It was time to restock, which

meant that I had the opportunity to place my system on an even more scientific basis by a careful choice of which papers we should stock for it.

Here my father absolutely shocked me, and very probably himself, by coming up with a useful idea. Since we had such a large quantity of paper to order, he said, might it not be useful to go to the mill directly, rather than through our usual wholesaler? We might be able to negotiate a good price, which would increase our profit without increasing the cost to our patrons. This was such a sensible notion that I was ashamed of not having thought of it myself. I made the preliminary inquiries by wire, and within two days had procured an appointment with a large manufacturer of paper goods just outside Altoona.

The evening before I went, I spent three hours or more making careful notes of my system. I rather pompously headed my first page "Bousted's Famous Graded Stationery," and below that heading outlined a series of twelve different sorts of paper, based on thickness and texture. I had twelve samples to go with my outline, and on each of them I had written a letter and a number, so that the sheets could be arranged in rows of three thicknesses and columns of four roughnesses. My arrangement looked so scientific that I had convinced myself of its merit. I was sure now that I was the Newton of the stationery trade: paper and paper's laws lay hid in night until the Bousted system came to illuminate them.

Absurd as it may seem, the two-hour journey to Altoona would be the farthest I had ever traveled in my life. The trains ran very frequently, Altoona being on the main line to Philadelphia and New York, so there was no need for me to make an overnight stay; but, nevertheless, the trip in my mind took on the aspect of a gay adventure. I looked forward to seeing Altoona, a grubby industrial town that had hardly existed a few years before, with the same fervor that a more seasoned traveler might reserve for Florence or Paris.

I remember vividly how crowded and stifling the Pennsylvania station was the day I left. This was the old station, the one that burned in the riots a few years later. It deserved that fate: it was too small and too dark, and it seemed as though the architect, having conceived a complete and implacable hatred for all travelers, had very cleverly designed every passage in such a way that it would carry the smoke from the engines directly into our faces. The whole place was covered in a layer of soot and grime that no amount of scrubbing could ever efface, assuming, of course, that any cleaning was ever attempted, which was doubtful. And for all that I was happy. For the first time a train would be

carrying me somewhere I had chosen to go, and
not merely from home to school and back again.
At that moment I loved the trains, and I loved
the bleak and crowded station where they waited
for me, a stable filled with magically swift iron
horses ready to do the bidding of any traveler
who could put down the money for the fare.

As the car I would be boarding came into
view, I felt a strange hollowness in my stomach.
This was an expedition that would change my
life. I felt certain that I was taking my first steps
toward the conquest of that business empire
which was my destiny. I had as yet formed no
clear notion of how I might take that empire beyond the walls of the store, but I was certain that
it would happen, and that my voyage to the fa-
bled land of Altoona would set that expansion in
motion.

The coach was filled nearly to capacity, and
the seats were uncomfortably hard; but I had a
seat by a window, where I could direct my gaze
outward, away from the filthy screaming children who seemed to make up half the passengers.
I had some dreadful yellow-backed novel with
me, but I did not read a word of it, caught up in
the marvels passing by my window. I remember
the feeling of wonder that passed over me as the
train eased away from the platform, shrouding
the station in smoke and steam. And then we
were clear of the station, and I could see the

mills and warehouses along the Allegheny; then, farther along, the land turned greener, and we passed into a winding hollow, the near vegetation blackened with the soot belched out by a hundred locomotives a day, but the upper hillsides covered with rich green forests. And then the open country, with the manor houses of the great men who had made their fortunes in the city. How long until I joined their ranks? A town or village here or there, with a stop to discharge a farmer returning from his business in the city, and then we were in the mountains, with their green hillsides, rushing brooks, and mysterious tunnels that plunged us into sudden darkness. The very approach to Altoona was full of marvels; surely the city of Altoona itself must be a place where miracles occur daily.

Altoona did not disappoint me. It was a grubby place, still only half-built, and occupied mostly with the business of keeping up the railroad. But it was the most delightful place I had ever visited, because there was a carriage waiting for me at the station. For me! In my entire life I had never been a person of such importance that a carriage met me at the station. There was one wretched wagon that conveyed me, and twenty or more other boys, from the station to the school,—but this was a carriage with a canopy and an upholstered seat, sent from the mill office solely for the purpose of collecting me and taking me the few miles remaining to the paper mill.

It was a delightful half-hour in the carriage, winding out of the town and over leafy hills, past pleasant little farms, until, as we began to descend into a little valley, the strong stench of sulphur struck my nostrils, and there below me, in the middle of a little town, was the Cargill Bros. paper mill, spewing odoriferous prosperity into the sky.

I was greeted by a gentleman who identified himself as an Accounts Manager. I liked him immediately: he did not seem at all surprised or disappointed by my youth, but merely inquired whether my journey had been a pleasant one, and then proceeded at once to the business at hand.

In my preliminary communication with the company, I had indicated the size of the order we intended to place; but I had suggested that considerably larger orders might follow if we were satisfied with the first order. I now explained my system in some detail, and showed him the examples I had brought. I also told him —perhaps with some exaggeration, but not straying too far from the bounds of truth—what a "sensation," as the businessmen would call it, our system was making among the fashionable ladies of Pittsburgh. Having heard all this, he seemed very favorably impressed, and he brought out a number of samples of the mill's own production, matching them as well as he could to the examples I had brought. He invited me to test each with pen and ink, which I did, rejecting two or three as not meeting my standard (which I did to make him think I knew what I was doing). Finally, he calculated a total for the order I had intended to place, and I was pleased to see that it was indeed a good bit less than what we would have paid through the wholesaler. And then he mentioned one thing that I had not considered.

"Of course," he said, "this will all be with our standard Cargill Brothers watermark. With a larger order, we can have it watermarked to your specifications."

"Really?" I responded, and I am sure that he could tell at once that he had hit a weak point.

"We can do any mark you like on a minimum order of twenty reams. Some of our larger customers find it very useful in building up their reputations."

I did some very quick thinking. Twenty reams of each of a dozen different grades of paper was quite a large order for our little store. It was exactly four times what I had intended to order, and it would cost us nearly every penny we had to spend on stock for the season. On the other hand, if we continued to sell my Graded Stationery at the current rate, we might make that back in a month.

For me, however, the question was answered, not by arithmetic, but by vanity. I wanted every middle-aged matron in Pittsburgh and Allegheny to be writing her vapid little notes on Bousted's Famous Graded Stationery. I made some show of considering the matter, but I had already decided.

Vanity! How we malign the passion that has accomplished more in the service of Progress than any other human feeling! I might have bristled then at the suggestion that vanity had aught to do with my decision; now I recognize the passion and applaud it as the engine of all improvement.

Necessity, they say, is the mother of invention. But is it necessary that we should write by gaslight (as I am doing now), or that we should fly across the country in trains that cover a thousand miles in a day, or that news from Europe should reach us by cable at the speed of thought? No, these are not necessities; they are vanities. The world went on for aeons before they were even thought of, and untold generations of men simply went to bed with the sun, or lit a dim candle, because illumination by coal-gas was in no wise necessary for their continued existence. But we have coal-gas, and locomotives, and telegraphs, because one man longed to shine out among his brethren, and to say "I made that," and earn universal applause. If I owe some of my success to vanity, and to a desire to rise above my station, I am not ashamed to own it: on the contrary, I rejoice in a distinction that makes me brother to every man who ever made something of himself.

Enough of vanity: I need only say (again) that I made some show of considering the question, but soon agreed to quadruple my order. Laying down a bank note for the deposit, I undertook to pay the remainder on delivery.

The carriage-ride back to the station was enlivened by conversation with another young man, a few years older than I, who was working in a department store in Allegheny, one of the leading establishments of that city. He had been sent to negotiate a purchase for their stationery department. My father seldom had any thoughts that went beyond the daily life of his store, and though he went to church regularly and dutifully, showed very little indication of any religious opinions; but he was certain that whatever eternal damnation he believed in had an especially unpleasant corner reserved for anyone associated with department-store stationery counters, which he regarded as dens of thieves intent upon putting honest men out of business. I, however, was willing to risk my immortal soul for a few moments of pleasant conversation with Satan's minion. Such a reprobate I had become already! If honoring my father was the foundation of ethical living, then I was certainly lost. At any rate, this other fellow—he has since risen to a rather high position in the department store, and he might be terribly embarrassed if I mentioned that his name was Snyder, and the store was Boggs & Buhl—was a pleasant companion. At least so I thought at the time; I believe most of my pleasure was in the fact that he treated me as a fellow man, not as a grown child.

"You get out to Altoona much?" he asked me as we rode back up the green hill away from the sulphur-belching mill below.

"This is my first time out here," I answered.

"Well, I'm not surprised. Nothing here but railroad shops, and the Cargill Brothers mill, of course. Still, a man can have a swell time here if he wants it."

"A swell time?"

"That's what I'd call it, and no lie. There's a saloon around the corner from the station where you can always find a few of the local 'heiresses'—that's what they like you to think they are, at any rate. Last time I was here I got such a soak on I can't remember half of what I did, but I'll tell you what, Bousted, I know it involved two of those girls. See, Altoona girls all come from railroading families that move around a lot and don't settle in one place, and I think they have a wider view of the world."

"Do they?" I had never really had a conversation with another man on a subject like this before. It was appallingly sinful, and I knew I ought to put a stop to it right away; but I wanted to hear more about Snyder's wicked experiences.

"Yes, I can show you the very saloon when we get there, if you'd like. Altoona girls are the best, Bousted. I've had a real heiress or two in my time, but nothing beats those Altoona girls. —But here I am talking about myself, and I haven't let you get a word in. What brings you up here?"

"Oh," I told him with an air of nonchalance, "I came up to arrange with the Cargill plant to manufacture Bousted's Famous Graded Stationery to my exact specifications."

"*That* Bousted?" he asked, as if the revelation had made a real impression on him. "Why, I've had three ladies in just this week asking if we carried something like Bousted's. My sister uses the Number Six. Says it's the best thing she's ever written on. You've got a thing going there, Bousted. How did you come up with it?"

"It's in the process of being patented," I said —a statement I privately justified because I had just conceived the notion that it ought to be patented so that people like Snyder could not steal the idea and take away my profits, and to conceive the notion must certainly be the first step in the process. "Naturally, the exact details

are a trade secret, but I can tell you that the
method of matching the paper to the writer took
a bit of hard study. We find, however, that our
customers invariably obtain better results when
their stationery is matched properly to their
penmanship."

"Well, I don't know anything about it—I've
got the most infernally awful penmanship—but
you must have something people think they
want, and that's the main thing."

"Yes, I think it's made what they call a sensation in Pittsburgh society." I felt a little guilty
about such shameless boasting, but it was delicious to be taken as a man of consequence; and I
also, I believe, had conceived the notion that this
Snyder might be useful to me, although as yet I
had no good reason to suppose so. "We have
multiplied our stationery sales several times
over. I believe the other stationers in town are
already conscious of being left behind in the inevitable march of progress."

Mr. Snyder continued to express a keen interest in the Bousted Method, and I was more than
willing to expostulate upon that subject; and by
the time we reached the station we were fast
friends. It happened that the train for Pittsburgh
was arriving just as we got there, and we agreed
to put off the adventure of the saloon for another
time—a good thing, too, as I should have had to
decline his invitation otherwise. It would cause

me no end of trouble, with my sisters at any
rate, to arrive home late and reeking of alcohol;
but I did not wish my new companion to know
that I labored under such childish restrictions.
We continued our conversation in the train for
the two hours it took to get back to Pittsburgh,
and we exchanged addresses. I was not aware at
the time how significant that exchange would be
a little later on.

Dear reader, does my little hint of future
events fill you with a desire to read on? It
amuses me to think so—to imagine a reader in
the distant future panting to know more, to discover why my possession of Snyder's address, or
his possession of mine, will take on such signifi-
cance. Shall I find him and murder him when I
become wicked?—for you already know, dear
reader, that at some point in this narrative I
must become wicked, and adopt as my creed
that very evil I had so scrupulously avoided hitherto. Or will he prove to be a long-lost relative, a
brother perhaps, who will reveal to me the mystery of my true parentage? Such things happen
every day in novels; perhaps they have happened
in my life as well. Will he bring me news of a
legacy that will make me rich beyond the
dreams of avarice (an expression that seems to
presuppose a very unimaginative sort of avarice)? O reader, how you must thirst for the answers to these questions—answers that I alone

possess, and can grant or withhold at my pleasure! My power is gratifyingly absolute. Had I
not made up my mind to be a merchant prince,
perhaps I should have been an author.

CHAPTER IV.

By a chance discovery, I a n induced to devote ny life to the pursuit of evil.

ON MY RETURN to the store, I suffered a reverse so severe that I hesitate even to narrate it. It gives me no pleasure to do so, except insofar as I recall that my triumph will be so much more complete for my having overcome an adversity that, in the end, changed the course of my life in a way that brought unfathomable benefit to me.

In short, because I do not wish to be long, my father utterly repudiated my negotiation with the firm of Cargill Bros. All my explanations, calculations, demonstrations, and remonstrations were in vain: he could not bring himself to spend that amount of money, and nothing would persuade him to do so. He insisted that I must wire

Cargill Bros. in the morning and cancel the order, and in this ridiculous intransigence he persisted adamantly, finally telling me in so many words, "I forbid you to spend that much money."

My sisters were simply delighted at my reversal. My father, who could never bring himself to be really angry with me, attempted to be pleasant through supper; I picked morosely at whatever Viola had boiled for the evening, and Viola and Camellia chattered incessantly and with uncontrollable glee.

"Really, Father," Viola said with her mouth full of boiled something-or-other, "what can you expect? You knew he was a noodle when you sent him out there."

This was a remark of unprecedented wit, to judge by its effect on Camellia, who spewed potatoes all over the table in front of her.

"You might as well have sent the cat," Viola continued.

"Or the goldfish," Camellia added helpfully, spewing more potatoes.

"Could you please pass the butter, Galahad?" my father inquired politely, as if he had not heard my sisters at all,—which probably was the case, his little mind being unable even to acknowledge the existence of whatever it could not comprehend, and my sisters' antipathy toward me being foremost among the things my father's mind could not comprehend. And this was how the rest of supper went: my sisters unrelenting in their attacks, and my father even more unrelenting in his pleasantness, which I honestly do believe was worse than the attacks of my sisters. I excused myself as early as I could, and retired to my attic.

Here again I sank into the profoundest depths of despair. At every turn my best plans were frustrated by the ignorance and folly of those around me. Must it not always be thus? My father was an oaf who did not understand the scale of modern business—but that was not a new discovery. To-morrow I should have to humiliate myself by sending a cable to Cargill Bros. canceling the order I had made, and then I should never again be taken seriously at that plant. Again I asked myself, what did I have to live for? It was not the particular reversal that was impossible, but rather the certainty that it would not be the last. There was a great world that lay beyond the little store on Wood-street, but my father could not see it, because he did not understand it. If my every attempt to break out into that world must be thwarted by my father's ignorance and timidity, then how could I grasp that imperial destiny that surely awaited me? And without the anticipation of that destiny, how was my life tolerable? But the result of my considerations was again the same: no matter how many different methods of ending my life occurred to me, each one was either impossible in my circumstances or too unpleasant to consider for more than a moment.

I felt a maddening impotence; there was simply nothing I could do. So I picked up a magazine and began to read.

The *Gentleman's Cabinet!* Dear reader, the time has come when that humble publication must take its place on our stage—must stand before the footlights, speak its lines, and advance our plot. How patiently it has been waiting on my little table, the one in the dormer with the old Windsor chair beside it—waiting to grant me its great revelation!

Yes, I took up the magazine, and, having exhausted the major articles, turned to the "literary" section in the back, where lesser hacks reviewed the works of greater hacks. Here I read a review of "Emmett Palgrave," the most recent novel by Mrs. Burton, who was then in great esteem, though I doubt whether a single one of her works is still in print to-day. I had intended to retire after that, but my melancholy state of mind was likely to prevent me from sleeping, and the title of the next review caught my eye:

THE WICKEDEST MAN IN FRANCE.

Well! That indeed was a distinction. I knew
nothing of France, of course, beyond what I had
read; but all sources seemed to concur in de-
scribing France as a country of extraordinary
wickedness. I believe my school geography, in
the map of Europe, had simply engraved the
word "WICKED" across the northwestern corner
of the continent. In popular literature, France
was not merely wicked: it was the source and
wellspring of wickedness, a sun of wickedness
from which rays of wickedness shone on an otherwise virtuous world. And, of course, like every
good American boy, I had in unguarded moments wished that I could be in France, where
the women were so unspeakably wicked that
their most characteristic acts always took place
between the end of one chapter and the beginning of another:—although, of course, I immediately repudiated that desire as unbecoming a virtuous young man. Now, if a man could be the
wickedest man in France, then he must be very
wicked indeed; and he must be a great deal
more interesting to read about than the insipidly
virtuous hero of Mrs. Burton's novel, which the
reviewer had praised as tending to the improvement of youth—a reviewer's kind way of saying
that it was the sort of book no one would willingly pick up. I began to read this new review,
which was not at all favorable, with sleepy and
half-closed eyes; but I was soon wide awake. But

why tell you, dear reader, about the review, when I can reproduce the review itself? I have preserved the magazine with as much care as a Mahometan might use in preserving his Alcoran: —for it is my holy text, and the foundation of my religion, though it has not the spare elegance of other holy texts. I copy it here and relish every word, although the reviewer plainly had no notion of the import of the work he undertook to review. Here it is, then, or at least the salient parts of it—for I shall copy while it is yet a joy, but cease when it becomes a labor.

THE WICKEDEST MAN IN FRANCE.

For all of history, men have questioned whether it is better to prohibit books that tend toward evil, or to suffer them to remain, and refute them. We speak not of books of obvious depravity, whose only aim is to excite concupiscence; but rather of those works which present an argument, the tendency of which, if it is followed to its conclusion, is to entice men to wickedness, and in a word to make wrong seem right. The general consensus of American and English thought has been that such books are to be allowed, on the grounds that their refutation will surely be forthcoming, if liberty of thought is granted equally to the wicked and the virtuous. It thus becomes the duty of good Christian writers to expose the specious and faulty rea-

soning by which wrong is made to seem right.
Whatever moralists may say of the state of literature in our own era, it is at least beyond
question that virtue never lacks defenders; and,
if their works are sometimes less read than the
works they refute, that is perhaps a fault to be
laid at the feet of the readers, rather than
charged to the writers' account.

Dear reader, I must break in here for a moment. If the works of the moralists are less read
than the moralists themselves would desire, what
right have they to complain of their readers?
Write a book worth reading, and it will be read;
but you give people stale bread to eat, and wonder that they prefer cake!

When we come to the work of the Comte de
Baucher, however, the ordinary Christian
writer finds himself at a loss. His business hitherto has been to make it plain where arguments
go astray: to show how that which was presented as tending toward the good tends rather
toward evil. Since it is acknowledged that good
is to be sought and evil shunned, the debate is
thus won, and the moral writer emerges
crowned with the laurels of victory.

But there can be no such victory against the
Comte. That his philosophy tends toward evil is
not an accusation in his eyes. He has called his
book *A la Recherche du nal*—*The Pursuit of Evil*
—and in it he argues, not that evil is good, but

that the superior man chooses evil, in accordance with the dictates of nature.

Here again I break in for a moment to point out how wonderfully this paragraph is calculated to make me prick up my ears. One thing I had grown to regard as certain was that I was, in the words attributed to the Comte de Baucher, a superior man. My difficulties were not in any lack of intellect or natural ability; they all came from the inferiority and stupidity of the obstacles that stood in my way—among which the foremost was my father, whose tiny mind was incapable of comprehending a great opportunity, simply because it was great, and there was no room in his mind for great things. The words "superior man," therefore, caught my attention, and, as the arguments in the first lines of the review had predisposed me to think of the reviewer as a man of no very keen intellect, I began to take the side of the Comte, as one who had something to say to the superior man. Ye simpering moralists, and ye pandering preachers who speak to us in apostrophe as "ye," see how quickly you mine your own lines, and destroy the virtue you would build up!

This is plainly not a proposition that can be refuted merely by saying that it tends toward evil: for if we said so, the Comte would be justi-

fied in replying, "*Et alors?*" Indeed, if evil is not
to be shunned, it is difficult to see on what
grounds the Comte can be refuted at all.

Our noble author begins with Creation; or,
rather, he begins by denying Creation, which
he dismisses at once as a superfluous hypothesis.
The universe, he says, came to be through collision and accretion of primordial matter according to natural laws. The primary law of nature
in this universe is not one of Newton's famous
discoveries, but rather what the Comte calls the
Law of Relative Strength, which may be briefly
stated thus: The stronger invariably destroys or
subsumes the weaker. Such is the law among
stars and planets; such is the law in the mineral
kingdom; such, most notably, is the law among
living creatures. The Comte gives two chapters
to the operation of this law in nature, but such
profligacy is hardly necessary. Big rocks crush
little rocks to atoms, and larger creatures eat
smaller ones; there you have his observations in
epitome.

When the Comte comes to consider human
history, he finds the same principle at work ev-
erywhere. A chapter on human origins is of the
most speculative turn imaginable, and yet the
Comte presents his speculations as established
truths. The wild surmises of Darwin, which
many of our most eminent authors have entirely refuted, are here accepted as unques-
tioned facts of science. In the time before
recorded history (for it is hardly necessary to

say that the Comte does not accept the inspired
works of Moses as genuine history), the Comte
imagines the Law of Relative Strength operating in such a way that the stronger man compels the weaker to do his bidding; and, having
thus subsumed, so to speak, the strength of the
weaker man in his own, employs this combined
strength to subsume the strength of another
man, and so on, until he has formed a tribe of
men who act under his authority, and whose
combined strength he calls upon to carry out
his will. Thus he sees the beginning of human
society, not as an association for mutual advantage, but simply as the result of one man's
pride.

Here it seems clear to me that the reviewer
misunderstands the argument. It is not pride that
is at work, but necessity. If the world is so ordered that the law of relative strength obtains—
a proposition that struck me as undeniable from
the moment I heard it—then it is as inevitable
that men should collide as that any other form of
matter must collide; and then the stronger must
either destroy or subsume the weaker. There are
degrees of strength in any group of men, and the
strongest, by repeated clashes with rivals, must
at last take his place. It is not a question of justice so much as a certainty of physics.

But what of that moral sense which distin-

guishes men from beasts? Whence did that
arise, and does it not refute the Comte's assertion that all human relations are merely the result of many collisions between stronger and
weaker?

This brings us to what appears to be the core
of the Comte's new system of philosophy. Moral
precepts, he would have us understand, are not
eternal truths of nature; nor are they laws given
to us by a higher and wiser power. They are
tools or weapons by which the strong control
the weak, and the greater the lesser. There is
more than one sort of strength: intellectual
vigor often prevails over mere physical power.
The strong-minded have devised moral principles in order to enslave the weak-minded, even
when the latter are men of great bodily
strength. One may be pardoned for surmising
that the Comte de Baucher is not a very healthy
physical specimen.

This feeble attempt at a sly dig in no way un-
dermines the argument, which is well-nigh unas-
sailable.—I really had no intention of interrupting so often, but I can hardly be expected to hold
back the thoughts I have kept to myself for
thirty years as I ruminated on these things. The
indulgent reader will forgive me—or, if he will
not, then he may find himself a dime novel that
will hold his attention.

As an example of the way in which those of
strong mind make use of moral precepts in order to bend the weak-minded to their will, the
Comte devotes an entire chapter to the Mosaic
law. This he finds riddled with absurdities and
extravagances that can have no other purpose,
so he says, than to keep the great mass of the
Israelites in subjection to Moses, Aaron, and
their successors. The Decalogue, which philosophers have often praised as the sublimest expression of the universal moral law, becomes,
on the Comte's reading, an arbitrary catalogue
of offenses against the authority of the superior
men who have subjected Israel to their rule.
Thus the first commandments enjoin exclusive
worship of the God of Israel, and obedience to
him, not because such a being exists and is
good, but because religion was the source of
Moses and Aaron's power over the tribes, and
any admixture of foreign religions must weaken
that power. The Comte praises the wisdom and
rhetorical skill of Moses: "for," he says, "the
man who can slaughter thousands of his own
people, and teach them 'Thou shalt not kill,'
must be extraordinarily persuasive." He devotes
most of the rest of this chapter to the provisions
of the law that seem most absurd to him, and
delights in counting up the number of occasions
on which a sacrifice will be required—a sacrifice that the priest shall eat, so that Moses was
able to assure perpetual abundance, not merely
for himself, but for his entire tribe, at the ex-

pense of the others.

In short, without giving any compelling reason for doing so, the Comte rejects divine revelation as a myth, and not merely a myth but a
deliberate fabrication, by which the superior
man—in this case Moses—assured himself of a
full stomach.

The rest of the Hebrew Scriptures are
treated in a separate chapter, which is not
worth summarizing here, except to say that the
kings and prophets whom the sacred authors regard as virtuous seem to come out as the villains of the piece: men who, when the people
had tasted liberty, enslaved them again, and
drove the inferior rabble back to that worship
on which the power of the superior men rested.

Once again, our reviewer has mistaken the argument. It is perfectly true that the "good" kings
of the Old Testament forced the people back into
servitude; but that makes them the heroes of the
tale, not the villains. To one who has correctly
understood the philosophy of Baucher—as I
seemed to do the moment I heard his ideas—a
hero is a man who bends other men to his will.

What, then, of the New Testament? Does not
the figure of Christ, the meek and mild Savior
who went to the Cross without offering the fee-
blest resistance to his persecutors, amply refute
the proposition that the Christian religion is

merely an imposition of the will of the strong upon the weak?

Here our noble author rather disappoints us.

He did not disappoint me! I clearly remember reading the lines that follow with a beating heart and an inescapable sense that hidden truths were being opened up to me. But let the reviewer carry on, and I shall interrupt him again if it amuses me to do so.

Instead of dealing squarely with the historical fact of the Incarnation, the Comte dismisses the entire life of Jesus as a fiction. Making that assumption—which we hope we may be permitted to doubt—the Comte proceeds to show how excellently the Christian religion is contrived for the purpose of keeping the powerful secure in their privileges. The poor are encouraged to believe that their poverty carries with it a special blessedness, that he who desires riches courts eternal damnation in the life to come, when the first shall be last and the last first. It goes without saying, of course, that the Comte admits no such futurity; he admires, however, what he calls "the audacity of the deception," by which not only are the poor induced to bear their lot with contentment, but also many accidentally wealthy men of inferior intellect are persuaded to sell all they have and seek poverty —leaving, of course, the superior men in possession of the good things of this life.

Now supposing all this to be true, would it not be the greatest folly for the Comte—who plainly believes himself one of these superior men who alone know the truth—to reveal these things to all and sundry? Here the Comte makes a most ingenious argument. It is no risk to the superior man, says he, to publish such a book as this, because it will reveal nothing to inferior minds. They will not see what they do not understand.

Is it necessary for me to mention that I thought of my father here?

Doubtless the book will come to the notice of a few inferior men, but few of them will read it, and of those few none will accept its truths. Such is the weakness of the inferior mind that, even when facing the undeniable truth, it prefers to retreat to its comfortable falsehoods. Only the superior mind will grasp the truth of what the Comte has written; the others will employ all their feeble powers to refute these truths; and will believe themselves to have done so, though all reason and logic be against them, because to admit that they have not succeeded would be to admit that every belief which they had been taught since early childhood to regard as inviolable, is false. This is an admission a man can make only at a point of crisis, when the beliefs by which he has regulated his life have brought him to an impasse.

Since the Comte himself has brought up the subject, and since we are at a natural division in his book, we may take this opportunity to inquire——

No, I shall not copy this next page or two. Our reviewer indulges in more sarcasm than I can stomach in narrating the life of the Comte—which, briefly, runs thus: he had an imbecile for a father, was miserable in school, and very early displayed all the signs of a superior intellect, which found no encouragement in his circle of acquaintances. I do not believe it is necessary for me to remark how closely the Comte's early life seemed to resemble my own life up to this point.

For the Comte, his "point of crisis" came when he was rejected by a woman. Our reviewer amuses himself, if not his readers, with remarks on the character of a Frenchman, and how different the philosophy of Baucher might have been had the woman been of that yielding character supposed to be so common in France. But is there any passion stronger than love, or lust if you prefer? and is there anything other than strong disappointment that can bring a man to the point of psychological crisis? It is, at any rate, sufficient to say that, whatever the opinion of the reviewer, I felt drawn to this Comte de Baucher as to a kindred spirit.

Let us resume the review two pages later.

Leaving the historical section behind, we come now to the second, and mercifully final, portion of the book, which the author facetiously labels "The Ethics of the Superior Man," but which may more accurately be called a frontal attack on ethics.

We are first taken through the many different ethical systems, philosophical and religious, by which men have regulated their conduct, and shown their fundamental identity. This is not a new observation: many other writers have pointed out the similarities in the ethical content of various religious and philosophical systems, and have found in that similarity evidence of an objective moral truth. This is not, however, the conclusion our present author draws. His survey of ethical systems consumes no fewer than three chapters, and takes him as far as China in his search for corroborative material; but, in the end, we are prepared for his great conclusion, which is that the similarity of all the ethical systems derives, not from natural moral law, but from the operation of the Law of Relative Strength in the human sphere. In short, all ethical systems are imposed by the strong upon the weak, and their purpose is to keep the weak in subjection to the strong—the inferior to the superior. How this subjection is variously accomplished the Comte describes in two more chapters; but we may summarize them by saying that prophets and philosophers

have taught honesty and gentleness the world
over, not because those things are good in
themselves, but because it is convenient for the
superior man that his inferiors should be honest
and gentle. That is a truth of nature: since even
the inferior man is, to some extent, an intellectual being, the dominance of the strong over
the weak must take an intellectual form as well
as a physical form. The superior man, in other
words, must control the beliefs of his inferiors,
as the surest means of controlling their actions.

But if ethical systems have no purpose but to
keep the inferior man subject to the superior,
then what are the ethics of the superior man?
He has none. This is the conclusion to which
the whole work has been tending, and therefore
it can in no wise be called unexpected. Yet it is
still something of a surprise to see it stated so
baldly. The inferior man must attempt to weigh
his actions against any number of ethical stan-
dards; the superior man, on the other hand,
asks himself one question only: Will this tend to
my advantage? No crime is beyond him, if he
can but persuade himself that it will make him
happier, or wealthier, or more powerful. The
good of inferior men does not enter into the
question, because they are inferior: they are
materials, which he uses for his benefit or his
pleasure, as he would use any other material.
The superior man owes allegiance to no one:
the state exists because it is useful that his inferiors should be governed, but the state no more

governs the superior man than a fence governs
the wind. He does what he pleases and takes
what he desires;—and this sort of behavior,
which we should not tolerate in a child three
years old, is the very mark of his superiority!
Obedience to the law, or to the precepts of religion, is, on the other hand, the badge of inferiority. The inferior man shows his inferiority in
his obedience, for by obeying he acknowledges
a power superior to himself.

In short, the conclusion, not only of this
chapter but of the entire work, is that the superior man proves his superiority by choosing
what is commonly called evil. He rejects the religion and the ethics of the inferior men who
surround him. He takes the course of action
best calculated to lead to his own advantage,
and if that choice demands that he rob or kill
his inferior neighbors, he does not hesitate to
carry it out. It is the mark of his superiority
that he refuses to acknowledge any law or principle as standing above him.

As I read these lines, I was keenly aware that
the scales were falling from my eyes. I was not
converted all at once, but for the first time I began to understand my own life. All my existence
had been bound by rules and laws which I had
done my utmost to obey; yet at school (by instructors and older boys) and at home (by sisters)
I had been subjected to all the most degrading

punishments, no matter how scrupulously obedient I was. For what reason? I had always thought
that, if I could somehow be even more obedient,
more perfectly virtuous, I might have avoided
the unjust punishments; yet, at the same time, I
always felt all too sharply the injustice of them.
Now, at last, I was free from the whims of instructors, but I had my father's ignorant intransigence to plague me instead—which was more
of a burden, because there was no set end to it.
Plainly I had the advantage in education, as well
as natural intellect;—yet I must submit to the
unfounded whims of an ignorant oaf, merely because he was my father.—But why? Because law
and tradition said that I must. Should I submit to
law and tradition? Or was not that certainty I
felt deep in my soul—the irrepressible knowledge of my own superiority—was it not, I say,
the signal that such things as law and tradition
existed far below me?

These things are called evil, not because they
are so in any absolute sense, but because it is
convenient for great men that lesser men should
be kept in check by their own consciences,
leaving the great man, who has no conscience
and does not acknowledge the existence of such
a thing, in control of the power and possessions
of this world.

The Comte gives us a number of examples of

great men who (he says) had chosen evil and prospered. Not all are men commonly held up for admiration. Alexander was, perhaps, a great man, and not without admirable qualities. The same may be said of Augustus. But when our noble author points out Nero, whose reign makes such a vivid impression in the pages of Gibbon, as an object of admiration, and indeed of emulation, we are compelled to acknowledge that the argument is at least novel, if not altogether convincing. In the Comte's view of Roman history, which differs in certain essential particulars from that of Gibbon, Nero was a capable emperor under whose rule the Empire prospered, and whose notorious excesses are pardonable because they did not tend to his own disadvantage. Even Nero's suicide, in our noble author's view, is not a failure. Having lived for many years with "unlimited liberty of action," as our author calls it, he foresaw the restriction of that liberty, and therefore took it upon himself to end a life that was no longer worth living—for the superior man, who in everything chooses is own way, does not hesitate to choose death when he cannot have the life of his own choosing as he would choose to live it.

This, then, is the essence of the Comte's philosophy: that morals and ethics are matters for the small and weak; that the great and strong wilfully choose evil, obeying the fundamental law of the universe; and that this deliberate choice of evil is the mark by which we recognize the superior man.

It is hardly necessary to say that the reception of *A la Recherche du nal* was not uniformly favorable. In France,——

Here the reviewer relates how the book was received in France, where the government of the hour quickly banned it; and in England, where the anonymous translation was greeted with derision, but nevertheless sold out its first run in just a few months. The book had not yet been printed in the United States, and as far as I know still has not been printed here. I took no interest in the reviewer's patriotic pride in the relative virtue of American publishers. To me, the philosophy of Baucher is not something that needs the approval of the American publishers in order to be true. Baucher's propositions are self-evidently correct. One has only to hear them stated to know that they are true—if, of course, one has a superior mind. This was the overwhelming sense I felt on hearing them: there was nothing, it seemed, that could refute them. I leap over the account of various small-minded attempts to prohibit the book, and the various equally small-minded attempts by imbecilic divines to refute it, and we come to the conclusion of the review.

Perhaps, however, each one of us is more capable of refuting the arguments of the Comte

than the ablest divines. For they must prove by
reason what is proved already in our own
hearts. Each of us is born with a conscience,
and that inner voice, if we will but listen, tells
us that the Comte is wrong. Virtue is not
merely for the weak; on the contrary, vice is a
weakness, which only strength can overcome.
Conscience tells us that the great man is great
precisely to the degree that he is virtuous: that
to be honest and obedient is an unfailing mark
of strong character. Our strength is given to
those of us who are strong so that we may render assistance to the weak, not so that we may
destroy or "subsume" them. The way that our
Savior has shown us is the truly superior way—
a way that requires strength, but strength
"made perfect" in weakness. This is what we
know to be true, because conscience, implanted
in us by our Creator to be our infallible guide,
speaks the truth to us in the inner recesses of
our souls.——

And so on: it blethers on for a page and a half
more, but without adding to the argument. I can
say only that I listened attentively and assiduously, and I heard no voice of conscience telling
me that traditional Christian ethical doctrines
were objectively true. All I heard was the complaint of my own soul, which told me that I was
enslaving myself to the folly and stupidity of an
ignorant oaf, and demanded to know why I al-

lowed myself to be treated in that manner. I could not formulate a satisfactory answer. I knew, in this case, what was the reasonable course; I knew also that my father's objections were unfounded; yet I had been prepared to allow my father to blight our joint prospects forever, and to prevent me from realizing my quite reasonable ambitions.

Now, however, I had a different way of looking at things. I had been prepared to obey my father, because I had been taught that I must obey my father. But if it were true that I was the superior being I had always known myself to be, then what business had I obeying my father, when I knew him to be wrong? There was, I said to myself, much thought ahead of me.

In fact I was completely incorrect in that prognostication. I woke in the middle of the night to hear the bells of St. Peter's striking two, and I understood, having somehow worked it out in my sleep, that I must take my place as a superior being. I was ready to be a great man, and to embrace the doctrines of Baucher. I was ready to give myself wholly to evil.

CHAPTER V.

I nake an awkward, but auspicious, beginning to ny life of evil by defying ny father, although not to his face.

EVIL IN THE abstract is all very well, but how does one put it into practice? I had not had the advantage of hearing the words of Baucher from the man himself; I had only an inaccurate and unsympathetic summary to go by. From this summary, however, I was at least able to extract the fundamental principle of evil, which is to say greatness, as a course of action. The evil or great man asks himself one question in every endeavor: Does this action tend to my advantage?

First, then, it is plainly necessary to decide in what one's advantage consists. As I dressed myself that morning, after a night that had been restless but productive of much useful reflection,

I looked at myself in the tiny mirror above my washbasin and asked myself very bluntly, "Do you know where your advantage lies?" My reflection, who was obviously a gentleman of parts, answered with wonderful alacrity, "My advantage lies in building this paltry store into a great commercial empire, in spite of the wretched ignorance of my father." "And of your sisters," I added, and my reflection nodded his enthusiastic agreement.

It was resolved, then: the order from Cargill Bros. must not be rescinded. For the first time I could remember, I had definite plans to defy my father's explicit command.

How to do so, however, was a more delicate question. I could, of course, simply defy my father to his face, telling him that I refused to allow the Cargill Bros. order to be rescinded, on the grounds that it was positively necessary for us to expand our business, and to strike, as they say, while the iron was hot. It would require considerable courage and conviction to do so;—in fact, it would seem almost virtuous, and it would doubtless end with my father, having thus been alerted that my loyalty could not be relied upon, removing the store funds from my reach, and perhaps even placing the money in the hands of my loyal and brainless sisters, from whose bony fingers no force on earth could extract it. No, open confrontation would not tend to my own

advantage, and therefore must manifestly be rejected.

I had, however, made good use of my sleepless
hours the night before, and I had formulated a
devious strategy that, if it were indeed successful, would circumvent my father's control of the
store funds entirely, by simply obviating the
need for me to spend any of them. Dear reader,
my scheme was so cunningly audacious that—
well, shall I tell you what it was? Oh, no! It will
give me much greater satisfaction to imagine you
panting for the answer, as pants the hart &c.,
and me withholding it from you; and if you complain at such treatment, then I shall say that, if
you did not desire to read a memoir by an
avowedly wicked man, then you ought to have
picked up a book of improving sermons by any
one of the innumerable ministers and doctors of
theology who warrant their prose entirely free
from wickedness of any kind.

I came down to the store that morning early,
as had become my habit; and my father found
me tidying up the place, as he called it when I
rearranged our stock for greater efficiency.

"Good morning, Galahad," he said with a sort
of tentative good cheer, as if testing to see
whether I might be harboring some sort of re-
sentment against him for his intransigence of the
previous evening.

"Good morning," I replied with a good cheer

that was entirely unforced. And then I set my plot in motion. "As you know, I have a little business to transact this morning. I was wondering if you might spare me until about noon or so."

"Well, I suppose so," my father replied—clearly unwilling to risk another unpleasant confrontation over a trivial matter of a few hours. He did not even inquire the reason for my protracted absence, but I gave him the explanation I had thought up even so.

"You remember, of course, that Camellia has a birth-day coming up, and I thought I might make use of this opportunity to buy her something without her knowing the reason for my errand." That was quite plausible, because it was absolutely true: I would make sure that, by noon, I had purchased some useless trinket that could be presented to Camellia as the culmination of weeks of careful thought.

My father's face lit up. I believe he desperately wished to believe that good relations obtained between my sisters and me, and I know it must have cost him some mental effort to maintain that illusion. Here, however, was concrete evidence that I was taking an interest in the happiness of Camellia, the ugly old horse, precious little Camellia who would soon be twenty-four but had the mind of a girl half her age.

"Well, of course, dear boy," my father said

with a great oafish smile contorting his whole face. He was a rather ordinary-looking man in most respects, but he could be positively hideous when he was happy. "First-rate. Kill two birds with one stone that way, won't you? Take as long as you need. Just be sure you're here by two, because I positively promised Mrs. Platt that you would assess her writing then. We had three more applicants yesterday, and they all insisted on seeing you."

I left the store soon after that, pleased that my father obviously suspected nothing of my plans. (And how could he suspect? Even you, dear reader, have nary an inkling of what happens next.) As soon as I was past Fifth-street, I nearly doubled my pace, walking briskly past the telegraph office, and then a while later joining the throngs crossing Liberty-street, with its shouting fruit vendors and imprecating draymen that made it seem more like an Oriental bazaar than a Northern thoroughfare; and then briskly to the Allegheny and across the bridge, and up Federal-street past Boggs & Buhl, which had not yet opened for the morning (which was part of my plan, you see); and then finally to the narrow residential streets north of the common, and in particular to a certain small house on Boyle-street, from which, in about a quarter-hour, a certain Mr. Snyder emerged.

"Bousted!" he exclaimed as soon as he

recognized me. "Well, this is a surprise. I was just thinking about you, you know. My sister had our aunt over for dinner last night, and my word! The conversation turned to Bousted's stationery, and they were both surprised to hear that I knew the inventor."

"In fact," I replied, "I came expressly to see you on that very subject. We have, as you yourself testify, achieved a certain degree of note with our system. People ask for it by name. I thought perhaps we might walk together to your store, so that we could discuss something that might tend to the advantage of us both."

"By all means," said he; and so we walked, and I laid my plan before him.

"Our obvious next step," I told him as if it were so obvious as to be beyond question, "is into the department stores. My father, of course, is all for Rohrbaugh's, but after talking to you yesterday, I had the distinct feeling that you had an instinctive grasp of the system. It is, of course, vitally important to us that the Graded Stationery should be handled only by establishments that will provide the service in a reliable manner. The reputation of the line depends on the accuracy of the analysis."

Oh, I was eloquent. As we traversed the common, I was already discussing terms with him. Mr. Snyder did not have sole authority in the stationery department; but he was sure that, in this instance, his advice would be followed. I explained how the system would be implemented: with an initial order of fifteen reams of each type, the store would receive complete instructions for performing the analysis, and (of course) the use of the Bousted name, which was already of great value in the trade.

I need not feign modesty in such a private memoir as this, but it does not amuse me to relate my whole conversation with Mr. Snyder, and subsequently with the manager above him. I need only say that I was entirely successful, so that, by half past ten in the morning, I had a signed agreement to supply Boggs & Buhl with an initial order of my Graded Stationery, with complete instructions for the implementation of the system, and—here is the absolutely brilliant stroke—payment on delivery. I even recollected my other errand, and did not neglect my dear sister, selecting a fine silk parasol for her that might effect some improvement in her hideous blotchy complexion.

Now, I thought to myself, is not Baucher marvelously accurate in his observations? The superior man, I told myself as I walked back down Federal-street toward the river, sees opposition as opportunity. I must write that down somewhere. It might be better phrased: one might say——

And all at once I completely forgot what I was

thinking about, because there, walking up the sidewalk toward me, was the most beautiful girl in the world.

I am not given to hyperbole, at least when the subject is something other than myself. I had seen girls who were beautiful, and I knew enough about beauty to know that my sisters did not possess it. But I had never seen *beauty* itself until that fleeting moment. It was over in an instant: I walked on, and she walked on; yet the image of her perfect face, her auburn tresses, her classical figure, was burned into my mind for ever. I can conjure up that image as fresh today as I could half a minute afterward. It was a trivial incident, but is not a man's life made up of such trivial incidents? At any rate, the sagacious reader will have divined already that, since nothing is introduced in this narrative without purpose (in this way, as in every other, I follow Nature), the incident will not be without consequence later. For the present I need only say that the sight of this woman so unsettled me that I very nearly forgot to stop in the telegraph office. I had walked half a block past it before I remembered what I was about and turned around. There I sent a wire to the Cargill Bros., directing them to deliver my order to Boggs & Buhl in Allegheny rather than Bousted & Son.

Having accomplished my errands, I returned to the store, carefully concealing the parasol in the back of the coat closet, since, if Camellia were to see the brightly wrapped package, she would doubtless guess from the shape of it—even with her limited mental capacity—that I had bought her either a parasol or a hunting rifle.

Immediately, I was positively besieged by women demanding to have their handwriting analyzed. Well, in fact, there were only four, but four all at once was an army in such a small store as ours. My father had them sorted out in order of their arrival; one of them had been waiting an hour and a half so that she would not lose her place. I had them all disposed of within half an hour or so, and it was another hour before another came in looking for the same service. Nevertheless, by the end of the day, I had analyzed eight feminine scrawls all told, which confirmed my most optimistic projection of our stationery sales. It was apparent that I had, at first unwittingly, discovered exactly what the ladies of Pittsburgh's merchant classes positively needed: an excuse for them to believe that their own precious correspondence was more proper and correct than their neighbors'.

"So, er, Galahad," my father began tentatively during a lull in the day's business, "I presume you—you had no—no difficulty at the telegraph office?"

It really was simply astonishing. He had just seen the ladies of Pittsburgh literally lining up for Bousted's Famous Graded Stationery, yet he still could think only of the money he didn't want to spend, completely ignoring the obvious opportunity right in front of his nose.

"Oh, no," I answered. "No trouble at all. I sent the wire to Cargill Brothers in plenty of time." And the observant reader will note that every word I spoke was literally true, though I flatter myself that, though speaking only truth, I was nevertheless able to create an entirely false impression in his mind.

"First-rate, Galahad. I want you to know that I have the utmost confidence in you, my boy." Which was a perfectly ridiculous thing to say, when his actions had demonstrated that he had no confidence in me whatsoever.

In the next few days, we had completely sold out of our stock of stationery. We were still taking orders, but with the understanding that delivery would be delayed until our new shipment arrived. At times the store was so busy that Viola and Camellia were forced to render some assistance, an inconvenience they heartily resented, and another injury they were at pains to add to my account.

At last came that fateful day when I must arrange for the delivery of sixty reams of Cargill Bros. paper, watermarked as Bousted's Famous Graded Stationery, from the Boggs & Buhl store in Allegheny;—or, in other words, when my fa-

ther must know what I had done. I might conceal
it from him that the paper had come from Allegheny rather than straight from the mill, but I
could in no way conceal the watermark. Oaf he
might be, but my father was intelligent enough
to inspect every delivery carefully, knowing that
what little reputation he had depended upon his
being able to vouch for the quality of his goods. I
might pass it off as a mistake, but it would not
be long before he heard of the Bousted name being used at Boggs & Buhl. Better to face him at
once, tell him that I had had dealings with the
hated department store, and suffer the consequences—which, given my father's oafish attachment to me, I calculated would not be permanent or severe.

"Father," I began as the wagon was already
rolling up Wood-street with my paper, "I have
not been entirely honest with you in regard to
the order from Cargill Brothers."

His face turned ridiculously pale. "What do
you mean?" he asked in such a sepulchral tone
that you might have thought I was the messenger
of death.

"I did abide literally by your prohibition," I
explained with some haste. "I did not spend the
money you told me not to spend. In fact, I did
not spend any money at all. Our entire order has
been paid for by Boggs & Buhl." I spoke the
name of the hated department store, the enemy

of all that was holy, with as little expression as possible, but I could not keep a certain quaver out of my voice.

My father simply gaped at me, his jaw hanging down in the most appalling manner, as I continued. I told him how I had met Snyder; how I had sold him the right to sell Bousted's Famous Graded Stationery, with our watermark, for a price that paid for our order and left us a tidy profit; how I had agreed to train a few of the clerks there in my method of analysis, and had specified that no one not instructed by me should be allowed to perform it; and that sixty reams of paper with the Bousted watermark would shortly be arriving at our door. Then I braced myself for the storm I was sure would follow.

Instead, my father slowly and silently closed his mouth. It was some time before he spoke; and when he did, it was very quietly.

"Do you mean that Boggs & Buhl will be selling stationery with my name?"

"That is the agreement," I answered cautiously.

"They will be advertising my name at Boggs & Buhl," he elaborated quite unnecessarily.

I nodded, having exhausted my stock of verbal affirmatives.

"But, Galahad, this is magnificent!" he fairly shouted, as a simply obscene grin washed over his face. "My name—our name—in Boggs &

Buhl! In all my life I never imagined anything so wonderful!"

This conversation was not going at all the way I had expected it to go, but I adapted quickly. "I wanted to surprise you," I told him, which was true as far as it went.

"And so you did, my boy! So you did! This is the most glorious surprise a son has ever given his father!"

He blethered on in that vein for quite some time, and when the paper arrived he must have spent at least half an hour, while the men and I unloaded it, holding sheets up to the light to admire the watermark. He talked of nothing else the rest of the day, and it was clear to me now what had happened. In his mind, I had not sold my soul to the devil: I had conquered the hated enemy and ground him under my heel.

Viola and Camellia scowled at me all through supper, and would not speak a word to me all evening. All in all, it was one of the most satisfying days of my young existence.

VOLUME II.

CHAPTER VI.

The rapid growth of the Bousted & Son firm effects certain important changes in our lives, of which our removal to Allegheny is not the least.

MY FATHER WAS so ridiculously pleased with me for the next week or so that I found myself wishing, on more than one occasion, that he could find at least one fault in me, so that at least for a quarter-hour at a stretch I might be spared that hideous simian grin of his. Outwardly, I continued to play the part of the devoted and dutiful son, because it was still to my advantage to do so. Inwardly, I could be as contemptuous as I liked. Indeed, one of my most delightful discoveries since adopting the system of Baucher was the freedom I felt inwardly. The outer man continued to abide by all the precepts of virtue, as far as anyone could see, even while the inner man was wonderfully wicked. There had been a time when I dismissed such seeming virtue as hypocrisy; now I called it expedient.

In that next week, I spent almost all my waking hours hard at work. Not a single day went by without the appearance of at least four or five ladies whose penmanship required analysis, and by the end of the week we were already coming near the end of our stock of paper in some grades. In the evenings I walked across the Allegheny—or, when I was feeling especially prosperous, rode the horse-car—to the great Boggs & Buhl establishment, where I trained half a dozen clerks in the Bousted system of handwriting analysis. Orders were coming briskly there as well, and it was not long before more of Bousted's Famous Graded Stationery was being sold at Boggs & Buhl than from our own store. That was good news, since we stood to make a healthy profit from the sales there with very little work, now that the clerks were properly trained. Very soon it was time to order more paper, which we did on the same terms as before— Boggs & Buhl to pay for the entire lot, and Bousted & Son to take a quarter of it, along with our fee in excess of the value of the paper. It amounted to being paid to take the paper we were going to sell—an arrangement of whose obvious advantage even my father was aware.

As all this was going on, Camellia had her

birth-day. I was careful to stay home that evening, giving myself a holiday from training clerks, so that I could make a show of interest in my horrible sister's happiness. As long as my father doted on his two hideous girls as much as he did on me, it was greatly to my advantage to give them as little real cause for complaint as possible. Camellia was in fact much pleased with the parasol I gave her, declaring it the "nicest" gift she had ever received. This in turn caused a simply delightful falling-out between her and Viola that lasted for days, during which Camellia went out of her way to be civil to me, which was very good, and Viola would not speak to me at all, which was better. She refused to smile for anyone except the silent clerk across the street, who appeared to melt into the curtain whenever she noticed him gawking at her and smiled at him.

I should also mention that, every time I walked up or down Federal-street, or rode the horse-car, I looked among the milling crowds for that girl. I never saw her, but I always looked for her. And you, dear reader, are perfectly well aware that I must see her eventually, or I should not have mentioned her in the first place. But for the present I did not see her, and that is all I can say.

Our next order of stationery was four times the size of the previous one; I won a substan-

tially lower price from Cargill Bros., but charged
Boggs & Buhl at the same rate. Since that remarkable day when Mrs. Rockland had blustered
into the store, we had made more in profit than
we had made in the entire previous year. My father was ecstatic, and gave me all the credit,
which of course was only my due. Camellia at
least affected to be pleased as well. Viola was
simply speechless with impotent fury, which is
the way I always like her best.

We packed bundles as carefully as we could,
but still there was no room for about a third of
the paper in the back of the shop. I refused to allow the excess to go down into the dank base-
ment, so it went up into my attic: I carried a few
reams at a time up three flights of stairs. Viola
was somewhat pleased by this inconvenience to
me, and even ventured a few cheerfully ill-natured remarks on the subject at supper before
my father's oafish pride in his son reduced her to
sullen silence again. As for me, I regarded the
carefully distributed bundles as trophies, and it
gave me distinct pleasure to gaze on them just
before retiring—though I must confess that my
thoughts, just before I drifted into the arms of
Morpheus for the night, were not of paper, but
invariably of that girl on Federal-street.

The parade of pretentious middle-class ladies
continued its unabated march through the little
store. A few men came in as well, but it was

plain that Bousted's Famous Graded Stationery (now advertised in large gold letters on the display window) appealed mostly to women. I suspected that most of our male patrons had been sent to us by their wives. My father was ridiculously happy almost all the time, and he found himself in possession of more money than he had ever seen in one place in his life, as he remarked at least once per diem. I was of course pleased as well, but I did not carry the thing to such loathsome extremes.

It was not long before we were in need of even more stock, and it was quite clear that, if we were to continue expanding the business this way, we should need to keep a larger stock, or continually be running short. Since there was no room for a larger stock, even with my attic taken up mostly by bundles of paper, we had to find somewhere else to keep it all.

"The difficulty," my father said, "is that the goods will have to be transported. That will cost us over and above the cost of warehouse space."

"There is an alternative," I said, seized by a sudden inspiration. "We could move ourselves, rather than move our stock."

"What do you mean by that, Galahad? Your sisters have already made it clear that they aren't willing to give up any space in their own rooms."

"No, I mean take a house. We could devote

this entire building to store and stock if we lived in a separate house."

My father laughed—not a jolly laugh, but a worried and uncertain sort of laugh. "That would cost a great deal of money."

"And we have a great deal of money, with more coming in every day. We could take—"

Here, all unbidden, the image of that girl on Federal-street rose up in my mind.

"We could take a house in Allegheny," I suggested. "The air is healthier, and the horse-car makes it a practical distance. All the better class of merchants are moving to Allegheny, or the newer parts of Birmingham. We might even expand the store—add a selection of maps, which I hear are very profitable, or children's books, for the children who already come in for their school things. The benefit to the store of a little more space must be obvious." And in my mind I added, "even to an oaf like you," though of course outwardly I was perfectly respectful.

My father thought for a moment, and the effort it cost him was painfully visible. "I don't think it's time for that yet," he said at last. "We've been doing pretty well, but I'd like to know that the money will keep coming in before I spend it all."

"Well, of—" I began,—and then I stopped. "Well, of course I shall defer to your judgment,"

I said in my best approximation of a dutiful son's expression. I had nearly said, "Well, of course it will keep coming in, you old fool," but I restrained myself. It was of great importance that I should appear to be a dutiful son. I had not yet reached my twenty-first birthday; as much as I had accomplished, I was still, in the eyes of the world, my father's son. The reputation of the store—the capital of my nascent empire—would be adversely affected by even the rumor of any falling-out with my father. I suppressed, therefore, the words I desired to speak, and substituted the words my father desired to hear.

It was an obvious necessity, however, that we should remove from the store to a separate residence. While we lived above the store, we were no more than shopkeepers, even if prosperous shopkeepers. My father might be content to live as a shopkeeper the rest of his life; and if there were shops in that dreary Methodist heaven he believed in, he might keep one there as well. I, however, was bound for greater things, and I must take the reins, while seeming to all the world to submit to my father.

The next shipment of paper arrived, larger than the last, and my attic was beginning to fill up with the bundles. I had little objection to the inconvenience, which was easily borne; but it did keep my father's shortsightedness ever before my eyes. I must find some way of overcoming it

—but without appearing to deviate from that filial obedience, the appearance of which was essential to my interests, even as the practical violation of it was essential to my advancement. Clearly it was necessary to bring in even more money, so that even my father could be persuaded that we had enough to take a house in Allegheny.

"Rohrbaugh's," I said suddenly at supper one evening.

"I beg your pardon?" my father responded interrogatively.

"We have given Boggs & Buhl the exclusive trade in the Graded Stationery for Allegheny, but nothing prevents us from making the same agreement with Rohrbaugh's for Pittsburgh, and thus doubling our income from the department-store trade."

"But would that not simply take patrons away from our store?" my father asked.

I said nothing, because there was (much as it pains me to say so even now) some justice in his objection.

"Really, Galahad," Viola added, "don't be a noodle." It appeared that she was speaking to me again.

I was sullen and dejected the rest of the evening, although to all appearances as cheerful as ever. It was not until I had nearly fallen asleep that night that I had my next sudden revelation.

Yes, it was foolish, and probably even fatal to my ultimate design, to give Rohrbaugh's the sale of my Graded Stationery. But there were department stores in other cities—in New York, Philadelphia, Boston, Baltimore, St. Louis. These stores would certainly not draw patrons away from us—yet there were dozens of them, hundreds perhaps. I quickly multiplied the profit we made from the Boggs & Buhl sales by one hundred, and idly calculated how large a house, with how many carriages, I could buy with that money.

The next morning, my father came down as I was marshaling my troops, as I called it—which is to say, arranging everything in perfect order, so that it could be retrieved instantly when a patron requested it.

"Good morning, Galahad," he said with his usual oafish cheer.

"If I double our income by Christmas," I asked without any preliminary greeting, "will you take a house in Allegheny?"

My father was silent for a moment; then he laughed briefly; then, when that also seemed to have failed him as a response, he asked me, "What sort of doubling do you mean?"

"I mean that December's receipts shall be twice last month's. No"—here a spirit of boastfulness entered my soul—"they shall be twice this month's, which are already a good bit more

than last month's. And we shall count the receipts until Christmas only, not any in the week
after Christmas. If the receipts from the first to
the twenty-fourth of December, from all our
various ventures—the store and the Boggs &
Buhl contract and anything else—if what we
take in then is double our receipts for the entire
month of September, will you agree that we
should take a house in Allegheny, and use our
rooms here to expand the store?"

My father smiled that empty smile that always
contorted his lips when the conversation ascended to heights he could not climb. "My boy,
if you can do that, I'll remove us to Allegheny,
and I'll stand on my head while I do it."

"I do not believe that will be necessary," I
told him. "The removal to Allegheny will be sufficient."

He laughed with an ear-splitting bellow, as if
he had just heard the most splendid *bon not* ever
spoken by the mouth of man. I made some show
of laughing, too, to show him that I was in good
spirits, because that, in turn, in his oafish devotion to me, always put him in good spirits. I was
rapidly learning that keeping my father happy
was essential to my success, for which reason it
behooved me, as a rational (which is to say evil)
man, to study his disposition and learn what
made him happy. The small effort it cost me was
an investment that would reap large dividends in

the future.

"I should be down long before we open," I said, heading for the stairway. "I have something to attend to upstairs, but it won't take long."

And then I ran up the stairs, doubtless thundering my sisters awake (which I am sure I did not regret in the least), and sat down at my little table in the dormer to draft a letter. I laid out the distinct advantages of the Bousted system of graded stationery, and what was far more important (I used the exact phrase "what is far more important") the appeal of it to ladies of a certain class, and their willingness to pay high prices for it; I mentioned the successful introduction of the line at Boggs & Buhl, and how ordinary clerks were, by a short course of training, fitted to perform the requisite evaluations; how the name of Bousted was already a household word in Pittsburgh and Allegheny, and was rapidly becoming so elsewhere as the letters written by Pittsburgh ladies made their way around the world (this I simply made up, or, to put it more kindly to myself, extrapolated from the facts known to me); and I concluded by inviting the recipient to join the small and exclusive society of dealers who carried the genuine Bousted line, by which they were enabled to double or treble their sales of high-grade stationery (this figure I also extrapolated, to use a term that sounds ever so much better than making up).

I did not have time in the morning to copy out
the letter, but I had written my draft. I faced the
parade of ladies coming in to scribble for me
with unforced cheerfulness. I was even polite and
pleasant to Viola at supper, which discommoded
her no end. In the evening I retired early and set
to work copying the letter a dozen times, writing
as neatly as I could. Here, for once, I was grateful for my schooling: I had been beaten mercilessly until I was able to write a very fair hand,
which (I thought) reflected very creditably on
the firm. I made sure, of course, to write on our
own watermarked stationery, and to choose the
grade that best matched my own penmanship.
And then, at the foot of each letter, I signed my
father's name, in a better-than-tolerable facsimile of his antiquated flourish. Yes, I suppose it
was deliberate fraud, but it was wonderful how
easily the system of Baucher met that objection
with the answer that it was a crime which it was
in my interest to commit. I was not insensible of
the disadvantage of my youth: howsoever much I
had accomplished already, I was still uncommonly young in the eyes of the world; whereas
my father, although I knew him as an ill-edu-
cated oaf, presented to the world the very picture of a respectable tradesman. It was of the
greatest importance, therefore, that, if any of the
gentlemen to whom I was writing should make
inquiries, he should discover only a respectable

stationer who had been in business for nearly two decades with an untarnished reputation.

Having finished copying, I looked at my pocket-watch. It was nearly midnight: I had been writing with such care that it had taken me more than three hours to finish the letters. But I did not feel at all fatigued. I lowered the gas, but I sat for some time in the darkness at the chair in my front dormer, gazing out at the empty street below me. From somewhere a street or two behind me I heard a group of inebriated revelers singing a rather ribald song about one Maisie, who apparently was lazy, and suffered the consequences of her lethargy, as detailed in a number of verses. As their voices faded into the low hum of steamboats on the rivers and trains along the shore, I reflected that I had never in my life been drunk that way. Until quite recently, I should have said, without thinking, that drunkenness was a sin; but now that I was living a life of sin, perhaps it was time to try the experiment. Those sturdy fellows down on Market-street, or wherever they were, sounded happy. I had only had wine at dinner—dreadful cheap stuff from New York, which my father considered a great luxury, and which he would buy only when he felt exceptionally prosperous. Since my father rightly attributed our current prosperity to me, Viola affected to disdain the wine, the palpable symbol of my success. "Where there's drink there's danger," she repeated as often as she thought of it, proving at least that she could read a temperance tract. At any rate, as I said, I had wine at dinner, but never in sufficient quantities to intoxicate me to any perceptible degree. Perhaps it was time to try some of that famous Monongahela rye against which the temperance societies railed so monotonously.

But not to-night. I had already used up half the night writing, and I was very much inclined to devote the rest to Morpheus. I undressed and lay down to sleep, closing my eyes and summoning up visions of that girl on Federal-street.

I shall not weary you, as I wearied myself, with the many expedients to which I resorted to obtain out-of-town newspapers and other references; but eventually I succeeded in finding a dozen addresses of great department stores in Philadelphia, New York, Boston, Providence, Washington, York, Cincinnati, Buffalo, and St. Louis. My letters were dispatched, and I had only to wait.

This waiting was an agony, the more so because no effort of mine could shorten it. I had to pretend that everything was going well for me, because I could not admit what I had done—not until I was certain of success. So I decided to get drunk.

It was, perhaps, the folly of youth that suggested such a course; but you must remember that I had no experience of drunkenness. It was said to be a vice, but I had turned away from virtue. My observations of the phenomenon from a distance suggested that it made men happy, and like any rational being I desired to be happy. My decision was a purely rational one, and I approached the implementation of it in a spirit of scientific inquiry.

My first step was to inquire into the popular methods of attaining that blessed state. I did not have far to go to do so. Viola had taken to leaving temperance tracts strewn about our little parlor, doubtless as a warning that my success (which enabled my father to buy wine for the table) would lead to damnation. I took up one of those tracts on Sunday afternoon and read it from front to back—an activity of which my elder sister coldly expressed her approval, which I know was really a gnawing displeasure, since, if I were converted to the cause of temperance, she must needs find some other vice in me on which to fasten her disapproval, and I had been very careful to conceal my devotion to vice under an impenetrable mask of false virtue.

The tract was nothing less than a complete manual of self-instruction for the novice tippler. In order to horrify the imagination of the female readers who were more than probably the only human beings besides myself who would ever read more than two lines of the thing, it described with wonderful thoroughness the scenes of appalling vice enacted in saloons throughout the land every Saturday night: how the poor lost soul, leaving his wife and children alone in the miserable hovel that was all he could provide for them (because, of course, his money went for drink), would walk into a saloon, where he was greeted convivially by other lost souls, demand rye whiskey, and begin an assault on his own mental faculties that did not end until well past midnight. I could not have asked for a better tutor. There was nothing for me to do but follow the detailed instructions in this comprehensive manual, and I could not fail at my enterprise. I wondered then, as I still wonder to-day, how many susceptible young men are led straight through the swinging doors by these temperance tracts. Perhaps the authors of them are all charlatans in the pay of the great distilleries. If it be so, I commend the inventor of the scheme.

It remained to find a place suitable for my experiment. The saloons were innumerable toward the Point, but their proximity made them unsuitable. I did not wish to be recognized. I must maintain that illusion of virtue in the eyes of my family and patrons which would allow my schemes to come to fruition. I was familiar with Allegheny, however, and in that happy city were many notorious haunts of demon rum. Since I was not well known there, it seemed quite rea-

sonable to undertake the additional quarter-hour
of walking, and the negligible toll on the bridge.
I fixed on the next Saturday as the date of my
expedition, since, if it proved necessary, I might
thus have Sunday to recover from my exertions.

That week was uneventful, except in that it
was our most successful week yet in the store.
More than once I had two or three ladies waiting
in the store at once for me to have a look at
their writing. In the mean time, no letters came
in from department stores. It was, of course, unreasonable for me to expect a reply within a
week, but knowing that my impatience was unreasonable did not make me any more patient.

Saturday we closed the store at the usual
time; and, as we ate supper, I announced that I
had plans to visit a friend in Allegheny. Viola,
that constant delight of my soul, expressed some
surprise at the news that I had friends, at which
Camellia snorted briefly in her usual way; and
then, recalling that for the moment she had
more grievances against Viola than against me,
abruptly silenced herself. My father, as was his
wont, either affected not to hear them or really
heard nothing, in his imbecilic way shutting out
what was too unpleasant to believe: viz., that
anything other than peace and inviolate affection
could prevail among his children. It was therefore not mentioned any more at the table that I
should be absent that evening; and later, when

my father said his offhand farewell to me as I passed through the parlor, I could not but reflect privately upon the immense difference between the great experiment on which I was embarking and the evening of dull fellowship which he doubtless imagined lay ahead of me.

The sun had set, but there was still a rosy light from the west as I set out on my walk up Wood-street. The streets of the city had an air of festivity, as they ordinarily had on a Saturday night; and I reflected that to-night, for the first time in my life, I was (in a sense) joining in that festivity, rather than simply watching it from four storeys above, as I had done on many previous occasions, or sitting in the cramped parlor and listening to Viola rail against it as she had done every week since she took up the torch of temperance. Men who passed me seemed genuinely happy. For most of them, this was the one time of the week to be their own men—not to be at the bidding of an employer, as they were six days of the week, or of a dour clergyman, as they were on Sundays (although I had heard shocking rumors to the effect that a significant number of the hired workmen did not attend church on Sundays, as though they cared as little for their supposedly immortal souls as I cared for mine). And it appeared that most of them were, like me, off somewhere to some saloon or other, where it appeared that happiness in fluid form was offered for a price even the humblest workingman could muster, provided he was not immoderately attached to his wife and children. The general gaiety was infectious, and I found myself walking with an unaccustomed spring in my step. The very air seemed fresher, with a steady breeze from the west to blow the smoke of the mills away and exchange it for what I imagined to be the fresh air of the Ohio countryside, though in reality it was doubtless merely the stale smoke from more distant mills.

Liberty-street was quieter; its pushcarts had been pushed home for the evening, and there were no saloons to attract the boisterous activity I had seen on Wood-street; but the activity resumed as I walked toward the river, along a street where there were not merely saloons, but music-halls that affected the name of "theaters" as well.

By the time I had reached the Allegheny bridge, the rosy glow of sunset had given way to the indigo of twilight; and the view from the river as I crossed the bridge was indescribably beautiful to me, with the innumerable bright gas lights of both cities reflected in the rippling water, and in the east the fire of the mills making almost a new sunrise against the darkening sky; the steamboats like fairy castles floating on the inverted sky of the river; the world infused with poetry and charged with romance. And I—I was a new Magellan, or a second Columbus, on my merry way to discover new worlds where none had even been suspected before.

Federal-street was bustling, but for some reason I decided to turn eastward on Ohio-street, which was also filled with Saturday-evening crowds. Here were many saloons, some of them euphemistically designated "cafes"; and, without having any reason to choose one over another, I rather unexpectedly found myself unable to choose one at all. I walked along the south side of the street for some distance, and then back along the north side, and I must have passed a dozen saloons at the least; but this one was too crowded, and that one too small, and the other too noisy,—so that it really seemed as if I was losing my courage. The moment I thought of it in those terms, the thing was done: no one should say that Newman Bousted had lost his courage. I simply walked through the next set of swinging doors I came to, and I did not stop walking until I had taken my place at the bar.

"What'll it be?" the gentleman behind the bar asked me as I sat on the stool.

"Monongahela rye," I answered readily.

"Straight up?" he asked.

I delayed answering for a moment, because I really had no idea what he meant by that question. On reflection, however, I concluded that the drink would be easier to handle vertically

than horizontally or on a slant of some sort, so I
answered in the affirmative.

The man nodded, and with seemingly impossible alacrity, and all in one fluid motion, poured a
small amount of brown liquid into a tiny glass
and handed the glass to me. In my eyes, it resembled nothing so much as an inkwell filled
with sepia writing fluid. Nevertheless, unappetiz-
ing as the appearance might be, I certainly could
not give up my experiment without a proper
trial.

I pressed the glass to my lips and took a tentative sip. At once my mouth was filled with burning bitterness, and rank fumes invaded my nostrils; and when, overcoming every instinct
pleading with me to spit the vile fluid out, I
swallowed, the burning continued down my gul-
let and into my stomach, where it began to
spread like an ink-blot to my chest and ab-
domen, and the rest of my frame.

This was not the pleasure I had promised myself. Nevertheless, I was preparing to take in the
rest of the abominable fluid, if only to get the
thing done with, when a sudden blow to my
shoulder nearly knocked me off the stool.

"Beauthted!" cried a voice, at once familiar
and unfamiliar, in my right ear; and I turned to
behold my old friend Snyder,—or, rather, what
remained of Snyder, the better part of him having been drowned already in a prodigious quan-

tity of alcohol.

"Mr. Snyder," I greeted him. I could think of nothing else to say.

"Ha!" he exclaimed, and he slapped my shoulder again. "My friend—my dear, dear, dear, dear, dear, dear, dear, dear,—what was I saying?"

"It's very good to see you," I said with as much politeness as I could muster under the circumstances.

"Yeth! Tha's it! Iss very good to see me! I mean you. Very good to see you. You have no idea the good you've done me, Beauteds! No idea whatsoever. No idea! You have no idea."

"I am always happy to be of service," I replied warily. At that particular moment, I might have paid a goodly sum in ready money to be somewhere else.

"Bothers' Famouth Graded Sass— Stationery —my idea to bring it in—you remember—my idea—introduced you to Mr. Whassacallit. Sales trebled—trebled!   Tee-tiddy-um-tum-trebled! Make me a minnager!—Ha! I mean to say, a managin. Salary, office."

"That certainly is good news!" And even here, in the noise and smoke of the saloon, I was drafting in my mind my next letter to a department store: "Already the man responsible for introducing the Bousted system at Boggs & Buhl has received a substantial promotion, which he attributes to no other cause..."

"Iss egslent news! Eskelent! Called me into office safternoon. Came here to celebrate! Happiest day of my life!" Here he suddenly began to weep with great heaving sobs. "Never been so happy—'sall your doing—you a ta-rue friend, Boatsaid—a true true true true friend!" He fell sobbing on my shoulder, mumbling the words "true friend" over and over again into my collar.

"Your friend has had too much," the barkeep told me. "He needs to go home."

I nodded in agreement, but the barkeep kept his gaze fixed on me, until he had made it clear to me that my friend was somehow my responsibility. Since the man was at least a foot taller than I was and twice my weight, I thought it best to comply with his unexpressed demand as expeditiously as possible.

"Come along, friend," I said, attempting to push Snyder into an upright position. "We'll get you home now."

My effort was mostly futile. I succeeded in rising to a standing position, but with Snyder's head still on my shoulder,—until all at once he stood bolt upright and declaimed, "Home is where the heart is!" Falling backward, he braced himself on the stool, which, toppling with him, made a loud clatter that turned every eye toward us. Snyder himself only narrowly escaped breaking his head on the bar, and that only by grasping my lapel and dragging me down with him. There was much laughter from the assembled crowd, and for the first time it began to dawn on me that the laughter I had associated with drunkenness was not a symptom of the happiness of the drunkard, but rather the ill-natured merriment of the observers.

"Home is where the heart is," Snyder repeated in a low but portentous voice. I stood and began pulling him up with all my strength; he rose slowly and almost majestically, solemnly intoning as he rose, "My heart is in my chest."

"Indeed it is," I agreed. "Now let me help you along home. You'll feel much better there, I trust."

"But do you grasp the meaning of it, Boorstep?" he demanded as we made our way, slowly and deliberately, toward the door. "My home is in my chest! How could I not have seen it before? My home is in my chest! Where my heart is!"

He continued in that vein for some time; then, as we reached Federal-street, he burst into tears again, and for the next two blocks he sobbed theatrically as we walked, slowly and deliberately. When we reached the common, he began to sing a rather lugubrious ballad, most of the words of which were indistinguishable to me; then he abruptly turned aside into the grass, fell on his hands and knees, and vomited. At precisely that moment, I lost all further desire to pursue my experiment in inebriation.

It was another half-hour before I succeeded in conveying Snyder to his own house, where a very pleasant young woman brought us both in. I briefly wondered why Snyder would leave such a wife as this at home to go out and make himself sick; but when she began to thank me profusely for my solicitous care for her brother, I understood the situation a little better.

"May I ask to whom we are indebted for my brother's safe return?" the sister inquired.

"Oh!" I replied. "Please forgive my ill breeding. Newman Bousted at your service, miss."

"Gertrude Snyder," she said, extending her hand, which I took politely. "I am very pleased to meet you, Mr. Bousted—Bousted! Surely not the Mr. Bousted of Bousted's stationery?"

"The same, Miss Snyder."

"Why, you must be a positive angel sent from heaven! Edward has told me how he owes his new position to Mr. Bousted—he has spoken of you as his benefactor every day—and now you appear here to bring him safely home! I beg you not to hold his weakness against him, Mr. Bousted. Edward only rarely indulges in strong drink. When he does, this"—she waved her hand in the direction of her brother, who by now was horizontal on the settee, snoring loudly—"this is the inevitable result. I worry so, Mr. Bousted!

How did you come to be with him, and yet so obviously sober? Oh, dear, I should not have asked such a question. Please pardon——"

"Not at all, Miss Snyder—nothing to pardon. I happened to meet your brother on Ohio-street" (which was perfectly true as far as it went, although I left out the pertinent detail of having met him in a saloon), "and I felt it incumbent upon me, as his friend, to make sure he returned home safely. I am certain that he would do as much for me under similar circumstances; although, as I am not myself given to strong drink" (well, not since this evening's experience of its effects, at any rate), "I suppose no exactly similar circumstances are likely to arise." I really do not know why I felt it necessary to make this veiled declaration of moral superiority, except that she was an attractive girl, and I was a man, and I thought it might dispose her to think well of me.

"Poor Edward!" she said with that tone, at once maternal and dismissive, that only a sister can manage. "You must have seen his good qualities, and please believe me when I say that those predominate. And I must say that he never drinks when he has an obligation the following day. But oh, Mr. Bousted, when he does drink, he is so terribly excessive! I wish he might take your example. You might have some salutary influence over him. I know he respects you a great deal."

"His respect," I said, "is very flattering, if perhaps undeserved, and I—"

Here Snyder interrupted with a loud cry of "Home is where the heart is!" before turning over and resuming his fitful slumber.

"I ought to be attending to my brother," Miss Snyder said, "perhaps with a pot of coffee. If I could offer you—"

"Completely unnecessary, Miss Snyder, I assure you. I need to be walking homeward myself now, so I shall detain you no longer. But I do hope I shall see you again soon."

Her expression told me I had hit just the right note: I did not presume upon the circumstances of our accidental meeting, but I expressed a hope of deepening our acquaintance at some future opportunity.

"Well, then, Mr. Bousted, good night, until we meet again, and thank you for your kindness to my brother."

I took her hand again briefly, and looked in her eyes as I bid her good night. She really was a very attractive girl—dark hair, flashing green eyes, a tiny nose that turned up just a little at the end. Perhaps something might come of our acquaintance. It occurred to me in that brief moment of touching her hand that a man might do much worse in a wife.

As I walked back down Federal-street, I reflected that the evening had not been entirely unproductive. I had not achieved my original purpose, but I had achieved something rather better than that: I had gained an education in the effects of drunkenness that has lasted me a lifetime. Furthermore, I had learned that Bousted's Famous Graded Stationery was held in high esteem at Boggs & Buhl, a fact which must be useful to me in some way. Finally, I had made the acquaintance of Miss Gertrude Snyder, who was already disposed to think favorably of me. She was an attractive young woman, and I could still feel the delicate touch of her hand on mine. I had little experience in the ways of women who were not my sisters, but it did not seem inconceivable to me that Miss Snyder might be willing to consider a more intimate acquaintance. As I crossed the common, my fancy painted a charming picture of Miss Snyder as my wife, waiting for me in our spacious mansion, greeting me with a bright smile, blushing prettily as I took certain liberties to which a husband is entitled—

And then, all at once, the picture of Miss Snyder was forgotten. In front of me, walking toward me, I saw that girl again—the most beautiful woman in Pittsburgh and Allegheny, and quite probably in the world. She was walking with another female, of whom I have no recollection whatsoever; and as they passed I raised my hat to her. She nodded, and for a fleeting moment looked directly into my eyes, while her friend continued her idle chatter. And that was all: she said nothing, and I said nothing, and we passed. But all the way home, and very late into the night, I thought of nothing but that perfect face.

Sunday afternoon, I walked back across the river to call on Snyder and inquire as to his health; his sister informed me that he was still sleeping, but otherwise suffering no more than the expected effects of overindulgence. I left my card, and we parted. I mention this visit only because it did in fact lead, by a series of events unknown to me at the time, to a more intimate acquaintance with Miss Snyder.

Monday I received—or rather my father received, but I intercepted and opened—two letters from prominent department stores. The first, from Lerner Bros. in Cincinnati, very politely thanked us for our correspondence, but regretted that the store had no need for our goods at the present. This put me in such a funk that I nearly tossed aside the other letter unopened; but at last I summoned up my courage and read it. It was from Carey's in Philadelphia: they had heard somehow of the success of my system at Boggs & Buhl, and urgently requested—urgently, they said!—a full order at the earliest opportunity.

More such letters followed, and within a week I had four orders. I shall not be prolix. I composed a short manual of instruction, of which I had a hundred copies printed by our regular printer, and sent it to each of the stores (with the warning to keep it strictly confidential, of course). As for the paper, I arranged for it to be sent direct from Cargill's. Meanwhile, I sent more letters to more department stores. By my twenty-first birthday, which was at the end of October, eight department stores were selling the Graded Stationery, and repeat orders were already coming in. On Christmas Eve, I presented my father with the figures, which showed that December's receipts so far were six and a half times September's. He said it was "first-rate" and danced. Right there in the store, in front of two baffled matrons waiting to have their writing examined, he danced what I think was meant to be a jig. At the end of January, we removed to Allegheny.

CHAPTER VII.

An unexpected suggestion comes from Snyder, and by acting on his advice I enliven my story with its first love-scene.

THE NEW HOUSE was on a fashionable street, as I should have called it then, in the western part of Allegheny, just west of the park, in a section that was but newly built. I was, of course, very satisfied to see the family of Bousted take what I considered its rightful place among the merchant princes—for so I thought of men who kept a house separate from their business establishment. Whereas I affected a becoming gravity, however, my sisters were delighted beyond measure. Viola attributed our new prosperity entirely to my father's sagacity; I can no more explain her conclusion than I can explain my father's entire lack of sagacity. Camellia had the gall to

suggest that my hard work might also have had
something to do with our success. This suggestion caused a coolness between the two harpies
that must have lasted for nearly five minutes,
until they were drawn together again by their
shared admiration of the bathroom. My father,
meanwhile, simply kept shaking his head and
smiling, unable to believe that he had passed
from the class of shopkeepers who live above
their stores to the class of merchants who keep
separate houses. The mere fact that we had a
garden now astonished him as much as any of
the fabulous miracles of the Old Testament
would have astonished him. It was, to be sure, a
tiny garden; but it was indisputably a garden,
and my sisters devoted a good bit of our first
week in the house to making and remaking plans
for what they would grow in it when spring
came.

A house like this, so much larger than our
rooms on Wood-street, clearly required a housekeeper; so I told my father, though he was unwilling to spend the little money a housekeeper
would require until the shrill voices of my sisters
drowned my own with their insistent expostula-
tions. Thus my father engaged the services of a
half-deaf German woman (or Dutch, as we said
in Allegheny in those days) named Mrs. Ott, who
was able to cook something that resembled food
more closely than Viola's productions did. She

was mostly silent, unless one of us attempted to give her instructions, in which case she would bellow in a voice like a steam-whistle that she couldn't hear us. It doubtless alarmed the neighbors for three streets in every direction, and we soon gave up attempting to give Mrs. Ott instructions, conforming ourselves to her schedule.

Every morning (except Sundays, of course) my father and I rode the horse-car into Pittsburgh, with a change at Federal-street; the trip was accomplished in less than half the time it would have taken us to walk, which was another source of astonishment to my father, whose capacity for astonishment was truly boundless. Often Viola and Camellia accompanied us, for there was much to be done in the store, and my father was not yet willing to hire a clerk; but just as often they did not, or only one of the girls came, leaving the other at home all day—an arrangement that would ultimately prove unwise, from my father's point of view, though it would be productive of considerable benefit to me.

With our old rooms above the store vacant, we were able to expand our inventory, and to keep enough of the Graded Stationery on hand to satisfy the demand. At the same time, I began matching pens to writers—almost by accident at first, since a patron had asked me what pen she ought to use; but by the summer we had a line of steel pens with our name on them, which we,

and the department stores that sold our line, offered along with the Graded Stationery, with a
discount (of course) for ordering both together.
Our profit continued to grow every month, and
in August we began extensive alterations to the
store, cutting through to the floor above to make
a balcony level, where maps and children's
books would be kept. I also began taking out ad-
vertisements in the Dispatch, which brought us
even more business. All this kept us, and especially me, very busy; but my father was still too
parsimonious to hire another clerk, let alone the
two or three we really ought to have had to take
care of both our patrons and our department-
store trade.

There: I have taken care of business, so to
speak; and now I may turn my attention to more
personal affairs.

I saw my friend Snyder about once every
week or so: although he was by no means possessed of a giant intellect, it was good for me to
talk to someone who was neither my father, nor
my sister, nor a pompous middle-class matron
with atrocious penmanship. We sometimes
strolled together in West Park, and on one such
occasion, an unusually warm day in March, he
began to speak to me of his sister.

"Gertrude thinks the world of you, Bousted,"
he said as we ambled over the bridge near the
monument. "She tells me so every time I men-

tion your name. 'Such a fine young gentleman,'
she says,—'such a good friend to you as well,'
she always adds. I think she wishes all my friends
were like you. It's plain as day she admires you."

"Oh, and I admire her, too," I replied. "She is
a young lady of uncommon good sense."

He stopped at the end of the bridge, and then
indicated by gesture that I should come with him
down to the base of the monument, which for
the moment at least was out of the way of the
milling throngs.

"Look, Bousted, this is—well, it's awkward,
that's what it is. I'm only speaking to you about
it because Gertrude—— I have to be a father to
her, you see, since our mother and father aren't
with us. I'm all the family she has. Now, she's at
the age where she ought to be marrying someone, and—and she's been seeing a fellow called
Hoffman, and, Bousted, I don't like him. Dutch,
or at least his father is. Do I have to say any
more than that? Now, I know how it is with girls.
Gertrude wants to be married, and although she
hasn't told me anything, it's clear this Hoffman
wants to marry her, and she's thinking of taking
him up on it because nobody better has come
along. But what if someone better did come
along?"

"I suppose she might change her mind," I answered cautiously.

"That's what I say," said Snyder. "If she had a

chance at someone respectable, I calculate she'd jump at it."

There was silence as a minister and his family walked past us on the promenade around the lake. We raised our hats and smiled politely; the minister raised his hat and contorted his features into an unnatural facsimile of a smile that almost chilled me to look at. When they had passed out of earshot, Snyder resumed his discourse.

"See here, Bousted, I know you're a young man yet, but you're only a year younger than Gertrude, and you're certainly in easy circumstances. Man to man, you should be thinking of a wife. I know I'm a big dub myself, nearly thirty and no wife, but I can tell you, you don't want to be in my position. Gertrude is a fine girl—you said so yourself—and a handsome one, too; everyone says so. You've got a good chance at her, if I'm any judge."

I smiled at him. "To be perfectly blunt, then, you mean that I should attempt to steal your sister away from this Hoffman fellow."

"You could say that," he agreed.

I considered his proposition, but it really took very little consideration. I was in the full vigor of my manhood; it was natural that I should long for a woman's attention. Gertrude Snyder was an attractive girl, and her face and figure had made more than a little impression on me. Now her brother, who was her only family, was more or

less offering her to me. I would have willingly
married her that afternoon, so that I could proceed to the characteristic business of marriage
that night. I delayed my reply to Snyder for
some time after I had made my decision only because I did not think it would be seemly for me
to say to him, "Yes, I have lusted after your sister, and I am delighted by your offer of the
means to gratify my lust."

"I cannot deny," I said at last, "that your sister has been in my thoughts on more than one
occasion. I am not insensible to her charms. If
your belief is correct that my attention would
not meet with her disapproval, then it will be my
privilege and honor to render her that
attention."

"That's splendid!" Snyder declared, grasping
my hand and shaking it vigorously. "First-rate!
There's no one I'd rather see courting my
Gertrude. You'll get started right away—dine
with us this evening—I'll speak to her beforehand—nothing definite—just a hint that you've
told me you admire her..."

He went on this way for some time, making
plans for my conquest of his sister as though he
were more enthusiastic about the prospect than I
was. In the end, after what must have been a
quarter-hour of Snyder's planning, we parted,
having made only this definite plan: that I should
dine with the Snyders, and that some opportu-

nity would be found for me to speak with
Gertrude alone.

I arrived at the Snyders' home precisely at six,
as I had been told to do, and Miss Snyder greeted
me at the door with her usual politeness, but
with more than ordinary reserve. She seemed
unwilling to look straight at me, and when I told
her I was delighted to see her, her whole face
was suffused with a hot rosy glow. It did not take
much imagination to deduce that her brother
had spoken with her, as he had purposed to do,
and that perhaps he had been a little too specific.

Dinner was awkward. Snyder was in good
spirits, but Gertrude hardly spoke. I did my best
to engage her in conversation, but she limited
her participation in our talk to forced smiles and
a few one-word answers.

When at last the plates had been taken up and
we adjourned to the parlor, Snyder excused himself rather clumsily, saying that he had something to do upstairs for a few minutes. That was
all he said, and he was gone; the rest was in my
hands.

For some time we both sat in silence, Miss
Snyder with her hands folded in her lap and her
eyes trained on a spot on the floor some distance
in front of her chair. I ought to say something,
but I could think of nothing to say. Plainly Miss
Snyder expected me to say something, but she
was not willing to say anything herself until I

spoke. At last, I broke the awful silence, and my voice sounded like a trumpet-blast in my own ear.

"Miss Snyder, I—I have something particular to say to you."

"Indeed, Mr. Bousted?" she asked without looking up.

"Well, yes. When I arrived here this evening, I could not but sense that you viewed me differently from before. It made me suspect that certain remarks I had made—foolishly, of course, and believing that they would not be repeated— might have been,—well, might have been repeated."

"I cannot deny that my brother did mention"—she was still gazing at that same spot on the floor—"certain flattering things you had said about me. I am very sorry if he has betrayed a confidence."

"Oh, no, there was no betrayal, I assure you, except in my unguarded speech; for if I did not specifically ask him to keep what I said in confidence, then he was under no obligation to do so, and I was the foolish one for speaking so thoughtlessly. But, Miss Snyder, what has been said cannot be unsaid, and perhaps in my embarrassment—— Well, what I mean to say is, Miss Snyder, that I hope you don't think ill of me for thinking well of you."

"I could not possibly think ill of you, Mr.

Bousted, and least of all for such a cause. It is"—
here for the first time she raised her eyes and
looked directly into mine—"it is surprising to
me that you should have taken any notice of me
at all, but I could never think ill of you for it."

This was my opportunity, and I could not fail
to make use of it. "Then permit me to say to you
openly what I have already said to your brother
when I thought I was speaking in secret. Miss
Snyder, you are very beautiful, but the qualities
of your soul which most evidently appear to anyone who has met you,—— No, this is—well, I'll
begin again. When I first saw you, Miss Snyder, I
admit that I was first—I mean—I was taken with
your beauty; but it was your kindness that won
my esteem, your attentiveness to your brother,
and— Well, Miss Snyder, I should very much
like to know you better."

She was silent for some time; I watched her
perhaps too intently, and she averted her eyes
before at last beginning to answer me. "Your
flattery, Mr. Bousted—no, I do not mean to ac-
cuse you of dishonesty, Mr. Bousted, for you are
far too good and honest—but your good opinion
of me is more than I deserve. I cannot deny that
my opinion of you is also—good. You have been
our benefactor in so many ways, and your kindness to Edward puts me in your debt to such a
degree, that—— My brother is almost a father to
me, Mr. Bousted, and I owe him all my obedi-

ence, and every consideration that I would owe to my father if he were alive. And I know that your attention to me, unworthy as I am——"

"No, say not so; I am unworthy of you, and it is——"

"Then I withdraw the remark, if it displeases you. I know that your attention to me meets with my brother's approval, for he has told me so directly; and what my brother approves, I cannot disapprove. That is what I meant to say."

She was smiling—not broadly, but smiling.

"Then, Miss Snyder, I do not ask anything more of you now than this: will you permit me—to hope?"

She turned to face me, and once again looked straight into my eyes. "Yes, Mr. Bousted. I will permit you—to hope."

I seized her hand and pressed it to my lips; and although I had, perhaps, been somewhat dishonest in some of my conversation, yet the joy I felt at that moment was quite genuine, and I would not willingly have traded places with any man on earth. Even today I can still conjure up the memory of her soft flesh against my lips with perfect accuracy. When I looked up, I saw her face glowing pink, and a single tear rolling down her right cheek. She was still smiling that enigmatic smile.

Neither of us spoke for some time after, until at last she said in a soft voice, "I suppose you had better call me 'Gertrude' from now on.''

Snyder had the decency not to interrogate us when he came back into the parlor, but his almost leering smiles kept a bright pink flush on Gertrude's cheeks until I left for the evening, bidding her as fond a farewell as seemed decent in front of her brother. I left at about nine, and I remember how confidently, as I walked back down Federal-street, I projected my future life with Gertrude by my side. I think I was truly happy for a short time, until I passed that girl again.

All at once the bottom dropped out of my stomach. Gertrude was pretty; but even the fleeting glimpse I had of this girl under the gas-light confirmed that she was quite simply the most beautiful woman in the world. She had no rival. I raised my hat; she nodded and looked away, as if I had been too forward with my eyes. We passed, and she was gone.

That night, as I lay down in my bed in my rather elegantly furnished new bedroom, I filled my mind with images of Gertrude: Gertrude at dinner, Gertrude strolling in the park beside me, Gertrude beside me in bed. Just before I drifted off to sleep, I realized that the imaginary woman beside me was no longer Gertrude, but that girl on Federal-street.

CHAPTER VIII.

*My courtship of Gertrude is interrupted by the ap-
palling behavior of my sister.*

THE NEXT MORNING I awoke, shaved, and dressed
as I did every day, but I felt like an entirely new
man. My success with Gertrude had, in my mind,
removed the last barrier to full adulthood. The
feeling was irrational; I had not really conquered
her, and perhaps if my mind then had reached its
current state of development, I should not have
felt any sense of accomplishment until I had entirely overcome her modesty. But she had accepted me without question as one who had
reached that state of life in which it was natural
that I should play the part of a lover. To her I
had always been a man, and never a boy; that in
itself was a singular success. Then, too, she had

permitted me to *hope,* and in doing so, I imagined, had confessed her feelings for me. For what
reason would a young lady permit a man to
hope, I asked myself, except to avoid seeming
too forward by giving at once the positive answer which must come eventually? These
thoughts were cheering in themselves; and then,
of course, the thought that some future day
would probably bring me the unhindered enjoyment of all Gertrude's charms was never far
from my mind.

As I look back through the years at my youthful self, I am struck by how little of the doctrine
of Baucher had penetrated into my notion of the
relations between the sexes. I was in most ways
utterly conventional, even moral. It was true
that I had been willing to engage in a minor deception in my declaration to Gertrude, leading
her to believe that her brother had spoken without my permission; but I had done so with the
object of persuading her to give me hope that she
might some day agree to be my wife. Courtship
—betrothal—marriage—so many steps between
me and what I really wanted from her! Today, I
should regard them as unnecessary hurdles; and,
were I not so fortunate as to be placed beyond
the need of doing so, I should not hesitate to seduce, ravish, and abandon the next attractive
girl who struck my fancy. How quickly, under
the tutelage of the great Baucher, my moral de-

velopment reached that advanced stage, you will read in the following pages. But, for a short time, our attention must turn to the monstrous follies of my sister Camellia.

My father and I rode in to Wood-street as usual the morning after my dinner with the Snyders, and on this particular morning Viola rode in with us, Camellia remaining at home. There was nothing unusual in this arrangement: we needed a third hand in the store, and since my father still refused to hire a man, one or the other of the girls might occasionally condescend to help out, as long as my father made it quite clear that he understood just how much of a condescension it was. We could easily have used the assistance of both harpies, but at least one of them always had a head-ache of the most incapacitating sort. So it was this morning with Camellia, and she was thus left alone all day with only the old half-deaf housekeeper, who was given to long naps in the afternoon. Presumably, my sister would fill the day with serial novels by illiterate lady authors; at any rate, it did not occur to us to imagine that she would do anything in the least interesting or unusual.

We arrived, Viola exchanging her usual furtive glances with the timid and rather bird-like clerk across the street, and immediately set to work. The whole day was chaotically busy, but my father, when I mentioned the possibility of another clerk to him, only repeated that he thought we might manage a while longer. I was very tired by the end of the day, though I had pleasant thoughts of Gertrude to sustain me; Viola, who had actually tended to two or three patrons herself, declared that she had never been so exhausted, and felt a terrible head-ache coming on. We had at least the day's receipts to console us, although Viola had no interest in how the money was accumulated as long as it was there to be spent when she needed it. As we rode back home across the river, the world seemed quite satisfactory to me, and it wanted only a good dinner and a quiet evening to make it completely so.

Alas, there was to be no such quiet evening for me. We had not been home five minutes when Viola favored us with a loud and theatrical scream and came thundering down the stairs at full steam, her right hand clutching a sheet of Bousted's Grade 7, and her left hand hoisting her skirts just enough to keep her from tripping and breaking her neck.

"She's gone!" Viola was wailing. "She's gone!"

"Mrs. Ott?" my father asked helpfully. Mrs. Ott was standing right beside him at the moment, enjoying Viola's performance.

"Camellia!" Viola shouted with angry exasperation, before returning to her previous wailing tone. "Camellia's run off—with—with a man!"

It was wonderful to see my father's reaction to this news. His usual policy was to ignore everything he could not understand, and for a few moments his face went utterly blank, as though he were trying an experiment to see whether this information could safely be ignored. Finding that it could not be—since Viola continued her dreadful wailing, and Mrs. Ott was beginning to join her—he next tried smiling, as if he had just "got" the joke and was prepared to appreciate it as much as the next man. The smile lasted only for a moment, however, before the tiny clock-works in his mind clicked in place, and he at last began to understand that here, for once, was an unpleasant thing that he could not ignore. "What," he said—"Camellia?" And having given vent to this pearl of wisdom, he stood frozen like a statue.

I, meanwhile, had also stood frozen, but only for a moment. My first reaction was to take the news like a brother:—that is, like a brother who cared for his sister's honor. Almost immediately, however, it occurred to me that I did not care whether my sisters lived or died, and indeed of the two alternatives I might prefer the latter. If Camellia had run off with some bounder, then I was down one sister, and had only to contrive some means of ridding myself of the other one to make my life infinitely better. But then the cool consideration of my own advantage which I had learned from Baucher came back to me, and I reflected that, in the eyes of the world, a blot on my sister's reputation was a blot on my own. All these things passed through my mind during those few moments when my father was running through his complete repertory of physiognomical contortions.

"Let me see that," I demanded, and I snatched the note out of Viola's hand. I read it aloud for the benefit of my father:

Dear Viola,

I am going to marry Charles and do not try to find me because we are going away and we will not be here. I am sorry that I will not see you again but I love Charles and I am going to marry him and we are going away.
———Love, Camellia.

"What, Camellia?" my father said again; and then he fell back on the settle and sat there immobile for, as far as I know, the next two hours.

"Who is this Charles?" I demanded.

Viola hesitated; I believe she was weighing the betrayal of her sister's confidence against the obligation under which it would place me. I am sure that betraying her sister would have given her great pleasure; but because I had asked her to do it, she was reluctant. At last, however, the pleasure of betraying a confidence vanquished the displeasure of obliging her brother.

"Charles Bradley," she said with a quavering voice. "Camellia has been seeing him sometimes during the day. He works nights at E and O."

"Where does he live?" I attempted to infuse my voice with a certain amount of menace, and —incongruous as it seems under the circumstances—I recall feeling with a distinct relish that, for the first time, I was successfully exercising authority over my detestable harpy of a sister.

"A boarding-house," she said, "at the corner of Sampsonia and Buena Vista."

"Take care of Father," I told her. "Bring him coffee or something. I'm going out."

I think she was saying something as I left, but it might have been to our father. I had no desire to hear it, at any rate. I was in a thoroughly black mood as I walked back out into the street. It was bad enough that my sister had run off with a shift-worker from the brewery, but she had ruined my dinner into the bargain! And now here I was, marching off to look for her, when she could be anywhere in North America by now. I had no notion whatsoever of how to go about retrieving a missing sister; the only thing that seemed certain was that it would be hard work, whatever it was I ended up doing. And for what reward? If my efforts were crowned with complete success, I should have my pestilential sister back—and doubtless she would be the more pestilential for having been thwarted in her heart's desire. If only she could have been married in the usual fashion, I might have been rid of her without the distressing complication of a blot on my own reputation. Such a foolish girl! Our father might not have approved of her choice, but did she actually believe he would have the strength of character to forbid the marriage? Yet she must run off, like the heroine in one of her dreadful novels—the heroine who, even in the world of fiction, usually comes to a bad end. How selfish she was! Since I am entirely selfish myself, I naturally despise selfishness in others, as a vice that tends to prevent them from giving due consideration to my convenience.

My only concrete plan, at any rate, was to inquire at the boarding-house, to see whether anyone there had some notion of where this Bradley fellow might have gone. Then I must pursue him, and, I supposed, find him and my sister, and tell him—tell him what? The absurd thing was that I had hoped for years to find some man fool enough to marry one of my sisters, and now that he was found, I must prohibit the very thing I had hoped for! If only he could have done the thing honorably! If only Camellia could have found a man with the means to support her, and the courage to face her father—now, really, how much courage would that have taken?—then I should have been rid of one sister, and I should not have been forced to expend all this useless labor on top of the wearying labor I had already spent because my father was too parsimonious to hire a single clerk. As I marched along toward North Avenue, these two injustices somehow conflated themselves in my mind, as if I had been forced to set out in pursuit of Camellia because my father had not hired a clerk.

Down North Avenue, still crowded with men returning home from stores and offices, hooves and wheels clattering against the stones; and then into the quieter residential streets; my mind still churning, still meditating on the injustices I had to suffer; until at last I came to the boarding-house in question, where a cab was waiting in front, and a weedy little man in patched trousers was carrying two valises down the steps.

At once I knew that this was Bradley. Only such an unprepossessing wisp of a fellow would have any use for Camellia. A quick glance at the window of the cab showed me Camellia herself, who had already seen me and was doing her best to melt into the upholstery. I almost burst out laughing at my good fortune, although I ought to have surmised that a man who was fool enough to elope with Camellia was fool enough to botch the elopement. I marched straight up to him and confronted him while he was still on the last step, which put our eyes on just about the same level.

"I believe you intend to carry off my sister," I said in a threatening tone.

The poor little man was petrified; he dropped the valises, one of which landed with a heavy thump on his own foot.

I had absolute power over him—the feeling was exquisite—and suddenly all the thoughts that had been turning in my mind fell into place, and I saw what I must do with perfect clarity.

"Well, I have no objection to that," I continued. "But I do demand certain conditions."

"Conditions?" he asked cautiously in a voice that sounded like a rusty hinge.

"Conditions which, if you adhere to them, will prevent me from blacking both your eyes," I explained.

"Ah," he replied sagely.

"First," I said, "you will abandon this ridiculous elopement. Second, we shall all go back in the cab to see Camellia's father and discuss with him the terms of your marriage."

"Oh?" he asked.

I picked up his valises and handed them to the driver, who heaved them up on the roof of the cab; then I graciously allowed Bradley to precede me into the cab, where Camellia was sitting with her mouth open. Her face was whiter than I had ever seen it before.

"Good evening, Camellia," I greeted her cheerfully, taking off my hat. "Mr. Bradley has changed his mind and would like to take us both home. —Oh, I don't mean that he has changed his mind about marrying you, but merely about the method of accomplishing it. I have persuaded him to ask Father for your hand."

Camellia looked uncomprehendingly at her beau, but he was as mute as she was. I had no objection to their silence, since, at this stage of the proceedings, it was difficult to imagine what either of them could say that would be of the slightest interest to me. I gave the driver our address, and he began the journey by the most circuitous route possible, hoping, I suppose, to increase his fare for the trip. It made no difference to me. I had my sister completely in my power. Two sisters in my power in one evening! I was sure that, at last, I was free of their domination. (In this I was quite wrong: it is a marvelous property of sisters that, no matter how much power and esteem he may win in the world at large, a man can never entirely free himself from their domination.) I had only to arrange for this marriage to take place under more auspicious circumstances, and I could be rid of Camellia; and Viola, I thought (incorrectly), would hardly dare assert her superiority after I had so clearly manifested myself as the tower of strength in the family.

"Now," I began, after what seemed to me a suitable interval of silence, "it seems to me that the one thing standing in the way of your nuptials, my dear sister, is Mr.—did you say his name was Bradley?—Mr. Bradley's complete inability to support you. How did you intend to address that?"

Bradley was silent, leaving Camellia to her own devices. "Two can live as cheaply as one," she said at last, tentatively.

"Yes," I replied with a great show of patience, "but *one* lives in a boarding-house for young men. You see the difficulty." Neither one of them spoke, so I continued. "In order to consider embarking upon your connubial existence, it seems to me, your Mr. Bradley ought to have a position that pays well enough to support, not only a wife, but children as well." Camellia blushed violently, showing, I suppose, that she was not entirely ignorant of the process by which elopement might lead to children soon or late. "Can you honestly tell me, Mr. Bradley, that your wages at the brewery are sufficient to keep up a household?"

Bradley was still silent; but his face fell a good six inches, telling me exactly what answer his own heart had given him.

Here was the moment I had anticipated with a relish that it took all my art to conceal—the moment when, from the most purely selfish motives, I should be able to play the part of the self-less, pure-hearted benefactor of my sister and her little weed of a beau.

"Then it seems to me that you ought to take a better position," I said, almost clenching my teeth to suppress a wicked smile. "Can you write tolerably well?"

Bradley just managed to squeak out the word "Tolerably."

"Then you will write out a letter of resignation, and, as soon as you are free from your obligations at the brewery, you will begin work at Bousted & Son."

I had been looking forward to the surprise and gratitude that I was sure would register on his face, but all he could manage was incomprehension. Camellia, however, was a study. I really do believe that every expression of which a girl is capable flitted across her face in a fraction of a minute. Surprise, confusion, joy, fear, doubt, gratitude, wariness—every one giving way in an instant to the next. Oh, if we had only had Kodaks in those days! At last she settled in with an expression of thoughtfulness, and asked, "But what about Father?"

"You leave Father to me," I told her. In truth she had hit on the one point on which I was uneasy as well. How would our father take to the notion of hiring as a clerk this Bradley fellow, about whom he knew nothing at all except that

he had attempted to carry off Camellia? Hiring a
clerk at all went against my father's inclinations,
and here I was about to ask him to hire a man
who must certainly be the object of his righteous
indignation. However, it was necessary to procure the agreement and his blessing, so that I
could at once lose a sister and gain a clerk,
which were my two fondest wishes at the moment. And it seemed to me that the best way to
secure my father's agreement was to lie to him.

I told the driver to wait when we arrived at
our house, showing him a handful of dollars and
implying that one or more of them might soon be
his. (I cannot pass by this opportunity to remark
on what a useful thing it is to have more money
than other people; and to every young man attempting to make his way in the world, I should
like to say that no investment brings dividends
more quickly than simply having five or six dollars to jingle together when it is necessary to exert one's influence.) Then I led Camellia and her
Lothario out of the cab and into our entry hall.

My father was still sitting immobile on the settle, with a cup of cold coffee beside him. But the
moment he noticed Camellia, he sprang up, bel-
lowed her name, and embraced her tightly
enough to interfere with her respiration. Then,
of course, he turned to me.

"You brought her back! Galahad, my boy, you
brought her back!"

"Oh, I had little enough to do with it," I said, and before Camellia could say anything (there seemed to be little danger of Bradley's producing articulate speech at the moment), I quickly began spinning out the lie I had thought up in the cab.

"Camellia," I said, "has been foolish, but a girl in love will do foolish things. Providence, however, has directed her affection to a most honorable gentleman. As soon as she arrived at his lodging, he at once summoned a cab to take her back home, and—though he is most sincerely attached to her—insisted that he would do nothing that would tend to her dishonor. When I arrived, she was already in the cab."

Bradley was watching me with what I already recognized as his usual expression of complete mental vacuity, but Camellia was staring with her mouth wide open. It was at this moment that Viola appeared at the top of the stairs; and, what with her thundering down like a herd of buffalo and screeching in delight as she embraced her sister, it was some time before I could continue. At last, when Viola had screeched herself out, I was able to resume.

"Mr. Bradley's intentions are entirely honorable," I told my father. "He would dearly love to marry Camellia, but was unwilling to ask your blessing because his circumstances would not permit him to support her in the manner he be-

lieves she deserves." I could have wished that
Bradley might have shown a glimmer of intelligence, but at least, as long as he was standing inert like a cigar-store Indian, he was not contradicting me. "Seeing, however, how much Camellia is attached to him, I persuaded him to come
back with us and ask you for her hand in spite of
those difficulties, and I hinted to him that there
might be a position for him with Bousted &
Son."

That, I thought, was a fine piece of work. If
there should be any young readers who happen
to light accidentally upon this book (for I am
sure your guardians will do their best to keep it
out of your hands), this tale of mine may serve as
a pattern of a profitable falsehood. A truly effective lie has always as much of the truth as it will
hold in it: we may say that it is but the truth
with a few convenient adjustments. By a simple
comparison of my previous narration of the
events in question with the redacted version I
produced for the ears of my father, the reader
may easily discern how such adjustments are to
be made, and thus may have the benefit of my
experience the next time there is a need for
bearing false witness. No skill is more necessary
to a life of wickedness, in my estimation, than a
facility with lying; and it would certainly be well
for you, dear eager young readers, to get in some
early practice in the art.

For some few seconds after I finished speaking, I was kept in suspense as to the success of my scheme. My father looked at Camellia, and then at the mute and ligneous Bradley, and then at me, as his tiny brain struggled with the mighty burden that had been laid upon it; then he suddenly lit up with a simian grin that displayed every one of his teeth, stepped over to Bradley, grasped his hand, and shook his whole arm up and down as if he expected to pump oil out of the man.

"My boy," he exclaimed, "there are no words —no words!" (And yet he continued to speak in words, ill-chosen though they might be.) "You've treated Camellia like the treasure she is, and, by heaven, if you don't deserve her, no one does!"

Privately, I wondered by what perversion of justice even the most hardened and unrepentant sinner could be said to *deserve* one of my sisters, but of course I let my father say what he liked.

"Oh, please excuse my manners," I said, since Bradley was still mute and staring at my father with eyes that might have been made of glass. "Father, this is Mr. Charles Bradley. Mr. Bradley, this is my father, Samuel Bousted, the founder of the firm." I am not certain why I added that last phrase, except that it sounded impressive, and it would (I thought) be a good thing to keep Bradley in awe of us.

My father greeted him heartily; Bradley mum-

bled something inaudible, which was enough,
since my father was still babbling. It was with
difficulty that I prised them apart, my father being apparently willing to accept this Bradley into
the family forthwith. At length, I reminded them
that a cab was waiting outside, and promised to
ride back with Mr. Bradley to make some arrangements in regard to his employment as our
new clerk. I left Camellia in the hands of Viola,
whose brow had begun to darken with envy until
I had the good sense to remind her that she and
her sister had a wedding to plan, at which her
eyes immediately lit up with excitement, and,
with Camellia in tow, she ran up the stairs to begin making lists.

I took Bradley back out to the cab and woke
up the driver, who woke up his horse, and we set
off for the boarding-house at Sampsonia and
Buena Vista.

"Well," I said to him as we clattered through
the dark streets, "I hope you were well and truly
set on marrying my sister, because there is going
to be a wedding. If you attempt to wriggle out of
it, I am not exaggerating when I say that there
will be hell to pay."

He nodded mutely without blinking, and I
continued.

"But of course it's foolish of me even to worry
about that, isn't it? I'm sure nothing would induce you to abandon a girl like Camellia. But

look here, Bradley, I want you to remember to
whom you owe your unimaginable good
fortune."

His face was an utter blank, and I realized it
was useless to be oblique with him.

"You owe it to me," I said rather shortly. "I
made things all right with her father because I
love my sister and desire her happiness. As a result I am now saddled with a clerk I didn't particularly want, but I am prepared to make that
sacrifice for my sister's happiness if you are prepared to do your best for me."

Once again, he nodded silently;—but it would
be useless to report any more of our conversation in these pages. In various ways, I attempted
to impress upon him how deeply he was obli-
gated to me, and each time he nodded vacantly.
If I had not heard him speak once or twice, I
might well have taken him for a mute. Nevertheless, it seemed to me that he had absorbed
enough of the general tendency of my remarks to
understand that he was greatly in my debt, and
that he would repay the obligation by giving me
his best effort as clerk. And I do believe he took
that admonition to heart;—with what effect, you
shall read in its proper place. I left him at his
boarding-house, and then had the driver take me
home again, where I gave him two dollars for his
trouble, which was doubtless more money than
he normally made in a day's work.

"Galahad," my father announced when I came into the parlor after putting off my coat, hat, and gloves, "I have something I wish to say to you."

"Really?" I asked, a little apprehensively. Had he had time to ruminate on the evening's events and comprehend that I had foisted a clerk on him against his will?

"Don't think I haven't noticed how much you had to do with all this."

"Oh, not really so much," I began, but he interrupted me.

"You needn't lie to me, Galahad. I am your father, after all—I know you better than most people."

Had I underestimated my father? Was he really a good bit more intelligent than I gave him credit for being?

No, of course not. "I only wanted to say, Galahad," he continued, "that, as happy as you've made your sister, you've made your father even happier. It's been hard, Galahad, rearing the three of you without your mother. I wondered sometimes whether I could do it. But to-day I looked at you and saw a man who will put his sister's happiness before his own—who will move heaven and earth for the sake of his family—and I knew, Galahad, I knew I had a son I could be proud of. You've been very successful in trade, and of course I have been proud of that, but this evening I saw in you everything that makes a man a man. Virtue, Galahad—no worldly success is worth a penny without it. You may yet be a rich man, but your real wealth is already in your heart."

I find that I have difficulty recording this speech without tears—hot tears of shame that I should have sprung from such oafish stock. But I have recorded it as accurately as I can remember it, to remind me how far I have come from such absurd notions as my father's. At the time, I dissembled my true feelings as well as I could, giving him some conventional reply to the effect that I could not possibly fail of learning some virtue with such an example as his before me. This reply pleased him, and I was thus at liberty to retire to the kitchen to see what remained of the dinner Mrs. Ott had prepared for us.

CHAPTER IX.

I resu ne ny courtship, and at the sa ne ti ne co n-nence ny training of ny new clerk.

AFTER A COLD supper, I retired to my room, but I had still one necessary duty to discharge. It was, I believed, incumbent upon me to write a love-letter to Gertrude. I had already allowed a day to pass since our *understanding*, as I thought of it; it was necessary that she should not think I had grown cold.

How to compose such a message was a matter to which I had given some thought. The letter must be exactly the sort of letter Gertrude would desire to receive—must make me appear to be exactly the sort of man she hoped for in a hus-band. But what did she want from me? I knew what I wanted from her, but I could scarcely put

that down on paper. It was my good fortune,
however (although this is probably the only occasion on which I have called it that), to have
sisters. They usually left a number of cheap novels strewn about the parlor, and I took one of
these with me—*Bertha's Beaux,* by Mrs. Traymore—in which I had found a suitable model.
My sisters, at least, regarded these dreadful tales
as infallible guides to contemporary mores, so I
reasoned that what Mrs. Traymore prescribed as
the ideal communication from a lover to his
beloved must meet with the approbation of most
girls Gertrude's age. I sat down at my writing-
desk, therefore, and began to compose the following letter on a sheet of Bousted's Grade *3.*

My dearest Gertrude,——

It is not within the power of mere written
words to express the joy that took possession of
my breast when I found that my addresses to
you were received with favor. No one is more
aware than I of how little that favor is deserved,
and my joy is naturally proportionate to the
condescension you have shown in hearing me.
Yet a letter can never say what I would desire
you to know: you see the ink frozen into words
on the page, but you cannot see the tears of joy
in my eyes when I think of you, or hear my
heart beat—although I sometimes fancy that
you can hear my heart beat, though half a mile
separates us. The hope of a closer acquaintance

with you sustains me throughout the day, and my last conscious act of the evening shall be a prayer for your happiness, which is now the chief end of my existence. You may be assured that, unworthy as I am, I have no other desire than to add to your happiness by whatever means are in my power; and I trust that, whatever shortcomings may be charged to my account, a want of readiness in your service shall never be among them. In eager anticipation of the moment when my eyes shall once again behold your face, I am

> Your most fervent admirer,
> Newman Bousted.

Some things in this letter were indisputably true: I did hope for a closer acquaintance with her, and in my rare idle moments throughout the day I had allowed my imagination to paint some very pretty pictures of that closer acquaintance. I was not aware of any tears of joy, but a brief look at Mrs. Traymore's wretched narrative assured me that such expressions were expected in any first-rate love-letter, and I did not want Gertrude to think that I had not given her value for money. I sealed the letter and left it with the post to go out, and felt that, on the whole, it was a very creditable effort;—nor am I inclined to judge it otherwise now, after an interval of two and a half decades.

The next day was a trying one, as indeed were the days following. Patronage at the store continued to increase, and it was evident that the reputation gained by our Graded Stationery had a salutary effect on our sales of other articles as well. Yet we had only the two of us to handle the constant stream of humanity flowing through our doors. Viola and Camellia were of course far too busy with wedding preparations to render any assistance; Camellia had determined that the wedding should be in six months, and if they spent every minute of every day until that time working on the arrangements, there might just possibly be time enough to get everything done. This is what Viola told my father, who of course acquiesced, and thenceforth refused even to ask whether one of the girls might come into the store for the day.

On the second day, I returned home with my father to find a letter waiting for me. I knew it right away because Viola did not suffer me even to hang my hat upon the rack before announcing the fact.

"A letter came for you to-day, Galahad," she said in a voice that was too impossibly saccharine to be anything but ironical.

"From a *lady,*" Camellia added, stressing the word *lady* as if it could bear the weight of a thousand innuendos.

"Thank you," I said, taking the letter from Viola's knobby fingers.

"Well, aren't you going to open it?" Viola demanded.

"Yes," I replied, "I am." But I made no move to do so.

"Who is it, Galahad?" Camellia asked with a revolting lilt in her voice. "Who is your secret lady friend?"

"No secret at all," I said as coolly as I could. "Miss Snyder is the sister of Mr. Edward Snyder, a manager at Boggs & Buhl and a good friend of mine. I dined with them a few nights ago."

Viola smiled an insufferable smile and nodded, if such a thing be possible, an insufferable nod. I also smiled, but I did not open the letter, placing it instead in my pocket, where I managed to leave it by a prodigious act of will. I did not wish my sisters to suppose that I was unusually eager to open it. Not until I went upstairs to dress for dinner did I have the opportunity to read it. It was short, but quite satisfactory:

Dear Newman,——

My brother holds you in such high esteem that, even if I did not know you myself, I could never doubt your character; and you have behaved with such propriety in all your dealings with me that I must regard myself as the unworthy one. I am deeply sensible of the honor you do me in writing to me in such affectionate terms; and, as it pleases my brother that I should receive your addresses (for he is invested with a father's authority over me), I hope that in time it may be possible for me to return your affection with a sincere heart. My brother has asked me to invite you to dine with us Thursday evening at seven, and if that time is convenient for you, I shall be very happy to see you. Until then, I hope you will regard me as your sincere friend, as I regard you as my greatest benefactor, next to my brother of course.

——With gratitude,
Gertrude.

Evidently Gertrude was not addicted to the same horrible novels that Viola and Camellia devoured with an insatiable appetite, since her letter was nothing at all like the response of Mrs. Traymore's heroine. It displayed a great deal more good sense; and, while her moral qualities were not the qualities I most desired in Gertrude at the moment, still, dim as my knowledge of the connubial estate was in those days, I knew that there was more involved in it than the mere satisfaction of my lust. It seemed to me that a little good sense in a wife would not come amiss.

Here, since I have mentioned that I did not reveal the subject of my correspondence with Gertrude to my father and sisters, I might be expected to explain my reticence. I do not know, however, whether I can articulate an explanation. I suppose I had some boyish embarrassment still in my constitution; and it might have been difficult to endure the congratulations of my father, and the studied incredulity of my sisters. And was there anything to tell? Gertrude had not yet agreed to marry me, but only to see me on terms that would probably lead to an engagement. We had—an understanding. It was a private matter between us; an engagement might be a public announcement, but did I not owe Gertrude the courtesy of waiting until she had decided that such an announcement should be made? So I said to myself at the time, and perhaps those were my reasons. Or perhaps I had already formed, in the dark recesses of my soul, some notion that I might wish to escape from Gertrude cleanly if a better opportunity came to me. I had no conscious idea of that sort; but it is true that, when I retired, and lowered the gas, and filled my mind with pleasing images of Gertrude, it was not long before I noticed that the girl in my thoughts was no longer Gertrude, but that Federal-street beauty.

We had several more days of hard work in the store while Bradley was still finishing up at the brewery. I did dine with the Snyders on Thursday, and Gertrude was friendly, though bashful, the more so because her brother treated us as though we had already set the date for our wedding. It made Gertrude blush prettily to hear him talk that way, but she did smile once or twice.

At last came the day when Bradley, free from his obligations at E and O, came to work at the store. I had anticipated this day keenly as the moment when our store would truly become a firm, which is to say an institution with paid employees.

Bradley, however, dampened my enthusiasm very effectively. He was an imbecile. Why was I surprised? Who but an imbecile would attempt to carry off Camellia—and fail in the attempt? The most elementary directions were beyond his capacity. I was patient with him—unfailingly patient and cheerful. How could I be otherwise? I would not be seen to admit that my hiring of a clerk had been in any way a mistake. My pride, I am sure, saved his life: for there were many occasions when I would willingly have killed him on the spot, had not my pride told me that to do so would be nothing less than an admission of failure on my part. If pride is the chief of sins, then it was very fortunate for Bradley that I was not more virtuous. I worked harder than I had done before: for now I had also to undo the damage Bradley had done. My only consolation was in knowing that Bradley could not possibly be as stupid as he appeared to be. It simply was not possible. The man clearly managed to feed and dress himself somehow. If he could do those

things, surely he could learn in time to distinguish a box of pens from a box of clips when I
sent him for one or the other. That blessed time
had not yet come, but surely it could not be distant.

The spring weather was warming, and the
cherry trees were blooming, and Gertrude and I
began to make it a habit to stroll in West Park
two or three evenings a week—often in the company of her brother, but sometimes just the two
of us. Gertrude was a little less bashful than she
had been, and as long as our conversation turned
on pleasant and indifferent matters, she could be
animated, and apparently happy; but she was
not yet ready to overcome her bashfulness if her
brother brought up the question of a wedding.
On these occasions, she would blush and look
away. I did not force the subject on her myself,
impatient as I was to enjoy those privileges
which, in my youth, I was not confident enough
simply to take for myself against her will, because it did appear that Gertrude was becoming
more and more attached to me. If my mask of
patience put her at ease, and made her more
likely to be my wife in the future, then patience
was good policy, however contrary it might be to
my inclinations. The truly evil man, which is to
say the enlightened man, does not prize conti-
nence for its own sake; but any virtue may be a
tool in the pursuit of that which he desires. This

is an important principle that every aspiring
evildoer ought to take to heart: the truly evil
man does not hesitate to practice virtue when
doing so conduces to his advantage.

Evening strolls with Gertrude gave me some
relief after days of dealing with Bradley. I was
very nearly ready to give up on him, pride or no
pride. In idle moments I sometimes thought of
killing him and Camellia together. But then an
entirely unexpected discovery showed me
Bradley in a new light, and made me think that,
perhaps, after all, his earthly existence ought to
be prolonged for a few more years. I could still
see the arguments against that proposition, but
now I could see that there were arguments in favor of it as well.

What happened was this: I had gone upstairs
for a few minutes, leaving my father and Bradley
in the store. When I came back down, my father
was occupied with a distinguished-looking gentleman who was in need of a mechanical pencil,
which left Bradley to deal with a middle-aged
lady who needed a blank book. Poor Bradley was
in a state of deep confusion, as he usually was. I
watched as he brought exactly what she told him
she didn't want, and then for some reason known
only to himself brought her a copy-book. At first
I thought I might simply push him aside and
complete the transaction myself; then I thought I
should watch, catalogue his mistakes, and casti-

gate him soundly once the woman had gone.

But as I watched, I noticed that the woman was not unhappy. Quite the reverse: however many mistakes Bradley made, she still smiled and addressed him in a manner that I might almost have called flirtatious. She was charmed with him. I had no idea why: he was as unprepossessing a specimen as I had ever seen in my life. Yet he had charmed the lady, who left with a morocco-bound journal much more expensive than what she had told him she intended to buy; and I reflected that he had charmed Camellia to such a degree that she had been willing to elope with him.

I experimented with Bradley several more times that afternoon, directing him to wait on female patrons and observing the results. In every instance, the lady was pleased. She did not always succeed in making the purchase she had intended to make, but she did make a purchase. One of our regulars congratulated my father on having found such a "nice" young man. There was no escaping the conclusion: Bradley was charming—inexplicably charming—to women, and to such a degree that he might very well be an addition of some utility to our firm. Formerly I had kept him as far away from the patrons as possible; now I saw that he might be put to far better use serving ladies than serving me. They at least were less likely to murder him.

I will not say that it was easy to teach Bradley. There were days when I thought I might more easily teach a goldfish to play the parlor-organ. But he was of great service to me in refining my instructional methods. By the time I had finished with him, I really do believe I could have taught a monkey the Bousted system of handwriting assessment. Though it cost me good money, I burned the remainder of the instructions I had had printed, and wrote an entirely new set of directions, which I had printed and sent to our next department store. These instructions are essentially the same ones that are still sent to our dealers to-day. I have often heard them praised for their simplicity, but the highest praise I can give them is to say that they were so simple that even Bradley could follow them.

My success in business continued, as more department stores picked up the Graded Stationery and the pens that went with it; our store, in fact, was now accounting for less than a fifth of our income. This prosperity was pleasing to me, of course; but I could not but think how much more satisfactory it would be with Gertrude by my side, to use a common metaphorical expression that fools no one but is necessary for the sake of euphemism. By June I had been seeing her regularly for three months, and I thought the time had come to pose that question which, in

spite of her bashful modesty, she must have expected from me.

It was a fine evening: the sun had only just set,
and the orange and peach in the sky were fading
to old rose; and Gertrude was walking with me
in West Park. The weather had been warm, but
not hot, and I remember that Gertrude looked
exceptionally pretty in primrose yellow. Bustles
were in fashion in those days; when I think back
on them, I think that they had a tendency to
make a plain woman look like a locomotive;—
but Gertrude was far from plain.

I do not know whether anything else I have
done in my life required as much positive
courage as what I was about to do. It is a strange
truth of human nature, that the fear of death itself is not greater than the fear of a rejected
marriage proposal. A rational man might tell
himself that the world is full of women, and another is bound to accept him if this one rejects
him. A truly wicked man might console himself
with the knowledge that he has the power to
take from a woman what she is not willing to
give. But a man in love is not rational; and since
wickedness properly understood is merely the
fullest development of rationality, he finds it
very difficult to be wicked. Nothing so effectu-
ally robs a man of his wickedness as this insidi-
ous passion: though lust be accounted a sin, it
too often proves a cunning trap that pulls a man

inexorably downward, away from his true self-interest, and toward that disinterested sort of love that desires the good of its object. The wickedest man in the world, giving in to his lust, may find himself positively virtuous before he knows it. Let this stand as a warning to our young people who desire to be truly evil: manage your lust carefully, lest it rob you of the devoted attention to your own advantage which alone leads to that state of perfect wickedness which is your goal. —The reader, if any reader there be besides myself, will forgive this excursion into moral philosophy, which he may well find applicable in his own life.

As I said, therefore, I was strolling with Gertrude along the carriage-drive in West Park, and Nature employed all her art to further my objective; I had but to find a private moment, and ask the question whose answer would assure my future happiness. Yet I hesitated. The moment was not opportune; we were observed, or we had to step out of the way of a carriage, or any of a hundred other things came between me and the question. Was I losing my courage? Merely to ask that question was to answer it: my stubborn pride would not allow me to confess, even to myself, that I was in any way deficient in the fortitude necessary for my success. I saw a likely spot ahead,—a shaded turn where we might not be closely observed,—and determined to ask her to be my wife when we reached that point on the drive.

We walked on, Gertrude's hand on my arm, my heart beating faster as we approached the spot. But I would not be deterred by timidity. As soon as we reached the point I had designated in my mind, I stopped and turned to face her.

"Gertrude, I——"

At that moment, I became aware of the sound of hooves and wheels. I led Gertrude aside into the grass, and a moment later a pair of perfectly matched black horses appeared, drawing behind them a victoria in the latest style, with the top folded down; and seated in that carriage, illuminated in the rosy light of the western sky, was the most beautiful woman in the world,—that girl whom I had first seen on Federal-street, and who had haunted my thoughts since that moment. The vision was brief, but ecstatic; in the time it took her carriage to pass us, every line of her face and figure was indelibly stamped on my memory.

I stood immovable and silent for a moment, but then Gertrude spoke.

"Oh, that was Miss Goode," she said with sudden recognition.

It took my mind a few moments to understand the implication of that simple statement. When I did understand it, I nearly jumped. It was all I could do to mask the sudden excitement that had nearly overcome me.

"You mean you know the lady?" I inquired, carefully keeping to an inconsequentially conversational tone of voice.

"Only slightly," Gertrude answered, "from the Workingmen's Improvement Society. She has spoken there a few times, and she has made some substantial gifts to the workingmen."

"She must have money to ride in that style," I remarked.

Gertrude smiled slightly. "She certainly has. Her father is Hiram Goode of Monongahela Glass, and Amelia Goode is his only child."

"That accounts for the carriage," I said. Not only beautiful, but immeasurably rich as well! "But why have you not told me about this society you mention? I had no idea you were so interested in charity."

So Gertrude began to tell me about her pet charity; and I allowed her to do so; and there was no proposal.

VOLUME III.

CHAPTER X.

My thoughts occupied with the beautiful Miss Amelia Goode, I return to the great philosopher for guidance.

I CAME BACK home that evening in a very agitated state of mind. I had hidden my agitation from Gertrude well enough; I was fairly certain of that. But I could not hide it from myself. I had set out that evening intending to propose marriage to Gertrude, certain that there was nothing in the world I desired more; the glimpse of that girl in her victoria had reminded me that there was indeed one thing in the world I desired more than Gertrude. But she was wealthy; absurdly rich, I might almost say. The Goode glassmaking fortune was almost legendary. She occupied a sphere as far above me as the stars are above the moon. What was the use of even thinking about her? Gertrude was a fine woman; no one could say that she was not. She had the good sense and even temper that make an excellent wife. No one ought to desire more than Gertrude—and yet I did desire more than Gertrude.

This agitation of mine persisted into the next day, as poor Bradley discovered when he brought me a box of blue pencils after I had asked for a pencil.

"Confound it, Bradley," I exploded, "will you put your brain to work for once? If I had wanted blue pencils, or red pencils, or green or yellow or lavender pencils, don't you think I would have specified the color? If a man asks for a pencil, he wants a black pencil, not a whole herd of blue pencils."

Bradley said nothing; he was simply inert, as if he were a rabbit hoping the hound might not see him if he stood very still.

"Well, take them back!" I shouted at him, after several unproductive seconds of silence between us. Bradley immediately took the pencils gingerly between his fingers, as if the box were a hot coal, and fairly ran into the back room.

Two or three minutes later, I realized that he was not going to come out again with the pencil I wanted. For some reason this particular stupidity annoyed me more than all the rest. I stood up and stormed back to where Bradley was standing like a Greek statue copied by a third-rate student.

"Where in blazes is that pencil?" I demanded in what was evidently the most terrifying tone of voice Bradley had ever heard. He stood straight and immobile, with eyes staring, and lips moving as if to form words that his frozen tongue refused to utter.

"Blast it!" I puffed to no one in particular; and I found my own pencil.

"Don't you think you were rather short with Mr. Bradley?" my father asked me a little later, when Bradley had stepped out for a moment.

"Yes, I was," I admitted, attempting an expression of contrition. But I was not contrite. Yes, I was indeed rather short with Bradley, who was doubtless much the better for it. His work improved, at any rate. It was apparent that he was terrified of me, and I suppose not without reason. After a few more days, however, I noticed that he was beginning to pick up some dim notion of how the stock was organized, and could, with some effort, retrieve a box of Esterbrook pens if a lady asked for one.

Over the next few weeks, I gradually learned more about Miss Amelia Goode—not by making inquiries so much as by simply keeping my ears open. It seemed that everyone in Allegheny knew of her, and the only excuse for my ignorance was my recent arrival in the city. For the people of Allegheny, she was not just a beauty; she was *the* beauty, or rather she was beauty itself. In every city there is one such girl whose physiognomy combines with her fortune to make her a kind of public institution; in Allegheny, that girl was Amelia Goode. Her engagement-book dictated the social calendar of the city: no ball or soiree or afternoon tea could be called "refined" unless she deigned to bless it with her presence.

Miss Goode was always at the center of a swarm of admirers, buzzing about her like bees, and with about the same effect on her perception as the buzzing of a bee or two would have. She treated them all with perfect civility and perfect indifference. She was the Vestal virgin of the social world. In women, she inspired envy and emulation; in men, desire and despair commingled. It was impossible to think of conquering her, as impossible as to think of conquering Beauty itself. She appeared to walk among mortals, but she had her true existence in the lofty realm of the ideals.

This creature's fortune came from the glass works her ancient father had founded half a century before; for she was the child of his dotage, conceived (I know not how) when he was already entering the hoary winter of life.

These facts I accumulated and stored in my memory over the course of some weeks; I did not at once possess the perfect knowledge I have imparted to you, dear imagined reader of the future. In that time I continued to see Gertrude, but I had not yet proposed marriage to her. I believe I had formed some absurd idea in my mind that marrying Gertrude would prevent me from pursuing Amelia Goode.

It was misery, this obsession with what must be unattainable to one of my station. I will say this much for myself, and you shall decide whether it counts toward the extenuation or the aggravation of my folly: that I never really desired Miss Goode's money. It was not that I had no desire to be wealthy, but rather that my lust for that perfect beauty was so intense that I simply forgot her wealth; or, rather, it was present to my mind only as a barrier that separated her from me. I am inclined to think it a case of aggravated folly when I look back on it at this remove: for money can buy the satisfaction of almost any lust, whereas lust almost invariably eats up money. To the young man pursuing a life of wickedness, I have this advice to give: always put greed before lust when indulging your petty sins.

I will say in my favor that the firm did not suffer. I was conscientious in my work in the store, and assiduous in discovering new opportunities for sales. It was during this time that I placed our first advertisement in Boli's, in which I offered attractive terms to canvassing agents in rural areas, where there were no department stores.

"Do you really think that farmers' wives and such will take an interest in expensive stationery?" my father asked when I announced my intention of taking out the magazine advertisement.

"I am sure of it," I told him. In fact I was not sure at all, but I was willing to make the attempt. We had, for perhaps the first time in the history of the firm, the luxury of allowing one of my ideas to fail if it were its destiny to do so.

"I think we'd do better to stick with the cities," my father said, cocking his head to look as if the opinion had cost him a great deal of arduous thinking. "Do people do much social correspondence in the country?"

"Are you going to forbid me to place the advertisement?" I asked directly, and a little testily.

I think he was taken aback by my exhibition of mildly ill temper. "No," he replied, "no—not forbid it. You certainly have as much right as I to make such a decision." (Here he admitted for the first time a principle that I had acted upon since the day after he had added the words "& Son" to the front of the store.) "I was merely making a suggestion, but of course if you have your mind made up, you might as well go ahead with it."

I ought to mention here that my faith in the vanity of rural women was entirely justified, and to this day canvassing agents make up a large fraction of our sales. There is nothing a farm wife desires more than to prove to the world that she is just as good as her cousin in the big city. In the instructions I have written for our agents, I dwell particularly on that vanity, telling them frankly to emphasize what a social embarrassment it is to have one's writing obviously out of date or incorrect, and that the Bousted System is the surest means of achieving correctness in correspondence. I give them a few cautionary tales to tell of ladies who lost their standing at church or in town because of a single ill-written, scratchy, blotted letter,—a catastrophe which might have been avoided if the letter had been written on stationery properly matched to the writer's penmanship. I have read an article somewhere attributing a rise in the quality of rural penmanship to the activities of our agents and those of our imitators. —This is, of course, a digression; I mention it to show that I was still productive of new ideas even when I was miserable.

And I was miserable—I repeat it. I was the more so because I could not form in my mind an answer to my misery. Should I forget Gertrude? But Gertrude might almost certainly be my wife, whereas the divine, the inaccessible Miss Goode was as far above me as the celestial regions. I might as well be in love with a statue in the British Museum.

In love! Yes—that was the heart of the matter. I was not really in love with Gertrude, and I was in love with Amelia Goode. —Now, I would not have you suppose that I mean what imbecilic popular novels mean when their imbecilic heroes talk of being "in love." I should say that I was in love with Miss Goode in the same way that the stallion is in love with the mare; and, as the fence is the greatest frustration in the stallion's life, so the great obstacle in mine was the insuperable barrier of Miss Goode's wealth. I had money—more money than my father had ever seen in his life, as he never tired of remarking—but it was a few pennies in comparison with the vast Goode fortune.

This state of things went on for months. From spring into summer I courted Gertrude, without making any definite proposal; and from spring into summer I longed for Amelia, without ever having been so much as introduced to her. I think, sometimes, that I shall always be more susceptible to feminine beauty than other men; when I write that I was miserable on account of having merely seen a celebrated beauty a few times, the thing hardly seems credible. Yet it was so.

I will not say that the misery did me no good. I

believe that my consciousness of the vast difference in wealth between the Bousteds and the
Goodes made me more assiduous in cultivating
the Bousted fortune, small as it was. Still, misery
is the thing I most remember from that time;—
misery and labor, which alone had the power of
alleviating my misery, and of which I did a
prodigious amount. I cannot conceive of how I
got along without a whole office full of clerks to
sort out the correspondence from department
stores and canvassing agents; but I did, though at
the cost of leaving the work in the store more
and more in the hands of my father and Bradley.

Eventually, worn down by my longing for that
which it was not possible for me to obtain, I returned to Baucher—not, of course, the book itself, which was probably not to be found in all of
Pittsburgh and Allegheny, but to that review of
it which had become my holy writ. What, I
asked Baucher, would the truly wicked, truly
evolved man do in my situation? His answer
shone clearly through the reviewer's scornful
irony. The man who is truly wicked lets nothing
stand between himself and the object of his desires. The superior man brushes aside, or destroys, whatever would prevent him from reach-
ing his goal. In the case of his relations with the
weaker sex, the simple fact of woman's weakness
gives man an immeasurable advantage.

It is true, however, that law and custom give

women considerable protection. A rational analysis of the problem reveals that the difficulty would not lie in the indifference or even outright refusal of Miss Goode, which might be overcome by a trifling application of force, but rather in the laws and customs that protected her. If these latter could be rendered inoperative in some way, then I might be able to fulfill my desire.

It is impossible to describe with what vigor this conclusion impressed itself upon me. It was quite likely that I could have what I desired, if only it could be done in such a way that the irrational virtue of the mass of mankind did not stand in my way. But it would require daring and determination. Had I the daring spirit necessary to succeed?

As always, the question was answered as soon as it was posed that way. I must succeed, because I had dared myself to succeed.

CHAPTER XI.

*How I contemplated and plotted a monstrous crime,
with the unwitting cooperation of Gertrude Snyder.*

WHEN I CONSIDERED the matter rationally, it appeared to me that Gertrude Snyder must be essential to any scheme I might form for possessing Amelia Goode. Indeed, she was my only tangible link to the celebrated beauty. Furthermore, I was under no illusions as to the probability of my possessing Miss Goode permanently. —No, it would be a fleeting deed of darkness; and then, if I were successful, I should be to all appearances the same virtuous young man as before. For such a young man, Gertrude would still make a pleasant and perfectly respectable wife.

I was therefore as assiduous in cultivating my courtship of Gertrude as I was in expanding the

firm of Bousted & Son, and I flattered myself
that I had equal success in both endeavors. Our
sales continued to grow week by week, and
Gertrude continued to meet me for walks in the
park and other innocent pastimes. That is to say,
they were innocent in her eyes; but I had a double purpose in each of our meetings. I so contrived these visits with Gertrude that we were
likely to catch at least a glimpse of Amelia
Goode. I quickly discovered that Miss Goode was
almost a slave to habit. If she passed a particular
spot in her carriage at seven in the evening on a
Tuesday, then she could be relied upon to pass
that same spot at seven the next Tuesday as well.
West Park was her favorite haunt, and she could
be found either strolling or driving there almost
every evening. I took great pains to learn the
patterns of her drives, for she was often alone
then, though sometimes she had a coachman for
the victoria.

There were times when it was difficult to conceal my keen interest in Miss Goode's movements from Gertrude, and I had to employ considerable art.

"Here is Miss Goode again," Gertrude remarked on one such occasion, as we saw the familiar victoria approaching. "Oh, isn't she splendid?"

"Why, Gertrude," I remarked gaily, "if I
didn't know you better, I might almost suppose

you were envious!"

"Perhaps not envious," Gertrude returned as the two perfect black horses came nearer, "but who would not wish——"

Here she stopped for a moment as the carriage passed, exactly on schedule, as regular as the Pennsylvania Railroad. When the noise of hooves and wheels had receded, she resumed, still gazing at the back of the victoria.

"Oh, Newman, shall I ever ride in a carriage of my own?"

I took her hand in mine, and she turned to face me. "Gertrude," I said, "it will always be my most cherished ambition to see that you have whatever your heart could wish for. If honest labor and intelligent investment can procure it, you shall have it."

Gertrude blushed prettily. We walked on, and she did not relinquish my hand. At such a moment, with her delicate hand in mine, and her lovely face bathed in a golden evening light, I could almost believe that I could be happy with Gertrude alone, and that it would cost me no sorrow to give up my hopes of possessing Amelia Goode.

We walked in silence for a while; and then Gertrude said, in a low voice, "Perhaps you ought to grow a moustache."

At the time I had no idea why she had made that suggestion, and I did not respond to it directly. But when I returned to my room that evening, I looked hard in the mirror and decided that Gertrude was right. My face, which I had kept clean-shaven, still had a certain juvenile quality; with a moustache, I might make a more impressive appearance on the world's stage. I resolved to begin the experiment in the morning. Meanwhile, sleep called me, and I retired with pleasant thoughts of Gertrude that soon gave way to less virtuous thoughts of Amelia Goode.

The next morning was trying, and the morning after even more so. When my sisters discovered that I had left my upper lip unshaved, not through negligence, but with the deliberate intention of growing a moustache, there was no end to their raillery. "Perhaps you ought to try growing some radishes as well," Viola suggested, which was so preternaturally witty that it caused Camellia to snort like a carthorse.

On the other hand, when I saw Gertrude three days later, she seemed pleased that I had taken her suggestion. "It will suit you, Newman," she said with one of her enigmatic smiles.

I might as well say here that, although I have known many women in my life, not one of them could out-enigma Gertrude. It was impossible to tell what her smiles meant, and as impossible to tell what her tears meant. She was a cipher to me. It was, however, satisfying to have her approval for the moustache, which in a few more days began to look more like an ornament than like an unfortunate error in grooming.

As I write these words, I have beside me a small leather note-book in which I carefully tabulated the movements of Amelia Goode as I observed them. Each page is headed with the seven days of the week; then, if during that week I happened to see Miss Goode, I noted under the proper day the time, place, and circumstances. If she had been seen in the same place, at the same time, on the same day of a previous week, then I marked the most recent sighting with a star. In this way I learned her habits as well as she knew them herself; and, indeed, it seemed that, the more I observed her, the more regular her habits became. After two months of observation, I was able to predict with almost astronomical accuracy where she would be three evenings out of seven, which was surely all I needed for my wicked purpose.

Although, with the accumulated wisdom of my years, I can see that my scheme was rash, and liable to a thousand mishaps,—yet I still wonder whether a crime of passion had ever been plotted with such scientific rigor before. This note-book of mine gave me great pleasure during those weeks when I was plotting my enormity; it was almost as though, in possessing the knowledge of her habits, I was already in possession of some part of Miss Goode herself. The note-book was kept under my pillow, and the knowledge it contained allowed me to imagine that, in a certain sense, Amelia was my companion through the sweltering nights of July and August, when sleep was impossible until well past midnight, and my loneliness might otherwise have been insufferable. Indeed, it is a truth that I have understood only gradually, that much of the pleasure of a wicked deed lies, not in the commission of it, but in the contemplation of it beforehand.

One incident did occur during this period that complicated my efforts. I was sitting at dinner one evening when Viola, a mean-spirited smile on her face, spoke up:

"Father, were you aware that Galahad has been seeing a lady?" she asked with a voice that dripped sweet venom.

"Really?" my father responded, sounding oafishly pleased.

"Yes, Viola and I saw them in the park," Camellia offered with the same honeyed poison in her tone. "We saw her only from the back, of course."

"Which was fortunate for our digestions, I'm sure," Viola added.

"Yes, do warn us next time you're seeing her, Galahad," Camellia said with a labored sneer, "so that we do not see her face by accident and turn to stone." Though the girls had not seen Gertrude's face, they knew by deduction from

first principles that any girl who associated herself with their brother must be hideous beyond
description.

"I suppose she has no more than six or seven
fingers on each hand," Viola remarked after a
brief silence.

At this, for some reason, my choler rose to the
boiling point at last, and I actually stood up from
the table. "By heaven," I declared, "if you were
a man, I'd——"

Here my father actually intervened.

"Now, girls," he said, "you really mustn't
tease Galahad so. I'm sure he's done nothing of
the sort to you."

This, I believe, was the only indication he ever
gave me in his life that he was aware of my sisters' mistreatment of me. He was, at least,
scrupulously correct in his assertion that I had
never been deliberately unkind to them,—not
out of any absurd notions of decency, but simply
because it was obviously wise policy never to be
seen as anything other than the perfectly dutiful
son and brother.

"I think it's splendid if Galahad has a lady
friend," he continued. "First-rate."

"Yes, perhaps she has a couple of aged uncles
for you girls," I added, and immediately regretted having spoken. But my father, having said all
he could say on the subject of family harmony,
said nothing more, and refused to believe that he

had not restored good feeling to the table.

At any rate, I continued to see Gertrude, and now my father and my sisters were aware of it. Their awareness was rather inconsequential, I suppose, since things continued pretty much as before; but I could have done without my sisters' relentless teasing, and certainly without my father's congratulatory wink every time I left the house for an evening stroll with Gertrude.

I have probably never labored harder in my life than I did that summer. My first responsibility, I had decided early on, must be to the firm; and I believe I may say accurately that I discharged that responsibility in such a way that the firm had no cause for complaint. Money was beginning to come in from our canvassing agents; the department-store contracts were gratifyingly profitable; and sales at the store continued to increase. After some weeks of work, I was even able to train Bradley so effectively that he could be left to handle the female patrons by himself. I grant that it might have consumed less time and labor had I trained a Labrador retriever to do the same work; but I had no Labrador retriever, whereas I did have Bradley. The ladies, as I have already mentioned, were fond of him, especially the middle-aged middle-class matrons who made up the bulk of our patronage. But my father took a liking to him as well, so that Bradley took on much of the burden of keeping him entertained during the day. It had never occurred to me how much of my time had been wasted on entertaining my father until the arrival of Bradley relieved me of some of that responsibility.

My work for Bousted & Son in itself was a heavy labor, but I had other labors as well. I had my courtship of Gertrude to cultivate; this was by no means an unwelcome labor, but it did consume two evenings and an afternoon out of the week. Finally, my pursuit of Amelia Goode was by no means the least of my labors.

I have already intimated that I approached the matter scientifically, as it were. As summer wore on toward autumn, and my sister's wedding preparations grew so fevered that it was advisable for me to be out of the house anyway, I began my campaign in earnest. I took to haunting some of those places where Amelia was known to appear at certain times, especially in the park. The arboretum afforded many opportunities for concealment, so it was natural that I should concentrate my efforts there. Consulting my notebook, I chose an evening when Amelia would be driving past in her carriage (not the victoria, but a wicker ladies' summer carriage, which she always drove alone); then I simply strolled through the park myself, endeavoring to time my stroll so that I should meet Amelia just as she passed a certain dark thicket that might ultimately suit my purposes.

I must confess that I thought my first reconnaissance a poor piece of work. I arrived several minutes before Amelia passed that point, and was therefore compelled to walk back and forth in a short path; although I did my best to appear as a casual evening stroller, I seemed to attract the attention of a large man with a big stick, who eyed me suspiciously each time I passed. When at last Amelia did ride by, the man and I had to step out of her way, so that we were standing side by side, each fixing a suspicious gaze upon the other. When the carriage had passed, I vacated the area as quickly as I could, and marched back home in a foul temper. But I did not abandon my campaign.

My next expedition was more successful, in that I did not lose my nerve, and must have seemed an ordinary young gentleman out for an evening stroll of no particular consequence. Amelia passed at her scheduled time; there was no one else to see her pass but me, and I was careful not to direct my gaze directly toward her, so that she should not remember or suspect me. I might easily have accosted her at that very instant, had I not promised myself that I should only reconnoiter that evening, and not succumb to the temptation to commit my crime of passion in the heat of the moment. Any crime, to be suc-

cessful, must be the product of long and careful
planning, and this is never more true than with
crimes of passion. Invariably the crimes of which
one reads in the press, where at least the crime if
not the criminal has been detected, are crimes of
the moment, insufficiently thought out, and
committed under the influence of a passion that
clouds the judgment. I confess that I was in many
ways unwise in the planning of my outrage, but I
did at least possess the wisdom to see that it required planning.

I repeated my expedition the next week, and
once or twice a week after that for several more
weeks. Darkness fell earlier each week, but (as I
had hoped) the fading light did not deter Amelia
from riding at her appointed times. It would soon
be quite dark when she passed my chosen
thicket, which would suit my purposes admirably.

Gertrude accompanied me on some of my ex-
peditions, quite unaware of their true purpose.
"Here is Miss Goode again," she remarked on
one occasion when the 7:23 carriage passed,
right on schedule. "I wonder that she still drives
alone, now that it is dark."

"Well, the gaslights are bright enough most of
the way," I said. "And would misfortune dare
accost a Goode? Surely fate must have favored
such an illustrious family." I did not tell her how
much I had been thinking along the same lines as

she. Foolish Miss Goode! Did she not know that
danger lurked in the darkness? Had she no fear
of the shadows? I found myself absently twirling
my moustache as I thought about it.

My next reconnaissance expedition (as I had
been calling them in my own mind) to West Park
went much as before, except for one disturbing
observation. As I waited in the darkness for
Amelia to pass, I saw once again that large man
with the big stick whom I had seen on my earlier
reconnaissance. He was standing in the shadows
several yards down the drive. In the darkness I
could see little of his face, but something in his
manner convinced me that he was surveying me
with deep suspicion. I stood my ground, deeming
it more likely to arouse suspicion if I retreated.
The large man stood his ground as well. Amelia
passed on schedule; and, when I looked again for
the large man, he was gone. I went on my way
forming vague suspicions in my mind.

On my next stroll with Gertrude, the large
man made another appearance. I did not call
Gertrude's attention to him, and I did my best to
make him believe that my own attention was entirely absorbed by Gertrude. I was always careful
to be modestly affectionate with Gertrude, and
in this case I felt a bit more secure with her by
my side as Amelia's carriage passed. Once again,
the large man vanished when the carriage had
gone.

He was there again on my next venture, and now I began to entertain the most extravagant suspicions. I very nearly persuaded myself that the large man was some sort of spy in the employ of the Goode family, and that he knew, or at least suspected, my dishonorable intentions. My rational mind told me that my doubts were absurd, but I could not rid myself of the feeling that the large man's appearances were more than coincidental. He was, at any rate, an inconvenience; he intruded on my privacy. How was I to concentrate on my evil plot if he kept popping up at the most inconvenient times?

He did not appear when I made my next expedition, and I persuaded myself that my suspicions had been groundless; but he was back the night after that, and all my fears returned with him.

In the mean time my sister and Bradley were married. We paid Bradley well enough that they were able to set themselves up in a small apartment on Resaca-street, and I was rid of one pestilential sister. Viola attempted to make herself twice as odious to make up the loss, but she could not completely succeed: there was only one of her, after all. I suppose if a woman were writing this narrative, she would fill it with details of the wedding; I have forgotten them all, except the undeniable gratitude I felt toward Bradley for ridding me of Camellia. If gratitude is a virtue, then I admit my weakness; but my

life at home improved considerably with one of
my sisters gone, and I resolved that, as soon as
my business with Amelia was brought to a successful conclusion, I should rid myself of the
other sister as well—either by marriage or by
murder, whichever seemed most practicable.

You, my dear hypothetical reader of the future, must be nearly out of patience with me by
now. I have been preparing my crime against the
beautiful Miss Goode for more than twenty pages
in manuscript, and you must be wondering
whether I intend to fill the rest of the volume
with this pointless dithering. I could do so; I almost have a mind to do it. But I will not. I
abridge the last few weeks of my preparations by
saying that I continued much as before, gradually closing my grip on Miss Goode until her
habits were predictable to me down to the
minute. Sometimes I went alone, and sometimes
with Gertrude; sometimes I saw the large man
with the big stick, and sometimes I did not. I
hated that man: he was the one uncertainty in
my plan, and nothing at all could be accomplished on a night when he made an appearance.
Twice, after I had decided that, at last, the time
for action had come, I was forced to abandon my
plan when he came into view just after I arrived
at my station. My frustration cannot be described to someone who has never been in a similar situation; and it is not necessary to describe

it to anyone else.

But at last there came a night when I was determined to act. The sky was cloudy, so that the darkness in my chosen thicket would be complete; Miss Goode was scheduled to pass at 7:23; I knew exactly where I should be and what I should do to accomplish my object.

The day had been unseasonably warm, but now a brisk breeze had picked up; and the air was decidedly cooler, with even a slight chill. I found myself keenly aware of every aspect of my surroundings as I walked into the park. The absurd thought occurred to me that I must be feeling what a condemned man feels on his last walk to the gallows—absurd because, of course, it was Miss Goode who was condemned, not I. Every sound was louder to me; every leaf on the ground had its distinctive crunch; the odors of the mills and the grass mingled and presented themselves to my nostrils; the breeze puffed against my cheek, and I felt every puff distinctly; I heard the sound of hooves on the cobblestones in the distance, and the quiet tapping and shuffling of my own feet on the drive. My every sense was enlivened to a degree I had never felt before and have seldom felt since. It was a delightful sensation; and to my distant readers, if any such there be, I would happily recommend the commission of some enormous crime to stimulate the nerves and encourage the flow of the blood.

When at last I took my position in the little thicket I had chosen as my blind, I had great difficulty in keeping myself still and quiet. Every nerve craved action; every sinew was coiled like a watch-spring. I stood still, absently twirling my moustache, and feeling what the viper must feel before he strikes; and at last, after what seemed to be ages or aeons of waiting, I heard the distinctive sound of Miss Goode's carriage approaching.

From my blind I could see her as she came down the drive. She was driving alone, as she always did at 7:23 on Wednesdays. It would be only a moment before I should leap into the carriage, take the reins, force the carriage into the dark alcove under the bridge, and——

——But suddenly I saw a large figure bolt from the shadows not more than ten yards from where I stood. The carriage lurched wildly, and there was a muffled scream;—I saw for an instant the outline of a large walking-stick raised against the sky;—and at that moment a blind fury, a rage such as I had never known, overcame me. That man with the big stick was attacking my Amelia! Damn him to hell! After all my months of meticulous preparation, he had the gall to try to steal my prize! Without even thinking I leaped on the carriage as it passed, my arm already swinging, my clenched fist connecting with the jaw of my opponent. He lost his balance

and fell to the ground just as the carriage
bumped to a stop in the grass, the horse having
decided that all this activity behind was excuse
enough for slacking off. Amelia was screaming;
the man with the big stick was righting himself
and starting to run. I leaped out after him and
caught him under a gaslight, knocking his legs
out from under him and throwing him to the
ground. He began to fight back with some vigor.
But his only encouragement was self-preserva-
tion, whereas I had months of frustration to ani-
mate me. Painful blows landed on both sides, but
I hardly felt them at the time. I knew only my
rage, and I pressed my advantage until my opponent fell back on the drive, striking his head on
the pavement. He was still, and a quick look in
the gaslight suggested that he had been rendered
insensible by the blow.

I stood over him for a moment, until it occurred to me that I should feel a great deal better sitting down; so I gently lowered myself to
the grass.

I heard an angel's voice above me. "Dear sir,
you are hurt," it said, and I felt the softest hand
in the world lightly touching my forehead—a
touch that, soft and light as it was, still carried
unexpected pain with it.

"Not very much," I answered.

I remember nothing after that until my eyes
opened in a palatial chamber I had never seen

before. A moment later, the beautiful face of
Miss Amelia Goode filled my vision; and for an
instant I thought that perhaps I had died, and, in
spite of all my evil deeds, a merciful God had admitted me to heaven.

CHAPTER XII.

I enjoy the fruits of my wickedness, but am confronted with a difficult choice.

IT WAS NOT paradise, but it was as close to paradise as I had come in my short life. "Oh, dear sir—thank heaven!" Miss Goode exclaimed, looking intently into my eyes. I might have happily gazed into hers forever if I had been offered the opportunity. "You were hurt," she continued after some time, having evidently decided that I was capable of understanding her now. "We brought you here—I hope you'll forgive the presumption, but we didn't know your name, and the alternative was the Sisters of Mercy. I owe you such an incalculable debt that I insisted we must care for you ourselves. Can you speak yet?"

I tried the experiment: "Yack," I said. I cleared my throat and tried again: "Yes."

"Forgive my not having introduced myself. My name is Amelia Goode."

"Galahad Newman Bousted," I responded, using up most of my breath. If I had not been so breathless, I should certainly have continued, "but I go by Newman Bousted,"—but I did not.

"Galahad!" she repeated. "What a wonderfully apt name! Are you a knight-errant in the service of every lady in dire distress?"

"Am I?" I asked, doubtless looking like a wandering idiot let loose from the asylum.

"You poor man!" Her voice was full of concern and compassion. "My rescue has cost you so dearly!"

Rescue! In my disoriented state, I had not yet put together what had happened to me. I had beaten off another pirate intent on seizing my prize—so much I remembered now. But in Amelia's eyes I had rescued her from a fate worse than death! The extent of her misapprehension was so great it made my mind whirl. And even as it was whirling, my mind was telling me that here was a turn of events which must redound to my advantage.

"Any man in similar circumstances would have done the same," I said weakly. In a manner of speaking it was true: any man who had plotted to have his way with a divine beauty, only to see the prize nearly snatched out of his hands at the very last moment, would have attacked the confounded interloper in a blind fury. I know that Miss Goode, however, took another meaning.

"Few would be so bold as to beat off a man twice their size," Miss Goode replied. "If there is any small way—nay, any great way—I can be of any service to you, I hope you will not hesitate to make me aware of it."

I began to sit up. "I should hate to put you to any——"

But suddenly sitting up lost its attraction, and my head fell back on the pillow.

"Pray do not exert yourself," Miss Goode said. "Let me inform your wife that you are here, and then you really must stay with us until you have sufficiently recovered."

"Oh, I have no wife," I told her, and I noticed a subtle change in her physiognomy that I interpreted as a favorable omen. Then I thought of my family, and added, "But I do have a father who may be wondering where I am."

"Tell me where he is, and Sheridan will be dispatched at once to inform him."

I gave her our address on Beech-street, and with a promise to return shortly she went off to do her dispatching.

Meanwhile, I was left alone with my thoughts, which were beginning to order themselves in a more rational manner. First, I was growing aware of a beating pain in my skull. I cautiously felt my forehead, and discovered that a bandage was wrapped around my head; the pain inclined me to believe that the bandage was the only thing holding my skull together. As long as I was gazing on the divine face of Miss Goode, the pain had not obtruded upon my perception; but now that it had the field to itself, it made the most of its opportunity.

In order to distract myself from the pain, I made a careful examination of the room, which was nearly the size of two of the bed-rooms in our Beech-street house put together. It was furnished in the style of the antebellum age, though with concessions to the more artistic modern taste in its hangings and wallpaper. From the lack of obvious personal belongings I deduced that it must have been a guest-room; doubtless the house that could accommodate such a room as this must have a multitude of guest-rooms. I had begun to speculate on the size of the establishment when the door opened again to admit, not the radiant Miss Goode, but an old man who must, I decided at once, have been her father, old Colonel Goode of the Monongahela Glass fortune.

"Well," he said with a surprisingly hearty voice for one who looked so fragile, "you're with us now! You gave us a little fright, my boy, with all that blood. Amelia's been taking good care of you, has she? Splendid. If there's anything at all you need, don't hesitate to ask."

"Thank you, sir," I replied weakly. The weakness was not altogether feigned, but I was also beginning to decide on weakness as a matter of policy. It might prolong my stay if I gave the impression that I was too weak to go, and if I had a chance of spending any more time near the divine Miss Goode, I was willing to exaggerate my weakness. I did not yet know what use I might make of this opportunity, but I did know that it was not to be squandered.

Since old Colonel Goode will have something to do with the rest of my story, I suppose I ought to describe him. Of course everyone knows something about Pittsburgh's first millionaire;— the first of many, and perhaps the most beloved by the ordinary people of Pittsburgh and Allegheny. No scandal has ever sullied his fame, and I could honestly believe that the man's mind had never formed an impure thought. —But these things will come later. As for what I saw from my bed in the guest-room that night, he was an unusually small man, frail in construction, but quick and lively in his movements, with an admirably straight posture. His face showed no especial intelligence; a wispy beard adorned but did not conceal his chin, and his eyes sparkled under neat brows, but sparkled only with a na-

tive vivacity, and not with any unusual perception. He had lost most of the hair on his head,
and what remained was snowy white. Not a thing
was out of place on him: his collar was exactly
right, his jacket exactly symmetrical, his watch-
chain draped with apparently unconscious preci-
sion. He was the picture of prosperous virtue.

I am sorry to sweep him off the stage so soon
after introducing him, but Colonel Goode hur-
ried off to his next duty after only a few more
pleasant words of gratitude. He will return more
than once in these pages, however; we shall not
miss him long.

For a short time I was left alone again, but I
had scarcely had time to ponder my stratagem
for making use of my presence in the Goode
household when Amelia reappeared and drew a
side chair up to my bed.

"I have sent Sheridan to your father, Mr.
Bousted," she told me, "and now I shall not
leave your side until the danger is past."

"Danger?"

"Dr. Andick was very particular that you
should not be moved for at least four hours after
you regained consciousness. After that, he said,
the danger would be past, and you might be permitted to walk with caution—with *caution,* he
stressed. He thought you should not leave this
house until at least to-morrow morning."

"I do hate to be an invader, Miss Goode." I

did not hate it at all if it brought me so close to this incomparable beauty, but I believed that conventional politeness would conduce to my advantage.

"My champion will never be an invader in this household!" she replied with a radiant smile. O! reader, you may suppose that you have seen a radiant smile;—you may speak of the smiles that adorn the faces of the most celebrated beauties of your own age;—yet you have seen nothing worthy of that description, for you have not seen the smile of Amelia Goode!

For an hour or so more, Miss Goode spoke of inconsequential things—as though any word that dropped from such perfect lips could possibly be inconsequential—and I remember every word. I also remember that even then I felt a vague sense that Miss Goode was leaving something unsaid. I shall not burden you with the rest of the conversation, however; you, dear reader, who are most likely myself at a later age, would probably lose patience with me, though I confess it still gives me considerable pleasure to recall that first evening with Amelia.

It gave me no pleasure at all to have it interrupted by my own father, who burst so suddenly through the door that, had I been a man of weaker constitution, I might well have succumbed to some sort of nervous fit. He was followed closely by my sister Viola, and at only

slightly less distance by old Colonel Goode. My
father made the most appalling show of concern
for my welfare; and Viola attempted, if possible,
to outdo him, as if she really did prefer that I
should live rather than die.

This ugly display of sentimentality made me
wish I could slip back into that unconscious state
from which I now regretted awakening—especially when old Colonel Goode very graciously
introduced himself to my father, and my father,
having ascertained that this was indeed the same
Colonel Goode of whom all Pittsburgh and Allegheny spoke in reverent whispers, replied with
the most oafish forthrightness, "You know, I'm a
businessman myself."

I must, however, confess that I felt a secret
thrill when Amelia immediately asked whether
he was the Bousted of Bousted's Graded Stationery, and my father, in the full flush of his
ridiculous paternal pride, told her that it had
been entirely my invention. She knew my
Graded Stationery—nay more, she used the
Grade 8 every day, or so she said. Every day,
those impossibly delicate fingers swept over the
smooth, perfectly sized surface I myself had
specified. It was almost as if she had been touching me for months without my knowing it. What
bliss it would have been just to be a single sheet
of paper!

I shall not weary myself with recounting every

fatuous word that dribbled from my father's lips. Miss Goode was very gracious to him, telling him that the father of such a son must be something of a hero himself; my father at least had the sense to blush at that remark. My sister Viola was mostly mute, which is certainly the way I prefer her; I believe she was overawed by her surroundings, since she had never before been in a building as large as the Goode house unless it was holding a temperance meeting.

My father and Viola stayed far too long, and my father was far too profuse in his gratitude to the Goodes when Amelia made it clear that she would not allow me to be moved until the morning. At last, however, my father took Viola away with him, and (old Colonel Goode having retired) I was left alone with my nurse.

By this time, but for the roaring pain in my head (which a bit of Colonel Goode's excellent brandy had blunted somewhat), I had recovered most of my vigor, and I was far from ready to go back to sleep. Miss Goode was also invigorated by the excitement of the evening's events. She was ready to talk, and I was more than ready to hear her voice. Yet as she spoke of this and that, I was more and more certain that there was something she wished to say beyond the inconsequential trivialities that made up our conversation. I believe that the weather has never been more thoroughly observed, catalogued, and subjected to the minutest analysis than it was during the hour after my father and hers left us alone. But at last we had exhausted even the endless conversational possibilities of temperature and precipitation, and we both fell silent for some time.

"Mr. Bousted," Miss Goode said at last, "I believe I owe you—a confession is what perhaps I ought to call it. I feel a certain—a certain responsibility for your injuries."

"Certainly any decent man who happened to see what I saw—an innocent woman assaulted by the basest ruffian—would have reacted the way I did. It was mere chance that I happened to be the one who——"

"But it was not mere chance," she declared with a sudden rush of feeling. "I was responsible —more responsible than you know. It was not chance that placed you in harm's way. It was my own—my own folly."

I made no answer; I simply gazed at her with incomprehension.

"I was imprudent," she continued. "I exposed myself to more danger than—than a young lady ought to be exposed to."

"Surely a young lady has a right to take a drive through the park without molestation," I said. How wonderfully sincere I sounded!

"But it is not prudent for her to drive after dark, except that—except that—Oh, Mr. Bousted, I have been such a fool! I ought to have listened to my father's gentle admonishments, but I —but I wanted to see you."

These last few words were spoken so softly that at first I was not at all sure I had heard them correctly. "But, Miss Goode, what could you mean by that? Until to-night——"

"Oh, doubtless you do not remember it, but you have seen me before. We passed in the street and I saw your face. Such a kind face! I remembered your face, though I saw you only a moment. And then I saw you again, and—and then I began to see you walking in the park. So then —and, oh, I know it was unpardonable folly—I came back the next evening at the same time, and you were there again. And I went back again, and again, and I began to discover your habits. You were as regular as clockwork, Mr. Bousted! I began—oh, I am sorry, Mr. Bousted! —I began to keep a note-book, and I recorded the times when I had seen you; and then I would go back at those times to see you again. So, Mr. Bousted, you would not have been exposed to danger had it not been for my folly, and I cannot expiate my sin except—except by asking you to forgive me."

Twice in my short life up to that moment, the world had turned upside-down: the thing I had always thought was the floor had turned out to be the ceiling. And, marvelous to tell, both times

had been in the same night. I had supposed myself to be an abductor, a defiler of innocence,
and found myself a hero; I had supposed myself
to be the hunter, and had found myself the prey.
I am sure that Miss Goode had an unobstructed
view of my tonsils as I recovered from the shock
of her revelation. For some time, there was silence in the room; then, when she spoke again,
she was on the verge of tears.

"Oh, Mr. Bousted, what have I done? I can see
that——"

"Nothing could be more flattering"—I hastily
interrupted her before she could say anything I
might regret—"Nothing could be more flattering, or—or more gratifying, and if I hesitated to
forgive you, it was because I could find nothing
to forgive. How could any man with blood in his
veins be displeased to find—to find that—well, I
mean to say, Miss Goode, I am not displeased."

She smiled slightly, although she would not
look at me directly. I had succeeded in putting
her a little more at her ease, and now it was time
to turn this astonishing development to my advantage. My brain was whirling, and all thoughts
of the pain in my head had vanished. Opportunity was here for the grasping.

"Indeed," I continued, "I do recall having
seen you on more than one occasion. You do
yourself an injustice if you suppose you could
pass by a man with eyes in his head, however

briefly, and make no impression upon his memory."

At this she did turn to face me, and her smile is impressed so deeply on my recollection that I can even now close my eyes and bring up the picture of it like a magic-lantern show.

How I should love to linger over this first encounter,—to savor each subtle change in Amelia's expression, each musical syllable of her delightful conversation! Yet I could fill a book with this night, and still not be done with it. I must therefore reduce my narration to a brief epitome. I talked with Amelia until two in the morning, at which the striking of a little clock on the mantel reminded us both that it was very late. Bidding me good-night with a fondness that would, to an uninformed observer, have suggested a longer acquaintance, Amelia promised to see me in the morning, and turned down the gas as she left the room. In the darkness I made some attempt to order my thoughts; but sleep overcame me almost immediately, and I slept a sound and blissful sleep until just before eight in the morning.

When I woke, it took me some time to recollect where I was. Not being in the habit of paying overnight visits to millionaires, I had no previous experience of waking in such a luxurious chamber as this one, which bore a very different aspect with the morning sun streaming in

through the tall windows. I began to recall the
events of the night before, and the sweet face of
Amelia Goode rose up in my mind's eye. But
then I was suddenly seized with an irrational terror that I must have been found out: that somehow, as I slept, the true motive for my presence
in the park must have become apparent. I tried
to use my reason to reassure myself, but my reason was not responding well to my commands. In
fact my mind was trying to find its way through
a fog of pain, the worst head-ache I had ever suffered. I could only imagine the fury of the
Goodes; perhaps even now they had summoned
the constabulary, or an angry mob with torches
(why they should require torches in bright daylight I cannot say, but in every novel with an angry mob torches were an indispensable part of
the equipment). I very nearly leaped straight up
from the bed when the door to the hall swung
open, and I fully expected to be either taken into
custody or beaten to death with sticks.

"Good morning, sir," said the voice from the
doorway. It was not the voice of one who intended to bludgeon me. An older man, impecca-
bly dressed, with another suit of clothing draped
over his arm, was observing me benevolently.
When he could see that he had my attention, he
continued. "Miss Goode hopes you will pardon
the liberty, but we have pressed your trousers
and coat. There are one or two spots that will re-

quire the attention of your tailor, but you should be quite presentable in the mean time."

"Thank you," I said a bit uncertainly, as I adjusted my mind to the thought that I was not to be haled away to the gallows.

"If you feel well enough to rise, Miss Goode has held breakfast."

"I'm certainly well enough to rise," I said with more good cheer than I felt. No head-ache, however severe, would induce me to miss breakfast with the angel of Allegheny.

"Very good, sir," the old man replied. He stayed there, almost but not quite smiling, and it gradually became clear to me that he intended to remain while I rose and dressed. And so he did. He was an active participant in the dressing: for the first time since I had learned to dress myself, I allowed myself to be dressed by someone else. This was what it was like to be truly rich: to have someone to attend to one's most inconsequential needs—not even to have to dress oneself. I was even more certain now that I must have that life for my own.

Breakfast confirmed me in that opinion. The most delightful part was the presence of Amelia, of course, but I was not immune to the other pleasures of a table laden with what I then considered luxurious delicacies. Nor was I dead to the delight of being conveyed back to our little house in a carriage nearly the size of our parlor.

"Such a grand house," Viola said a little later on, as we sat in the dining-room for luncheon. My father had left Bradley entirely in charge of the store, which was not a comforting thought; but I resolved to put off my worries for the day and enjoy, for once, the favorable attention of my sister, who insisted that she must nurse me until I had recovered.

"Yes," I agreed, "it is an elegant place."

"And what an impression you made on Miss Goode!" she continued. "It's obvious she thinks the world of you."

"She is merely grateful for what, after all, any gentleman of spirit would have done." I suppose I hoped she would disagree and insist that I had been heroically brave: by now I had really begun to think of myself as Amelia's rescuer, rather than the man from whom, but for the timely intervention of fate, she would have prayed to be rescued. But Viola would not give me the satisfaction of contradicting me.

"Oh, she is very grateful," Viola continued. "The way she looked at you, I should have said she was a good bit more than grateful. Oh, dear, what will your poor Gertrude think?"

I give you my word, dear reader (though you must know by now that my word is worth nothing), that, until that moment, I had not thought of Gertrude since I set out on my fateful expedition the night before. What, indeed, would

Gertrude think? And what was I going to do about her?

CHAPTER XIII.

Gertrude or Amelia?

THE CHOICE THAT faced me was difficult, but only because so much of the knowledge I wanted for making my decision was unknowable. I had to choose between Gertrude and Amelia; and, put that way, the choice must obviously be Amelia. Gertrude was pretty and pleasant, but Amelia was both the most beautiful girl in Allegheny and the richest. In my foolish youth I found her face more attractive than her money;—but I was not insensible to the attraction of her money.

Gertrude, however, was a bird in the hand. Was it reasonable to abandon the near certainty of Gertrude for the distant possibility of Amelia? It was certainly true that Amelia had said some very encouraging things to me; but was not the difference in our position an insuperable barrier to any hope of marriage? And, now that I was definitely known to her, the alternative to marriage that I had proposed to myself was clearly impossible. It was marriage or nothing. (Here the alert reader may have noticed that I did not consider the possibility of seduction. So little did I know of the ways of women in those youthful days that I supposed what I desired would never be willingly given, and must be taken either as a duty of marriage or by force.)

Yet, as I retired that evening, visions of Amelia's beautiful face crowded every other thought out of my mind. I tried to summon up Gertrude to give her defense in the court of my imagination, but she refused my summons. Amelia was all I saw; Amelia was my only thought. In the darkness I was certain that my choice must be Amelia; and if perhaps it could have remained dark, I might have made my choice. But daylight brought back rational thought, and rational thought brought back doubts. Or perhaps the truth was simply that I had not yet given my soul completely over to darkness.

Daylight also brought an end to my brief respite from responsibility for the store. It was bad enough to have left it momentarily in Bradley's hands, but I was certainly not such a fool as to leave him holding the reins two days running.

But in fact my worries were groundless.

I greeted him with my usual "Good morning, Mr. Bradley," and he greeted me with his usual glassy gaze and inarticulate grunt. But then I turned immediately to the ledger, and I discovered that the receipts from the day before were not a whit diminished. In fact, we had done better than usually.

"We did very well yesterday," I said to Bradley.

He looked at me, and then at the ledger, and nodded, or perhaps merely twitched his head.

"I ought to say, *you* did very well, Mr. Bradley," I added, trying to encourage him to say something. But there was no sound from him.

"Well, I'm very pleased," I continued. "Father, look at this. The store did quite well with Bradley in charge."

"First-rate!" my father opined, without really looking at the numbers on the page at all.

So I began to discover one more facet of this Bradley: he was very much less of a fool when I was not near by. In fact, as the day wore on, two regular patrons stopped in to tell me how well "the new man" had done in serving them yesterday. The thing puzzled me a little at first, but I suppose I had no reason to be puzzled. I had taken care that he should fear me at our first meeting. The stratagem was perfectly justified under the circumstances, but I ought not to wonder that the impression I had made on him then had lingered. At any rate, I resolved to experiment a little more with my brother-in-law. He might prove more useful than I had anticipated.

As for Gertrude, it astonishes me now to relate that I actually lost sleep over her. I even felt some remorse—I blush to recall it now, but I did —at the thought of rejecting her after having given her every indication that I intended to marry her. In extenuation I can only plead my extreme youth. I had assumed the responsibilities of a life devoted to wickedness at a time of life when the temptations to good are multifarious and incessant.

All day in the store, my mind revolved the one great question: Gertrude or Amelia? —I do not mean to say that I was negligent: none of the clerks' wives and superannuated spinsters who came to have their writing classified would have surmised that my mind was elsewhere. I gave them the service they expected, looking directly into their eyes as I explained to them where their writing fitted on the Bousted scale. Yet still I was plagued by that dreadful indecision. Gertrude or Amelia? Amelia the perfect beauty, or Gertrude the delightful companion? Amelia the rich and far above me, or Gertrude the poor but within my grasp?

I continued my inward battle as my father and I rode the horse-car back to Allegheny, and I

had nearly reached the conclusion that it must
be Gertrude. In my young and inexperienced
mind it seemed the more reasonable choice.
Taking into account my own more and more urgent desires, a speedy union appeared to be almost a necessity; it could very probably be effected with Gertrude, but with Amelia I had only
begun an acquaintance which, reason told me,
could not be very likely to terminate in marriage, so insuperable did the gap between us
seem.

Such were my thoughts when I returned to
our house to find a letter from Amelia. I knew at
once that it had come because Viola accosted me
as I was still taking off my coat.

"A letter came for you," she announced with
that artificial lilt that I verily believe can be produced only by an older sister, "from your *friend*
Miss Goode." She pronounced the word *friend* as
though it could carry a heavier load of innuendo
than any other word in the English language.

"Probably inquiring after my health," I
replied; and I took the letter with a great show
of indifference, nor did I open it until well after
supper, when I was alone in my own room.

She did inquire after my health, but there was
more to the letter than that. I have kept the letter, and I will insert it here at length, so that, in
my own future perusal of this chapter in my life,
I may feel yet again the thrill of reading Amelia's

own words.

Dear Mr. Bousted,——

In a moment of weakness, I made a confession which I ought perhaps not to have made; but since I have already laid indiscretion upon imprudence, it would be futile to pretend I had said nothing. Nor would I be showing reasonable gratitude to one to whom I owe so much—perhaps my very life—if I were at all dishonest with you.

I write to express that gratitude to you once again, but also in the hope of continuing that acquaintance which my imprudence has so happily purchased for me, though at such a painful cost to yourself.

Oh! Mr. Bousted, you must think me the most selfish creature in the world, but I am glad that such a ruffian accosted me—I dare even to say that I am glad that you were injured, if it gained for me the privilege of tending to your injuries. Of course I hope you are well now, and I could never truly wish you harm; but I struggle to express how much I hope for another visit from you. If you can find it in your heart to forgive my folly, and now my impertinence as well, I pray you write to me, and tell me that, somehow, you will see me again.

This marvelous, this astonishing letter was written on two sheets of Bousted's Grade 8 and signed simply "Amelia Goode." The No. 8 is a very good match for her careful, yet confident, writing, showing that the sales clerk at Boggs & Buhl (where she must have bought it, since I should certainly have remembered if she had come to my store) had indeed mastered the elements of my system.

Until I read Amelia's letter, I had been very nearly certain that the victory must go to Gertrude; now it was quite clear that Amelia must be my choice. If she was of such a mind as to write such a letter as this, surely my battle was already half-won; the walls were breached which a moment before had seemed impregnable.

I did not hesitate, therefore, but immediately took pen in hand and dashed off a reply. I have not a copy by me, for in my haste I took no time to copy it out; but I recall telling her that I was as glad of our meeting as she was, and that I had not ceased to be astonished by the singular good fortune which had brought us together; and, having subjoined such words of flattery as came most naturally to my unskilled pen, I closed with a wish to see her at the earliest possible moment.

After that letter, I composed another, this one addressed to Gertrude Snyder. This second letter was very short: I said nothing but that I should like to see her the next evening, as I had something particular to say to her.

In these transactions it is very possible that my youth and inexperience served me well. If I were doing the same thing to-day, I should not have let go of the bird in the hand until I had definitely captured the one in the bush. I should have kept Gertrude supposing that I was within days of asking for her hand. My eagerness to pursue a connection with Amelia, however, led me to cast Gertrude aside; she was now an encumbrance of which I wished to rid myself at the earliest opportunity. How fortunate it seemed now that I had not made any definite proposal to her!

Yet it was not a pleasant prospect to me, this meeting with Gertrude. I received a note from her the next day agreeing that we must speak, and suggesting a walk in the park as suitable to that purpose; and it was, if you can credit the assertion, only as I read her note that I realized she must be expecting me to propose marriage at last! "I had something particular to say to her," I had told her in my letter. What else could such words indicate to a young lady?

It was therefore my mission to dash Gertrude's hopes just when I had raised them to the highest peak. That seemed very hard—very hard indeed. Only a fortifying dose of Baucher gave me the courage to keep our appointment.

It was an unseasonably warm afternoon in October, and the park was more than usually filled with strollers and promenaders. Gertrude was waiting for me at our usual meeting-place on the south end of the bridge. I could not help seeing that she was a beautiful girl; if there had been no Amelia, I might have considered myself uncommonly fortunate to have Gertrude. But there was an Amelia;—I reminded myself of that.

"It's a very fine afternoon," Gertrude remarked as we began strolling together.

"Very fine indeed," I agreed.

"I think it's uncommonly warm for so late in the season," she added.

"It is," I said; and then, feeling as though I ought to say something more, I added, "but it might well be the last warm day before the cold weather sets in."

These observations are exceedingly dull to record, but the weather furnished us with the theme for our discourse over the next quarter-hour or so; and to talk about the weather with a beautiful girl on a fine October afternoon, with the colored leaves tumbling through the air all around, is as great a pleasure as any I can think of at the moment,—if only the sword of Damocles is not hanging over your conversation.

At last we came to the base of the monument, which, from its situation away from the main-traveled paths and somewhat below the bridge, afforded us a little measure of privacy; and here I had determined to make my speech, which I had prepared and rehearsed beforehand.

"Gertrude," I began, "when I wrote to you yesterday, I said that I had——"

"Newman, please," she said suddenly, quite uncharacteristically cutting me off. "I know already what you intend to say to me."

"I really don't think——"

"I do, Newman." Her words began to pour out in a torrent; she was more animated than I had ever seen her, and there was simply no possibility of interrupting her. "Did you think I hadn't seen you working up your courage—thinking over what you would say to me? Oh, Newman, I have seen how you look at me, and heard how your voice changes when you speak to me, and though you may think your heart has secrets, I know them all, my poor man! And I knew that this moment would come, and I struggled with myself—what would I say? how would I answer? —and, oh, how I wished, how I prayed that I could make you happy, for I never met a man more deserving, more worthy, but oh!—Newman, I cannot marry you! I ought to marry you, I ought to love you with my whole heart, but— but I love another!" At this her tears began to flow, but she went on with hardly a pause for breath. "I love another! I have been false to you all these months, hoping and praying that my heart would change, that I could give you the answer you deserve, and the answer all reason tells me I ought to give you, but no,—my heart will not obey reason, and it must love one who I am sure is infinitely less worthy, but,—but he is a good man, Newman, and I do love him!"

At this her tears overcame her completely, and she hid her face in her hands, leaving me standing at sixes and sevens for the moment, wondering what the passers-by must be thinking of me.

But on the whole the conversation had been completely satisfactory from my point of view. Instead of cruelly dashing a young girl's hopes, I was now in a position to show grace and nobility in the face of rejection.

"My dear Gertrude," I said gently and quietly, as though my heart were breaking but I had determined to suppress my feelings, "no man worthy of that name could ever wish anything before your happiness. I don't deny—it would be futile to deny—my own feelings of disappointment. But that same strong regard for you which causes my disappointment compels me always to put your happiness before my own. If you are happy, I am happy; and if my happiness is admittedly imperfect, still it is genuine for all that."

This was a very pretty speech, don't you think? I was quite proud of it. It had its desired effect on Gertrude, who wept all the more and declared that I must be some sort of angel, and perhaps she ought to——but here I cut her off,

lest she be tempted to reconsider. I told her
frankly that she must follow her heart, and that,
if she had any regard for my happiness as well as
hers, she must not allow any mistaken sympathy
for me to cloud her judgment; for surely I could
never be happy in possession of a heart that
could never be truly mine, and it was better for
me in the long run to endure disappointment
now, however it might sting, than to live a life of
misery.

When at last we parted, she had recovered
marvelously, and was actually smiling that rare
and beautiful smile of hers, which for a moment
almost made me regret that I had got rid of her
so easily. She promised that she would ever be a
true friend to me, and of course I promised her
the same. Then she turned and left me.

I did not walk home with her as I usually did;
but I did stand and watch as she walked away,
calculating that it might be better to be seen
gazing after her with regret if she should happen
to look backward. In the event, however, she did
not look backward.

Thus did I rid myself of Gertrude, and I was
free to turn my attention completely to the conquest of Amelia. And so I did;—or, rather,
nearly completely. I was distracted for some little time by a scheme for disposing of my elder
sister.

CHAPTER XIV.

How I disposed of my pestilential sister Viola, and how I prevented my friend Mr. Snyder from behaving as a gentleman.

I<small>T</small> <small>DID</small> <small>NOT</small> take my sister Viola a long time to discover that there had been a definite break between Gertrude and me. I told her as much of the history of our parting as was suitable for her to hear: viz., that Gertrude had confessed to loving another, and that I of course had acted the noble part and refused to stand in the way of her happiness. Gertrude certainly believed that version of the story, and why should not Viola believe it as well?

She did believe it, since it fitted neatly with her prevailing assumption that her brother was of no account in the world. "My poor brother," she said when I had related my sad tale. "Your Gertrude found a better man—one of the beggars on Liberty-street, perhaps, or a ragpicker from the Point. It is very fortunate for her, of course, that she discovered her mistake in time. But how sad for you to lose the only girl who would even look at you! You must be broken-hearted."

Thus she alternated between congratulations to Gertrude on her fortunate escape from my clutches and the most nauseatingly saccharine and ironical expressions of sympathy for my disappointment. Viola had a way of blighting even my triumphs;—and in this case she had all the more opportunity to be a blight, since my very triumph in ridding myself so easily of Gertrude must be presented to the rest of the world as a bitter defeat.

Not for the first time I considered how much better my life might be without Viola than with her. But how to be rid of her? Murder might be simple and direct, but as an answer to my difficulties it seemed to present too many difficulties of its own. I had read in various novels of poisons that could not be detected, but as a general principle it looks odd if a young person suddenly falls dead when up to that moment she has been as healthy as an ox—an animal with which Viola shared divers other attributes as well.

No, the only means that presented itself to my attention of ridding myself of Viola was the same one by which I had eliminated Camellia. Some besotted oaf must marry her and take her away with him.

Where does one find besotted oafs? It has been my experience that there is no sister so loathsome but that some fool will think her a perfect angel. One has merely to be observant. In the case of Viola, I recalled the timid, if not positively ghostly, clerk across Wood-street from our store. Something might be made of him, though it might take a crowbar, or blasting-powder, to set him in motion.

In the mean time, something must be done about Amelia. I considered what I might do and how I might do it, when lo! I came home and discovered that it had all been done for me. Viola was waving a card almost in my face.

"An invitation!" she almost sang. "An invitation to a ball! At the home of Colonel Goode and his daughter!"

She swirled around as if she were waltzing, making me cringe when I thought of the damage she would do to her partner's feet.

"First-rate!" my father responded with a tooth-baring smile. "I can see you're happy about it."

"It's the Goodes' ball!" she crowed as she continued to swirl through the entry. I braced the hall-tree in anticipation of a collision as she swept past it. "Only the very best families of Allegheny go to the Goodes' ball! Oh, and you're invited, too. I must have a new gown!"

Indeed the entire family had been honored with this invitation, but of course Viola saw it as her very own triumph, an acknowledgment, tardy but welcome, that society had at last recognized her worth. That her new position was owed entirely to me in every possible way seemed not to have occurred to her. On the contrary, it was quite apparent to her that she had achieved her elevation on her own merits;—an accomplishment made all the more admirable for having been achieved in spite of her being saddled with a brother like me.

At any rate, she was triumphant, and must have not only a new gown for the occasion, with a bustle of absurd if not positively dangerous dimensions, but also—as she thought more about it—new shoes, new gloves, and everything else she could think of to spend money on. For that reason, she rode into town with us the next morning, intending to pay visits to all the purveyors of feminine equipment on Wood-street. And when we reached our store, there was that clerk across the street staring out the window at Viola; nor did I fail to note her secret smile when she briefly met his gaze. I took the opportunity to ask Viola directly whether she knew that young clerk across the street; she answered in a very quiet voice that she did not, and blushed the most violent shade of purple.

Soon Viola set off about her business, and our own store filled up with the usual assortment of schoolmarms and shopkeepers' wives. My own mind, though I tended to the customers with my usual assiduity, was filled with thoughts of Amelia. I imagined myself taking her aside at some opportune moment during the ball and pouring out my heart to her; and, of course, in my imagination she reciprocated my affection, and, after some reluctance, accepted a chaste kiss which promised more fervent expressions of affection to come. How my imagination differed from the reality you shall see soon enough; but it was a very pretty picture I painted for myself, and it kept the greater part of my mind occupied, while the lesser part examined one dreadful scrawl after another.

I happened to look up after sending one difficult matron on her way with a set of Grade 3 and a dozen pens to match, and by merest chance I saw a quite unexpected sight. It had been a grey day all morning, but just after noon the sun began to appear, and by about two it was shining with as much force as it could muster so late in the year on the storefronts on the opposite side of the street. In the one directly across from us a patch of sunlight made part of the interior clearly visible, and with widening eyes I beheld my own sister in earnest conference with the clerk. It was certainly not one of the stops in her expedition to conquer the purveyors of finery and frippery; this store sold lamps and lamp-oil. She could have only one reason for being there.

Now, I might simply have allowed nature to take its course, but nature had not the desperate desire that I had to see Viola married as soon as possible. At that moment I decided that I must intervene and give nature a helpful shove.

The scheme I contemplated was cruel, deceptive, and altogether wicked; but my conscience was learning to bow to my will, and the wickedness of it was now rather an attraction than otherwise. For the rest of the day, even as I tended to the customers, I formed in my mind the exact words I would use, so that, by the time we had ushered out the last schoolmarm and closed up the store, I had already played out the scene a dozen times in my imagination.

I sent my father, my sister, and Bradley off with the explanation that I had a few things I wished to arrange, and would follow them on a later car. They left, my father and Bradley both laden with bundles enough to outfit a regiment of Violas, and Viola between them carrying nothing but her umbrella. As soon as they were on the car and out of sight, I locked up the store and marched across the street, where I pushed my way through the lamp-dealer's door just as the young clerk was about to lock it.

"I'm sorry to say we're closed for——"

I cut him off. "I have no interest in lamp oil," I told him. "I came to speak to you personally."

"To me? I'm afraid I don't——"

"Look here, man, I don't have time to shilly-shally, nor would I if I could. I came to find out what the devil is going on between you and my sister." Here I looked him straight in the eye, and moved close enough that he could feel my breath on his face. I had read a novel once—I have no other memory of it now—in which the hero was much intimidated by feeling the villain's breath upon his face, and it was necessary that I should intimidate this fellow.

I believe I created the desired impression. "Your sister?" the man croaked out, looking altogether like a thief caught robbing the poor-box.

"I don't know what your intentions are toward Viola," I continued, "and to be quite frank with you I was ready to snap you in two." By this time he had his back against the counter and was perilously close to knocking over three or four bottles of whale-oil. "My sister, however, seems to be fond of you,—with what reason I am sure I cannot say,—and my sister, sir, means the world to me. I cannot bear to see her unhappy."

At this I stood up—for he had been leaning backward until his back was nearly flat on the counter, and I had been lowering over him—and stepped back a little to give him a sudden sensation of release. "So you are very fortunate," I continued. "in that, for the sake of my sister's happiness, I have decided not to snap you in two, —provided that your intentions are honorable."

"Oh, of course——they——I mean to say that I——"

"And by 'honorable,'" I added, interrupting his stammered assurances, "I mean that she must have received a proposal of marriage by no later than closing-time to-morrow. If she has not, I shall be forced to assume that you had no other intention than to trifle with a young girl's affections." I did my best to breathe on his face again for a moment before adding, "—which I am certain is not the case. There should, therefore, be no difficulty whatsoever about our arrangement."

"Oh, none whatsoever," he agreed, with a sickeningly forced smile.

"Splendid," I said with an equally forced smile. "And one more thing: it is imperative that you say nothing to my sister of my visit here. If she supposed that your asking for her hand proceeded from any other motive than pure love for her, it would naturally break her heart." I spoke the words "break her heart" in such a way as to remind him that I stood ready to avenge any unhappiness he might cause my sister.

"I understand perfectly," he assured me.

"Very good." I grasped his limp hand and shook it heartily. "Then I look forward to congratulating you both to-morrow afternoon." And I turned and left the store.

How delightful it would be to feel as confident as I had endeavored to appear during this interview! The clerk—I have called him "young," but in fact he was several years older than I was—was not a small man: slender, but quite tall, with a shape rather like that of a heron. If I had misjudged his character, the encounter might have gone very badly for me. Even as I left the front door of his store, I wondered whether, once the direct intimidation of my presence was removed, he might reconsider his promise. I should not know until the morrow.

Meanwhile I had an evening to get through with my father and my sister. Without Camellia in the house, poor Viola was forced to regale her two male relations with tales of bargains in silks. I noted that she was silent with regard to the lamp-dealer's store, and I could not resist the opportunity to watch her turn purple again.

"I wonder you didn't remember to pick up some lamp-oil while you were running up and down Wood-street," I said with studied diffidence. "I don't think we have more than a week's worth left. Perhaps if you go shopping again to-morrow——"

"I certainly can't carry a gallon of whale-oil," she said crossly. "It must weigh a hundred pounds. You might as well ask me to carry the whale." But I noted with satisfaction that her face had achieved the desired purple shade.

That evening, when I retired to my own bed-room, I spent some time composing a letter to Amelia; but, after crumpling five or six sheets successively, I gave up the attempt, put out the lamp, and turned down the gas. I had been para-lyzed by the idea that whatever I wrote to Amelia must be perfect of its type, and each of my attempts fell short of perfection. I mention these failed letters only to illustrate the agitated state of my mind at the time.

It does not amuse me to prolong the narration of Viola's abbreviated courtship. It is enough to say that, the next afternoon, she appeared with her clerk beside her, who very nearly choked himself before he succeeded in asking my father for his daughter's hand in marriage. When the question was finally posed, I saw my father hesi-tate for an instant; but I rushed forward to con-gratulate both Viola and her clerk. My father, caught up in the general good cheer, readily gave the assent I had already taken for granted, and the betrothal was accomplished.

It was certainly a happy day for me;—the more so because, when we all came home, a letter from Amelia was waiting for me. Viola was too full of her own triumph even to notice that I had received a letter, and immediately after supper she went out to confer with Camellia on the wedding plans, my father accompanying her so that she would not have to walk alone in the dark. That left me alone to read the letter from Amelia; and I had just opened and unfolded it when there came a most horrendous pounding at the door.

An ordinary knock I might have left for Mrs. Ott to answer or not, according to whether she affected to hear it, but this pummeling was so insistent, so incessant, that I felt sure it must betoken some desperate emergency. I leaped from my chair in the front parlor and strode quickly to the entry, where I flung the door open and stepped aside as my old friend Snyder fell into the room.

He did not fall flat on his face, but he avoided that catastrophe only by a wonderfully intricate series of steps that a French dancing-master would have envied. He braced himself on the settle, set down a small case he was carrying, and recovered himself for a moment. Then he whipped around to face me.

"Bousted!" he shouted, much too loud, so that he seemed to be taken aback by the sound himself. He lowered his voice, but not by very much, and tried the experiment again. "Bousted! You have traffled with my sister's afflictions!" He stopped and thought about that for a moment, but appeared to conclude that he had made his point, and continued. "You are a scad and a coundrel—— a skid and a candle! You are also a scad. What do you have to say for yourself?"

"Now, Snyder," I began—although it was a foolish endeavor trying to reason with a man in his state—"you know that your sister was the one who rejected——"

"She's gone back to that Friedrich or Hiffman or what-have-you, that blasted Dutch fellow! Do you think I'm sooch a foal as to behave—I mean believe; of course I mean believe; did you think I didn't mean believe? Of course I meant believe. But I don't believe it. That's the point."

He turned away muttering.

"Believe what?" I asked at last.

"That she would pick a fat Dutchman over you!" He attempted to fix me with a steely eye, though not with a great deal of success. "Of course she told me it was her choice—she is the dearest, sweetest girl in the world, and she would rather fling hersilf from a bredge than say anything against you. But I say through her faceed!"

"I'm sure that if we sit down and talk for a little while, we can——"

"A pilpable lay!—I mean a lie; of course I mean a lie. Why do you always twist everything I say? I said it was a lay, and I meant it was a lay. I mean a lie. There you are again, twisting my words!"

"I'm sure you know that I never——"

"Are you calling me a layer? Of course you are, because you are not a generalmin." He reached behind him and fumbled on the settle, at last finding the little case he had brought. "So I will thank you to take a walk with me down to the river."

He opened the case to reveal a pair of pistols.

This alarming development put me in a very conciliatory mood. I had no particular wish to shoot Snyder, and I had a very particular aversion to being shot myself. "I'm certain we can come to some rational agreement," I said in my calmest tone.

"Rational?" he sputtered. "What has raisin to do with a woman's honor?" He snatched one of the pistols from the case and pointed it at me. "You will come with me to the river," he said very sternly, "or I will shoot you here."

If those were his conditions, then it seemed far the wiser course to accompany him to the river; and so I agreed.

Here I cannot forbear remarking what fools our sense of honor makes us. Here was Snyder, a man who, in his inebriated state, was far more

likely to fall into a ditch than to hit anything
with a bullet; yet he was challenging me—a man
who had not touched a drop of spirits since that
evening when I met Snyder in the saloon on
Ohio-street. How did he know that I was not a
crack shot? In fact I had never discharged a pistol in my life, but he had no means of knowing
that.

Our walk to the river was one of the strangest
experiences of my young life. It was not yet particularly late; but it was dark and chilly, and the
streets through which we walked were almost
deserted. We proceeded in almost complete silence, though all the way my mind was filled
with the most absurd thoughts. I desperately
wished to think of some way to avoid this ordeal,
but my mind gave all its attention to ridiculous
irrelevancies. If this was to be a proper duel,
should there not be seconds? If I did kill Snyder,
whom would I inform? Is there some sort of city
department or private service charged with collecting the corpses of defeated duelists? I wondered all these things, yet I spoke not a word to
Snyder. His threatening me with immediate an-
nihilation had made me wonderfully silent, even
though he had long since replaced the pistol in
the case.

Snyder's face maintained an expression of perfect steadiness and deadly determination. The
rest of him, on the other hand, was not steady at

all; and about halfway to the river, as we were passing the rope-works, he suddenly thrust the pistol-case into my hand with a garbled "Hold this," and then fell to the ground and vomited in the gutter.

He remained for some time in the attitude of a worshiper supplicating the gutter-gods; and all at once my brain, which had hitherto been useless to me, formed a delightfully simple scheme; a very wicked scheme—perhaps too wicked. I decided to remove the bullet from one of the guns, so that I should be certain not to be hit. It would, perhaps, have been more virtuous to have removed the bullets from both, at once saving Snyder from his drunken folly and myself from all danger;—except that Snyder's pointing a pistol at me had made a deep impression upon my imagination, and at the moment I regarded the man as my deadly enemy, whom it would be safer to kill at once than to leave alive to plot a more effective attack. What, after all, could I do if Snyder discovered my stratagem?—and was he not bound to discover it, even in his present state, when both pistols failed to fire? No, my own course might be wicked, but it was the most rational. The safest thing was to kill Snyder.

At any rate, I did remove the bullet from the lower pistol; at least I removed something from it, which I assumed must be a bullet, although it was hellishly dark, and I had only the scantiest theoretical knowledge of such weapons as these. Then I stood, the pistol case in one hand, the other hand absently twirling my moustache, until Snyder was ready to continue.

When Snyder had emptied himself sufficiently, he laboriously resumed an upright stance and rather roughly took back the pistol-case, as if his vomiting were one more fault to be added to the account of resentments he kept against me. At length we reached a deserted spot by the river, a long cobblestone plaza where the gaslight was at least sufficient to make out the outline of a man. Here, still in complete silence, Snyder opened the case, and I, after making a show of indecision, chose the upper pistol.

To this day I cannot explain what happened next. Perhaps I chose the wrong pistol, in spite of my care; perhaps I had misjudged what I was doing earlier in the dark by the rope works; perhaps any number of perhapses. When Snyder announced "Ten paces" and counted them off—he counted very slowly and counted eight twice—I turned, raised my arm, and pulled the trigger. I felt nothing in my hand, but at about the same time there was a loud report, and my hat flew off my head.

Human nature is an unaccountable thing. Certainly one of the great arguments in favor of a life of evil, which is to say of rational self-interest, is that a life devoted to good involves a man

in a mass of ridiculous contradictions. No sooner
had the bullet taken my hat off—leaving my
head quite unharmed, I hasten to assure you, my
dear trembling reader—than Snyder was running toward me, demanding to know whether I
was "all right," and protesting that he would
rather die than harm a hair on my head. He fell
on the ground before me and quite literally embraced my knees, doubtless to the great detri-
ment of his trousers, and repeated something
over and over, which I was eventually able to in-
terpret as "You didn't fire."

"No," I told him, making a very advantageous
use of the truth, "I had removed the bullet from
the gun. I did not expect that you would be able
in your state to come as close as you did to hit-
ting me; but, for my part, I am sure that death
would be preferable to harming a friend to
whom I owe so much, and who (moreover) is the
brother and protector of a woman whom I must
always hold in the highest regard, however she
may have disappointed my own hopes."

This pretty speech silenced him for half a moment; then he repeated, "You didn't fire!" after
which he decided that the phrase bore repeating
a few dozen more times.

Such was the issue of my one and only duel;—
for no rational man would willingly indulge in
such a folly. Dueling is a poor substitute for assassination. It is an attempt to clothe our basest

and most primitive resentments in a cloak of honor and virtue; but after all it is only a curiously inefficient sort of murder, with an unwelcome element of risk added to soothe the conscience of the murderer. For my part, I find a simple secret assassination, perhaps by means of poisoning, much more rational. A duel, after all, opens up the very real possibility that the wrong man may be killed. Then there is the likelihood of being found out, even if one is the successful contestant; and success in a duel, however honorable it may seem in the eyes of certain gentlemen, is still murder in the eyes of the law. Taking all these things together, can anything be more absurd than to begin the enterprise by placing every possible obstacle in the way of its success?

——This is a digression, you may say; I admit it, but I make no apology. I may choose to write what I like in my own book, and you may choose whether to read it or no. But I shall end the digression here, merely repeating that I should prefer poison as a means of ridding myself of anyone whose continued existence had become an inconvenience to me. Indeed, I have preferred poison, as the course of this narrative will show. Do you tremble, dear reader? Do you shudder and wonder what monstrous outrage I may already be plotting? Shudder as much as you like: I shall not tell you until the time comes, except to say that it will very probably be even more monstrous than you imagine.

The excitement of the duel sobered up Snyder considerably; I accompanied him on the long walk home, but he was able to remain upright without stumbling, and even to carry on a conversation of a sort. When we reached his house, his sister was waiting for him, along with a man I took to be Hoffman. Gertrude embraced her brother and expressed her inexpressible joy—so she called it, although clearly it admitted of some expression—to see us both alive, and apparently on good terms; it was obvious that she had had a clear idea of her brother's intentions, and had spent the evening fretting herself half to death.

Hoffman watched her with an awkward concern. He was a short man, not slim and not stout, with a spherical head, his hair parted in the center with perfect symmetry and disciplined with a prodigious quantity of macassar oil. The only thing remarkable about him was the extraordinarily luxuriant moustache that weighed down his upper lip. My own moustache had achieved a respectable growth by this time, but clearly it would never equal the magnificent proportions of Hoffman's It occurred to me that perhaps Gertrude, for all her good sense and domestic virtue, might judge a man by his moustache; and by that criterion Hoffman was clearly the better man.

While Gertrude tended to her brother, Hoffman and I introduced ourselves. His Christian name was Magnus, which I still think is just about the most absurd name ever applied to a human child, with the possible exception of my own. I did not even tell mine to him, introducing myself merely as Newman Bousted.

Apart from our respective names, we could find little to say to each other, and it was with some relief that I parted from him when Gertrude asked for a word with me in the parlor. I followed her into the little room; she slid the pocket door closed, and then turned to face me.

"Newman," she said, "my brother has told me what you did for him tonight. I—I have no words to express my admiration for someone who would rather risk his own life than his friend's"—here she lowered her eyes—"especially when his friend has behaved very badly."

"Now, Gertrude," I responded (thinking that what I said might later be repeated to Snyder), "I would not have you think that of your brother. His fault was a misapprehension, and everything he did was done from love for you. He loves you as never a brother has loved a sister; and if his conduct is at times excessive, recall the motive, and forgive him. You are his

dearest treasure, and his only wish is to protect
you from every harm."

Was this not a pretty sentiment? I thought so,
and Gertrude did as well. "Oh, Newman," she
replied, "at times I think you are something better than a man: for here I had made up my mind
to plead with you to forgive my brother, and you
are begging me to forgive him! And I do forgive
him—I do, Newman, only—Oh! how I wish he
wouldn't drink so!"

At this I lowered my eyes in acknowledgment
that I could not excuse her brother's drinking
quite as readily as I could excuse his dueling. Indeed I wished he would give up strong drink almost as heartily as she did, though from a somewhat more selfish motivation.

Gertrude's admiration of me had never been
higher; but it was a purely moral admiration
that did not engage her passions. Hoffman was
the moustache she loved. A certain competitive
instinct in my heart resented his success; but my
rational mind successfully overcame that resent-
ment, reminding my heart how much easier her
attraction to Hoffman made it for me to court
Amelia.

Amelia! At the thought of her, I suddenly recalled the letter I had left open on the little table
in the front parlor. What news did it bring? And
had my sister been reading it? It would be an ir-
resistible temptation to her if she found the

thing. I was consumed simultaneously with eagerness to read the letter and dread of my sister's having discovered it. Hoping I might get back home before Viola returned from her conference with Camellia, I made my rather hasty apologies to Gertrude, who agreed that it was quite late and saw me to the door. There she took my hand and told me very seriously, "Magnus—Mr. Hoffman—he is a good man, Newman. I hope you will come to know him."

I have to this day no clear notion of why she said that. It was one more enigma from Gertrude, a girl from whom I had learned to expect enigmas. I expressed the hope that I would indeed come to know the man of whom she thought so highly, although in fact I could see no reason why I should desire any further acquaintance with him. Then I walked out into the chilly night.

The bracing cold was very pleasant, filling my lungs and rasping at my face as I strode briskly through the narrow streets of modest rowhouses, and then along North Avenue opposite the park, all the while turning over the events of the evening in my mind. Sometimes the duel presented itself to my imagination almost as if it were happening again; and only now, when the danger was over, did I come to realize how fearful the danger had been. In those moments I forgot about the letter from Amelia; but then the thought of it sitting there open on the table would come back to me, and I would quicken my pace again.

As soon as I reached the house, I flung my hat on the hall-tree, and I think I dropped my over-coat on the floor. Then I rushed into the parlor —and there was Viola, reading my letter from Amelia.

This was the realization of my worst fear. But the scene was not as I had imagined it. Instead of the smug self-satisfaction I had expected to see on her face, I beheld an expression of consternation I had never seen before on my sister. Her face was bright crimson, and I could hear her breathing in short gasps.

"Viola," I began uncertainly.

Suddenly she started up—it appeared that she had not even noticed my entrance until I spoke —and dropped the letter on the little table where she had found it. She stood gaping, her eyes wide, her face turning a deeper purple with every tick of the clock. She must have stared at me open-mouthed like that for more than half a minute; then she suddenly turned and ran from the room, and I heard her shoes clattering noisily on the stairs.

VOLUME IV.

CHAPTER XV.

I am introduced to polite society, and I find that it suits me very well.

SOMETHING APPALLING MUST be in that letter. In all my life I had never seen Viola in such a state. I had seen her furious; I had seen her seething with hatred; I had seen her frightened half out of her mind by a spider; but I had never seen that look of—of what? I supposed it must be horror, because I could not imagine what else it might be.

What could be in that letter? My mind whirled through every possibility, each more frightful than the last. But the general tenor of all of them was that I had been discovered: somehow—I knew not how—Amelia must have found out the truth about my lying in wait for her in the park;

she must have denounced me in that letter in terms so scathingly explicit that even my dullard sister could understand them and be horrified.

Now, at this point in the narrative, if any readers besides myself ever peruse these pages, I suppose they must be just about evenly divided into two camps. The one group asks, "But why does he not simply read the letter? It is there before him on the table where his purple-faced imbecile of a sister left it. Why does he speculate on the contents when the thing itself is there, waiting to divulge whatever secrets it holds?" So say the readers who possess no imaginative faculty, and I think I should find it unutterably wearisome to write for such readers as those. —In the other camp are the readers who already know what it is to be paralyzed by such a fear; who even now dread turning the page and making the terrible discovery along with me. To you, dear sympathetic readers, I address myself, since it is so much less laborious to write for you than for those others. You have already, without my telling you, felt the near impossibility of even lifting the letter from the table, as if it were something a thousand times heavier than lead; you know how my shifting eyes lit on every other object in the room, but shunned the letter as if it were as painfully bright as the sun itself;—because your own eyes would have done the same. You see the blackness of the future along with me; you wonder as I do how I shall continue to exist in a world in which all my hopes are dashed.

Yet I did read the letter, because I dared myself to read it. "What," I said to myself, "are you such a coward that a few sheets of paper terrify you? What would Baucher do under like circumstances? He would read the letter, and then, no matter what doom it portended, he could contrive to turn it to his advantage."

I therefore took the letter in hand,—and almost immediately burst into laughter: audible and doubtless very undignified laughter. The greeting alone was enough to show that I had entirely misjudged the cause of Viola's consternation. As I read on, however, my laughter soon subsided, and by the end of the letter I believe I must have been nearly as red as Viola had been. But I need not delay you any longer, dear sympathetic reader: I have given you so much description of my mental agitation only because I desired to point a valuable moral, which is how easily irrational feelings of guilt can assault a man who is only just setting out on a course of pure evil. I have the very letter before me now, and I shall transcribe it faithfully for you, the ideal reader in my imagination.

My dearest Galahad,—

If you have any regard for my reputation, or

any sense at all, then you will burn this letter—
but oh! I find that I hope you have no sense,
and treasure it next to your heart. It would be
something for me to know that my words lie
there in your bosom, where I long to lie myself.
No virtuous girl would ever commit such
thoughts as mine to paper, and our short acquaintance should make me doubly reserved.
But I cannot write anything at all without
telling you how I long for you, how I burn to
feel your lips pressed to mine. Shall I say more?
When I retire at night, I long for the time when
you should retire with me; I long to lie in your
arms and feel your gentle strength pressing
against me; I long for things no proper girl has
even words to name. I have dreamed of these
things night after night since I first saw you. Do
you see now why I say you must burn this letter?—And yet, if you have not the heart to
burn it, oh, Galahad, how happy it would make
me!—Then you must keep it next to your heart,
and let no one ever see it; and if your father or
your sister should ask what I wrote to you, you
shall say with perfect truth that I asked after
your health, and had forgot the name of that
book we talked of when last I saw you. —How
is your health, Mr. Bousted? And what was the
name of that book we talked of when last I saw
you? I seem to have forgot. —Now you have no
need to deceive your family, for I am sure that
deception is not natural to you. They need not
know that I have committed to paper such

thoughts as no respectable girl ought even to think; but oh! Galahad! I could not do otherwise: the thought that you might hesitate from not knowing how I might receive your addresses—— Galahad! You must not hesitate! I have placed myself at your mercy; my very life is in your hands. I will see you very soon, and then you must tell me—you must, or I shall die —that I have not been a fool. Farewell, Galahad, my valiant knight, and when you retire tonight, take me with you in your thoughts, and know that I should give almost anything to be with you in body as well; and that I long with all my heart for the time when you shall call me

Your own
Amelia.

Reader, you may be quite certain that I did take Amelia with me in my thoughts—but also Viola, who came all unbidden into my mind. The letter was my greatest triumph;—but Viola had read it. Would she blight this triumph as she did every other success of mine?

Viola said nothing about the letter the next morning. She went through the ordinary business of breakfast in the usual way, except that she avoided meeting my eyes. I avoided meeting hers as well, and I am sure we were both quite happy to be spared the trouble of looking at each other. But whether she was mortally embarrassed at having been caught reading a personal letter, or whether the contents of the letter had shocked her conventionally virtuous little mind so deeply that she could not bring herself to speak of the matter at all, or whether her own betrothal had inclined her to take a more indulgent view of her brother's amours, she said nothing.

As for myself, I had changed my opinion of Amelia considerably, and rather for the better. Her letter had taught me something that (absurd as it may seem that I should have been so ignorant) I had not yet known: that women can have desires comparable to those of men. I wonder now what I had imagined before that letter: across the distance of so many years, it is impossible to reconstruct my ignorance. I think I believed that a woman's love was pure and spiritual, whereas a man's love must always be admixed with a certain quantity of physical desire. If, as it seems, I had a higher opinion of women than they deserved, it was doubtless owing to the innumerable dreadful novels I had read, most of them written by females who never permitted the least suspicion of an impure thought to cross the minds of their heroines. Even the fallen women in those novels had fallen by directing their pure and spiritual love toward the wrong sort of man; there was no suggestion that the female herself had desired the act by which she had fallen, but rather she had permitted it in the mistaken belief that it would bind the object of her love to her. But in one letter Amelia had taught me, or at least begun to teach me, that women are not such fools as they appear to be in popular novels. I suppose I ought to have learned the same thing from the classical literature of my school days; but the love of Dido and Aeneas does not make a lasting impression on a boy's heart when it is presented in terms of ablatives of means.

Preparations for the ball and the wedding (though Viola had decided on a June wedding, which was months away) occupied Viola completely for the next few days, and I was happy to have her out of my way. I had a letter to Amelia to post; again, I kept no copy, but you may be sure that it was filled with expressions of delight at the content of her letter, and assurance that I loved her all the better for her candor. Yes, I told her that I loved her, although the words could hardly have come as a surprise to her after the sentiments we had already exchanged.

The great night came at last: the night of the ball that Viola regarded as the crowning event of her life so far, hardly to be exceeded by her own wedding. A man can dress himself tolerably well in half an hour, but I think Viola had been dressing for a solid week. The ultimate effect was splendid in a horrible way: the dress was expensive, the gloves perfect, the jewelry at least tasteful; but in the middle of it all was my odious sister, and no amount of painting could make her a lily. The bustle she had chosen was huge beyond all measure, and no end-table or hall-tree was safe when Viola was in the vicinity. I have listened to many arguments in favor of the proposition that civilization is continually improving, but the most convincing evidence I have seen of any advancement in human happiness is the disappearance of the bustle.

As for myself, I had dressed as well as I could. I believe I looked respectable if nothing else. My father, on the other hand, was dressed in a style that might have been quite respectable in the time of Andrew Jackson, for aught I know; but it was not calculated to win him any admirers in the present day. He might just as well have worn knee-breeches and a powdered wig; it could not have made him look any more embarrassingly absurd.

We had hired a carriage for the evening: it was an expense my father considered ridiculously extravagant, but Viola insisted that to arrive at such an event without a carriage would be as improper as to arrive in one's night-clothes. How Viola knew such things she never revealed to us. She was not in the habit of arriving at millionaires' balls, but she set herself up as an expert on the subject. Her opinion carried a certain amount of authority, because she was blessed

with the ability to make life, or at least domestic
tranquility, completely impossible if we did not
accede to her wishes. The carriage, therefore,
arrived promptly at the time specified, and then
had to wait another half-hour while Viola made
the final adjustments to her appearance, at the
end of which she was still Viola. Then at last we
ascended into the carriage: it smelt equally of
must and of horse manure, and I recall wondering why the wealthy classes put up with the
stench of carriages when they could walk in the
open air. (The answer, of course, is that a carriage properly maintained has no disagreeable
odor; at least none of mine have, and a coachman who allowed my carriage to deteriorate into
such a deplorable condition would not long remain in my employ.) Viola took up most of the
interior with the imposing edifice of her bustle;
my father and I were forced to compress ourselves into the smallest possible dimensions. I
should have been much happier walking; my father,—well, there is no telling whether any
thoughts were blowing through the howling
wastes of his mind, but he seemed as idiotically
pleased with the world as he generally was. Viola
was entirely satisfied with her choice of the carriage, and found it impossible to contain her satisfaction, expressing it in a continuous stream of
blether without taking a breath the entire length

of the short ride from Beech-street to the Goodes' house on North Avenue.

And here we were, in a swirl of activity like nothing I had ever known before, with a line of carriages (none but ours the least bit musty) discharging splendid ladies and fine gentlemen into a blaze of lights, laughter, and motion. Somewhere inside the house music was already playing. And this was how I was to spend the evening —among the aristocracy of Allegheny! A sudden fear gripped me. Would I have the courage to walk through this press of humanity, to present myself as if I belonged there? Well, of course I must. I was ashamed that I had ever doubted. Truly enlightened men do not ask what belongs to them. They take what they desire, and that is the end of it. Strange—it took as much courage to enter that crowd as it had ever taken to do anything in my life, and I do not except the duel with Snyder.

By the time I had set my feet on the ground, I had worked up the courage to go in; but first we had to extract Viola and the bustle from the carriage. I worked from the front, and my father took up his position in the rear; our efforts were greatly hampered by Viola's worry that we might somehow mar the gown, or dislodge a bow from its exactly proper place in the composition. I was ready to call for a carpenter to take the carriage apart, but Viola at last extracted herself and her bustle from the thing, and we were on our way into the house.

What a house! The walk through the grand entrance hall and into the presence of the Goodes looms in my mind like a half-remembered dream of a pilgrimage. I know that we were met by Sheridan and announced, and I know that he conducted us to the presence of Amelia and her father; but their house was so enormous, and the crowd so pressing, that the journey thither seemed as full of peril and incident as the voyages of Ulysses, and my courage was tried as sorely as if I had to face a dozen of Homer's choicest mythical monsters. Viola was struck absolutely dumb by the spectacle, which was a great improvement in her; but my father was struck with an unquenchable loquacity. I do not remember a single thing he said, although his remarks followed one after another in a ceaseless torrent: I remember thinking only that, if there were indeed a benevolent Providence, my prayer that he would shut his mouth before we reached the Goodes would be answered. It was not answered, which was just as I ought to have expected, but which was a severe disappointment nonetheless.

And then we were before the Goodes themselves, father and daughter, and if I had not been speechless before, I should certainly have been struck dumb by the vision in front of me. I knew

now that my journey had been so arduous because I had at last been admitted to the heavenly
mansions, and here before me was an angel.
Amelia was dressed in the latest French fashion,
all classical drapery, with her shoulders bare,
displaying more of her captivating flesh than I
believed it was possible for a girl to show in public, and with absolutely no bustle at all. It was
fortunate for me that she took it upon herself to
begin the conversation, because I should not
have been able to form articulate speech.

"Miss Bousted!" Amelia greeted my sister as
though she were genuinely pleased to see her,
which of course was impossible. "How delightful
to see you again! I hope you have been well."

Viola murmured a few syllables in what might
have been Chaldee for all we could understand of
it.

"And Mr. Bousted—the elder and the younger,
of course," Amelia continued with a bright
smile. My father returned her greeting with an
old-fashioned bow that would have made John
Quincy Adams proud; I very properly took her
hand for the approved length of time and no
more.

"You must remind me to show you the
gallery," Amelia said to me. "Father is very
proud of his collection, and I know what an admirer you are of Boucher." —In fact I had never
heard the name Boucher before: in the noise and

music, I had almost thought I heard her say
Baucher, and my blood froze for an instant before I realized that Boucher must be some picture in her father's gallery. It was still a mystery
why she thought I was an admirer of Boucher;—
but there was no time to think about that: more
guests were arriving, and Amelia was introducing me to a pleasantly plain young lady, a Miss
Weatherly or Wherewithal or some such name.
And then I was talking to Miss Wherewithal, and
Amelia had gone on to the next guest;—I saw
out of the corner of my eye that my father was
still babbling at Colonel Goode, and was evidently prepared to continue babbling until the
poor old man's ears melted into a puddle in his
collar.

Then there was dancing, and for once I was
glad that my father had paid the dollar and a
quarter extra to have me trained in the art at
school. There was also much drinking; but I
avoided any alcoholic liquors, the example of
Snyder being still fresh in my mind. I danced
with several ladies who had already drunk a little
too much. I danced with Miss Wherewithal, who,
like me, had avoided spirits (or so she said), but
whose giddy awkwardness was as good a replace-
ment for drunkenness as one could wish for. At
last I danced with Amelia, and if all the divines
of the world could have the same privilege, they
would cease to manufacture imaginary heavens

and acknowledge that paradise can be found on earth.

The music came to an end, and, as Miss Wherewithal appeared to be approaching, Amelia quickly said, rather louder than necessary, "Oh, Mr. Bousted, I did promise to show you the gallery, didn't I?" This was enough to stop Miss Wherewithal, who turned away and began searching the room for other prospects. "Father appears to be engaged"—Amelia's eyes flitted toward her father, who (*nirabile dictu!*) was now talking to mine in a happy and animated fashion—"so I suppose I shall have to take on the duty myself. It's right through this way."

She took my arm and led me to the edge of the room, nodding and exchanging greetings with various guests along the way, until we reached a pair of sliding doors, one of which she slid open just enough to admit the two of us, and then closed again.

We were in what was evidently the back parlor. The sounds of the ball were muffled, and the gas was turned down to a dim suggestion of light; but Amelia spoke even louder than she had done before.

"I venture to say there are few finer collections in Allegheny or Pittsburgh; one or two larger perhaps, but none chosen with such good taste. I think you will be favorably impressed, especially by some of the larger works."

She was almost shouting in my ear, and I was filled with a sense that something very odd was happening. By the time we reached the pocket door at the other end of the room—which was only a few steps, but an infinite number of mental revolutions—I had persuaded myself that, whatever our true destination might be, it was certainly no picture gallery.

Amelia had fallen silent now, and she released my arm and pushed the door back. The room beyond was even dimmer, but as Amelia turned up the gas to a great chandelier in the middle of the room, the darkness dissipated, and the place revealed itself as—a picture gallery.

The walls were crowded with pictures of every sort, from every era. Old Colonel Goode might or might not have taste in art: I was no fit judge of that. But that he had money any fool could see. I knew nothing of paintings or artists (a deficiency I have since remedied), but merely in canvas and paint this gallery had to represent a considerable expenditure.

"The Boucher is over there," Amelia said, speaking very softly now; and she walked over toward the opposite wall, with me following her closely. She stopped in front of the largest canvas in the room.

"*La Belle Anglaise,*" she announced, turning to face me.

It was a picture of a reclining nude, which in itself was very shocking to me at the time. Such things were not publicly exhibited in Allegheny or Pittsburgh at that remote era. I had heard of such pictures, but I knew them only by verbal descriptions. It was also more than a little embarrassing to look at the picture of a nude woman with another and far more beautiful woman judging my response. I tried not to show any of my discomfort, of course: instead, I attempted to absorb certain details that I might be able to mention from an artistic perspective. I remember especially noting the drapery: the woman was on a couch draped with abundant red velvet, and the texture of the velvet had been rendered with great skill. There at least was something I might be able to mention if called upon to render an opinion. More red was in the curtains behind her; a subtler, deeper shade of red, indicative of shadow.

"She was the mistress of a French duke," Amelia explained. "He loved her passionately; but so, they say, did Boucher. I think from her expression you can tell which one she preferred."

It was even stranger, and somehow deeply thrilling, to hear a woman talk of such things as the young men I knew—with the exception of Snyder, of course—mentioned only in hushed whispers.

"My father," Amelia continued, "keeps the gallery closed off when we entertain. Some of the ladies are easily offended, and we have not seen the O'Haras for five years, because the mother and daughter both refuse to set foot in a house where such a picture exists. But you are not a prig."

"No, of course not," I agreed, stepping closer to the picture and examining it in detail, as if I were admiring the brushwork.

Amelia turned and stood close beside me, taking my arm. "I am not a prig either," she said.

Suddenly I felt myself whirled around to face her, and a moment later her lips were pressed to mine with such force that I nearly stumbled backwards. My first instinct in the face of this unexpected assault was, absurdly, to raise my arms to defend myself; but in the event my arms rose only half way, and, as saner instincts took possession of me, my arms encircled Amelia, as hers did me, and we tightened our embrace. And all the while my mind was filled with the most ridiculous thoughts. Is this how kisses usually begin? Are my hands correctly positioned on her back, and should they be moving in some fashion? Are my lips what she was hoping they would be? Is my breath pleasant enough? Does a kiss normally involve quite so much of the mouth? Is it proper for me to break the contact first, or do I wait for her to move away? Will I be expected

to make some appropriate remark afterward? Do
I dare touch the bare flesh of her shoulder?

At last Amelia withdrew her lips from mine;
but she did not break our embrace, and she
rested her head on my shoulder. "Oh, Galahad—
oh, dearest, dearest Galahad—I love you so
madly! It's foolish, absurd—I've known you such
a short time—but I do love you; I loved you before I knew your name! When you wrote that
you loved me, I kissed the letter a thousand
times;—and then at night,—at night I laid it on
my pillow, and kissed it a thousand times more.
And I wished—how I wished!—that the letter
might have been you. I don't know what has
made me the slave of passion, but I had to snatch
this precious, fleeting moment to do what I've
longed to do since you first passed me on Federal-street.—We must return to the ball soon—I
can't be missed—but, oh, Galahad, when you
dance with Miss Weatherbee and all your other
female admirers, I want you to remember
this——"

She pressed her lips to mine once more, with
less violence, but with growing ardor; and I certainly cannot say that I was passive in our embrace.

When at last she withdrew, she led me by the
arm back to the doorway; then, just as she was
about to turn down the gas again, she turned for
a moment and looked back toward the Boucher,

and spoke a few words that engraved an indelible
picture on my mind:

"I should like to be your *Belle Anglaise*."

CHAPTER XVI.

A consu n nation devoutly to be wished.

AMELIA WAS A perfect hostess for the rest of the
evening, which meant that I saw very little of
her except from a distance. She took special care
of Viola, so that she always had a dance partner;
I suppose she thought it would please me. And so
it did, but only because it showed Amelia herself
in such an attractive light. Otherwise, nothing
would have pleased me more than to see Viola
perfectly miserable. I danced with a number of
fine ladies, not one of whom made the slightest
impression upon me, although I was told later
that my good humor and scrupulous courtesy
made quite an impression upon them. To Amelia
I spoke only once more, briefly, as we were de-
parting, and with her father beside me, she could

not communicate anything particular to me
other than a secret glimmer in her eye;—but
that was enough to make my heart beat faster
and my breath come shorter.

The brief carriage-ride home afforded Viola
the opportunity of a monologue on her great success as a member of proper society. I remember
nothing of it except a few of her remarks about
Amelia herself. Viola thought that "she was very
charming, to be sure. But that gown!" (Here she
looked rather pointedly at me, probably recalling what she had read in Amelia's letter.) "I suppose even a fortune like the Goodes' is no guar-
antee of correct taste. No bustle at all! And the
—well, I won't say it was indecent, but my
word! I wouldn't be seen in public that way." Although I had a very different opinion of the gown
in question, I was in such good spirits that I
could not even bring myself to feel offended by
Viola's malicious babbling. After all, whatever
else might be said about the relative merits of
one style or another, there could be no question
that a gown with Amelia in it was worth a great
deal more than a gown with Viola in it. I sat and
smiled the whole time Viola was babbling, and
even though she did not shut her flapping jaw
until we arrived at our house on Beech-street,
for probably the first time in my life I was not
annoyed by my sister's incessant chatter. Even
the considerable effort required to extract her

from the carriage did not put me out of temper; and when my father paid the coachman, I added a considerable gratuity from my own pocket— not, I hasten to explain, from foolish notions of generosity, but because I thought it behooved us, as a family worthy to mix with such as the Goodes, to keep up the appearance of prosperity.

It was absolutely necessary for my purposes that I should keep the flame of love burning bright in Amelia's breast. In spite of the late hour, therefore, I sat at my desk to compose a love-letter before retiring, so that it should be ready to go out with the morning post. I put some considerable effort into this composition, although it was by no means an unwelcome labor. Under the influence of the lingering memory of Amelia's lips, her touch, her gown—all things that are even now so fresh in my memory that hardly a day seems to have passed between then and now—the words poured out of my pen. Nevertheless, I wrote three drafts before I was satisfied with the result. In particular, I wavered over the greeting, before deciding at last that Amelia's conduct had given me ample license to dare all.

When I had finished the letter, I took care to copy it in a rapid but elegant hand, so that it should appear to be a work of haste rather than deliberation, an outpouring of my passion rather than a carefully considered essay. Since I took that precaution, I have the original here before me now, which does not differ in more than two or three words from the letter that Amelia read:

Ma chère Belle Anglaise,——

I cannot sleep. The memory of your touch, of your lips on mine, will give me no rest. I did not know that it was possible for love to grasp a man's whole being and leave no room even for thoughts of sleep, but I find that it is so. And to know that my love is returned with equal intensity is almost more than my heart can bear! I close my eyes and feel the impression of your lips on mine, and my heart beats so wildly that I imagine it must wake the whole household. I know that you have heard your beauty praised often enough, if indeed perfection can ever be praised often enough; but beauty alone could never have left such a mark upon my heart. It is, after all, the soul in which beauty resides;— and yet I must confess that I find myself wishing that Boucher were alive today to paint you. What a masterpiece he would create! He could never capture the essence of your true beauty, —but I should very much like to see what he could capture.

And now, my dearest, my love, my own Amelia, one question consumes me:—When shall I see you again? To you, perhaps, it is merely a question of the clock or the calendar; but to me it is life or death. I live if I see you; I die if I do not. Remember, then, when you reply, that you hold my life in your hands, and be merciful to

                                Your devoted servant,
                                Galahad.

I signed the letter with that ridiculous name my father had given me because Amelia seemed to enjoy thinking of me as her Galahad, her invincible knight and protector; and I was not such a fool as to allow my distaste for the name to stand in the way of my winning the greatest prize I had ever fought for.

I copied the letter, as I mentioned before, and I do recall making at least one change: I changed "wishing that Boucher were *alive* today" to "wishing that Boucher were *here* today," because I could not say with absolute conviction that I knew Boucher to be dead. Then I sealed the letter, confident that it was as perfect as I could have made it. How assiduously I applied myself to my work in those days! To-day I have a secretary to attend to my correspondence, and a messenger-boy waiting to carry it off if it is urgent; but in those days I had only myself—slender enough resources, it seems to me.

The next day was Sunday, but I was not willing to allow the superstitious indolence of the postal service to delay my letter to Amelia. I went straight out after church and took the letter over to the Goodes' house myself, handing it to the boy who answered the door along with a very fresh-looking dollar, and giving him strict instructions to deliver the letter only to Miss Goode. The magical gleam of silver made him my eager co-conspirator; and it was not more than two hours later that the same boy appeared at our door with a note for me, which Viola peevishly but wordlessly delivered, since Mrs. Ott took Sundays off. I wish I could describe to you the delightful expression of haughty disapproval on my dear sister's face as she handed me that letter: her eyebrows rose to such a peak that I thought they might fly off her forehead. Yet she still said nothing, dropping the letter into my lap as if it were some particularly unpleasant insect and turning with a slight snort to leave me alone in the parlor.

Of course I did not delay a moment after her departure: recognizing Amelia's hasty but tidy hand, I broke the seal at once. Here is the letter itself in the box with the rest of them, and what sweet joy it is even now to read it!

My valiant knight,——

It is not possible to express the joy I felt last night when we were able to snatch a few precious moments in the gallery; but I too am consumed with the longing to see you again. A day has not yet passed, but an hour apart is too long

—oh, that you were with me now! I must be content for the moment with your letter. But if you will come to-morrow evening to the meeting of the Workingmen's Improvement Society, I am speaking there, and I shall certainly find a way to spend a few moments alone with you afterward. —Oh, Galahad, how I wish we never had to part again! But I know I shall dream of you to-night; and we shall not truly be apart if you will also dream of me, perhaps even as

Your passionately devoted
Belle Anglaise.

With this letter, which I read over three times, she had enclosed a program for the meeting of the Workingmen's Improvement Society, which was to be held at the parish hall of St. Andrew's Episcopal Church, and at which the principal event was a speech by Miss Amelia Goode on the Condition of the Working Poor in the Cities of Pittsburgh and Allegheny. Now, the Working Poor had ceased to hold any interest for me the moment I ceased to be one of their number; but merely for the opportunity of gazing on Amelia I was willing to endure any number of pious platitudes about the duty of Christian charity toward our most useless citizens. I would certainly attend the meeting.

In the evening I retired with my thoughts of Amelia. I lay awake for quite some time after I had turned down the gas, forming lovely images of Amelia as Boucher might have painted her. I remember hearing the hideous clock in the front parlor striking eleven, and then half past. I did not, however, dream of Amelia. For some reason I dreamt of legions of shopkeepers' wives filling the store on Wood-street.

My dream was not far from the reality. The next day was an extraordinarily busy one, and but for the invaluable assistance of Bradley, I think I might have given in to despair. I took the trouble to congratulate Bradley on his performance, because I had good reason to hope that a few words of praise might serve as an inducement to even more dedicated work on future occasions. I did not, however, make use of the word "invaluable," since I feared that it might provoke him to ask why, if he was truly so invaluable, we persisted in valuing him at only a dollar and a half per diem.

I had no time for proper supper in the evening. I informed my father that I had an appointment; he asked no questions, and Viola implied by her supercilious silence that she knew all the answers. A crust of bread from the kitchen was sustenance enough—that and a quarter of an apple pie.

Marching through the chilly darkness, I found my way to the hall where Amelia would be speaking. This was the old St. Andrew's, not the

much more elaborate Gothic edifice that has
since replaced it; but it was even then a good
step above the humble Methodist meeting-house
my father had attended since we removed to Allegheny. Crowds were gathering already, though
I was early by a quarter-hour. They were crowds
of the sort of people I had seen at the Goodes'
ball—indeed, quite probably many of the same
people. No workingmen were to be seen: clearly
they were not expected, and I wonder what reception one of them might have met had he
wandered in fresh from the mill, with his face
black and his coat reeking of coal-smoke. Indeed, I almost felt out of place myself. I had to
remind myself that my newfound prosperity had
elevated my social position to a level that placed
me on an equal footing with many of the other
gentlemen in attendance. And how many of
them had kissed the divine Amelia Goode?

I dropped a dollar into the donation box at the
door, for which I seemed to be regarded as a
prodigy of generosity; but I considered it well
worth the expense to establish my credentials as
a man to whom money was of no importance.
Exchanging a few polite greetings with random
strangers, I found myself a seat in the hall about
a third of the way from the front to the back—
close enough, I reasoned, for Amelia to see me
there, but not conspicuously close. I spent the
remaining few minutes examining the program,

which promised a positively excruciating evening
to everyone who was not fortunate enough to
have one of the speakers in love with him. Invo-
cation by the Rev'd Egbert Wheeze—Preliminary Remarks by the General Secretary, Mrs.
Henry W. Prattle—Report on the Moral Questions Raised by Public Bathhouses by Mrs. E. F.
Prigge (if you expected something a bit sensa-
tional from this report, you were very much mistaken). Then, at last, *The Condition of the Working Poor,* by Miss Amelia Goode. I sat through all
the edifying preliminaries with a fixed expression
of rapt attention, though I am sure I could not
have repeated a single word from any of those
speeches five minutes later.   But at last Amelia
appeared, and then my attention was no longer
feigned.

She wore blue, which suited her very well; she
was modestly and decorously attired, but there
was no concealing the beauty of her form. What
did she say? You may be surprised to know that I
listened as well as looked. She spoke of the duty
of employers to provide a living wage, and told
some very affecting tales of the difficulties faced
by those of the laboring classes whose wages did
not permit them even the bare subsistence that
was their natural right. And even the clerks in
stores—why, many of them earned no more than
a dollar and a half a day! It was enough for the
needs of a single man, perhaps, but hardly suffi-

cient for a family. How can we expect to suppress vice in the poorer neighborhoods if we make the state of marriage positively prohibitive for the ordinary workingman? Nay more, the inability of even the most diligent hired hand—and she laid especial stress upon the diligence, for she would not have us think that she spoke of idlers and wastrels—his inability to provide for his family is productive of a veritable cascade of evils, a cataract of vices. The sons turn to crime, and the daughters to infamy; the mother wastes away heartbroken, and the father finds his only consolation in drink. Oh, the affecting pictures she painted of gloom and ruin among the poor! It was enough to bring a tear of sympathy to every eye in the hall—for when Amelia speaks, she is invariably persuasive, and even I could almost find pity in my heart for the imaginary families her words conjured up so vividly before us. Yet though she warmed to her subject and gave it her all, when her gaze, wandering over the audience, rested on me, her eyes lit up with a secret joy, invisible perhaps to everyone else, but filling me with a warmth and ardor that made every word she spoke a golden treasure. This Amelia was the object of every man's longing, of every female's envy—and I possessed her heart! Oh, what rewards evil has in store for the patient!

When Amelia had concluded her oration and received much applause, the meeting was ended, as if it were impossible that anyone should command any attention after the divine Miss Goode had left the podium. I made my way forthwith to the front of the hall, where Amelia received me with decent and friendly warmth, introducing me to certain other members of the Society as "Mr. Bousted, of Bousted's stationery," and allowing me the infinite satisfaction of discovering that the Bousted name was by now well-nigh universally known among the better class of citizens in Allegheny. We made some inconsequential conversation on the subject of the workingman, and how fortunate he was to have such friends as we were; the others drifted away one by one, but I stayed, until at last it was impossible to stay any longer without inconveniencing the man who was waiting to lock up the hall. Then there was no one but the coachman to take note of my leaving the hall in Amelia's carriage.

It was a closed winter carriage, and it was a dark night, and as soon as the thing began to move, Amelia's lips were pressed to mine; nor do I believe she disengaged them for at least a quarter-mile.

"Galahad!" she sighed at last when her lips were free for sighing; and that sufficed for another quarter-mile's conversation. Her head resting on my shoulder told me more than a volume of extemporaneous remarks might have done.

At last she spoke again. "I told Henry to take the long way, because I have—things to say to you, Galahad. But first, I must tell you that I love you, with burning passion, and—and whatever else I tell you, please hear it in the light of this———"

She kissed me again, and there was another quarter-mile gone.

"I love you, Amelia," I said at last, "more than I thought it was possible to love. Nothing you say will change my love. If your father is an obstacle, let me prove myself to him—let him give me twelve labors, dragons to slay—what do I care, if you love me?"

"Oh, Galahad, I believe you, and I do love you. If you were any other sort of man, I'd never tell you what I feel I must tell you—but if you were any other sort of man, I shouldn't love you as I do, for I feel instinctively that you love honesty above all, and to a man like you I cannot lie."

She was silent for a moment, and of course my mind worked like a locomotive, trying to imagine what this revelation would be. It was only a moment, however; when she spoke again, it was in a lower voice, tinged with something that sounded like shame.

"Galahad," she said haltingly, "I am not worthy of you. A valiant knight's fair lady should be pure as snow, but—oh, Galahad, I am not pure!"

"Pure?" I repeated idiotically.

"I am not—not—unspotted," she explained. "You are a—a man of the world, I am sure. You know that there are men—men not at all like you—who seduce young ladies with false promises. I knew such a man,—I knew him, and—and —he took from me what can never be returned."

Well, that at least explained how she knew so much more about kissing than I did. That was my first thought. Almost at once, however, it was followed by the realization that Amelia expected me to be thinking something else. She feared rejection; she hoped for forgiveness; but she was certainly not expecting me to say, "Well, if he taught you to kiss like that, then bully for him!"

"Darling Amelia," I began in my softest and most love-besotted voice, "do you really suppose that any past indiscretion could diminish my love for you? I own that I should be very angry if I met the cad who dared to deceive you;—but angry for the pain he caused you, my love, for I can never bear to see you hurt. But, Amelia, do not class me with him! It is your heart I love, and I am sure there is no purer heart in the world."

"Oh, Galahad!" I had evidently said the right thing, because we lost another quarter-mile. I am not altogether sure that Henry did not take us by way of Beaver Falls; the man certainly took his business seriously when you told him to go the long way.

"Galahad," Amelia said when at last her lips were free to speak, "you're the only man I've ever known whom I could trust completely. And how I love you for believing that my heart is pure! But, nevertheless, I'm—I am a woman of the world now. I have lost my girlish innocence, and I can never get it back, and so—so I think perhaps it is not necessary for us to be over-scrupulous." She kissed me again, and then spoke just above a whisper. "My father has retired for the evening, as he always does promptly at half past nine; his bedroom is at the opposite end of the house from mine; and Henry is discreet to a fault."

I suppose it was quite obvious what she meant me to infer; but my mind was so entirely unwilling to believe my good fortune that I actually asked her, "What are you saying, Amelia?"

Again she pressed her lips to mine for a moment, and then she continued in an even lower voice, her lips almost touching my ear, "I mean that there is nothing to prevent you from spending to-night in my bed."

An indescribable thrill passed through me from the pit of my stomach up into my chest. I kissed her passionately. Here at last was the thing I had longed for since I first saw Amelia walking past me on Federal-street, the crown of all my schemes and the fulfillment of all my desires—a night of rapture with the most beautiful girl in Allegheny. And yet—and yet—while I kissed her I was thinking furiously. When I first began my pursuit of Amelia, I could imagine nothing beyond having my way with her; but now, with her lips on mine, and the experience of the past few days in my memory, I realized that I desired infinitely more than that. I could never be content with one night in Amelia's arms; I wanted her to have and to hold so long as I lived. I had also seen a glimpse of the wealth of the Goodes, and do not suppose that it had failed to make an impression on me. But of course the possibility of possessing Amelia and her fortune depended upon Colonel Goode's having a high opinion of me. He thought highly of me now. Would I risk that for one night's enjoyment?

What would Baucher do under like circumstances? Surely the truly evil thing to do, the enlightened course of action, would be to consider my own advantage in the long term, and not merely the present pleasure. It would be difficult; it would require discipline and self-control; but evil is not always easy. One must have faith that it will produce good results in the end;—and by "good," I mean (of course) redounding to one's own advantage.

"Amelia," I breathed in a half-vocal whisper, "my darling, my love, there is nothing I could possibly desire more than a night in your arms, —except a thousand nights, ten thousand nights in your arms. Beloved, hear me out. I am tempted—oh! how I am tempted!—but I feel I must control my passion, not because I don't desire you, but because I desire you infinitely more than that." As I spoke, I was aware of a change in Amelia, a hardening, some tightening of the muscles that suggested she might push away from me; so I very suddenly decided that I must dare all at once. "What I mean is this: I know that our acquaintance has been short, but I can no longer imagine a life without you. My darling Amelia, my one true love, will you be my wife?"

For a moment that seemed like an eternity, there was a silence like death in the carriage; then there was an explosion of emotion.

"Yes!" Amelia half-sobbed, half-shouted into my ear. "Oh, Galahad, yes!—a thousand times yes!"

My joy and relief actually made me laugh. "I think one time will suffice," I said, and Amelia laughed and sobbed at the same time and covered my face with kisses.

"I didn't dare hope—Well, I did hope, but— Oh! Galahad, my dearest love, I'll make you the best, most loving, most faithful wife there ever was!"

And that was the last we spoke—we were otherwise occupied—until Henry finally managed to bring the carriage into the porte cochere of the Goodes' mansion. The stop surprised both of us; we had paid no attention at all to the world outside the carriage.

"I suppose we must say good-night now," I said with unfeigned regret.

"I'll have Henry take you home," Amelia responded.

"No, I'll walk—I'm too happy to ride. Soon we'll never have to part again."

"It must be very soon," Amelia agreed. "I won't be content until I rest in your arms...You must speak to Father to-morrow!"

Yes—her father. There was still that difficulty to get over. We agreed that I should come after dinner the next day to see Colonel Goode, and I cannot say that I was completely confident of myself. The triumph of Amelia's acceptance counted for nothing unless I could persuade her father that I was the right man to marry his daughter. I believe Amelia might have run away with me if he had refused, but that would mean running away from the Goode millions.

As I walked back through the cold and silent streets of Allegheny, I cannot tell you how many times I reminded myself that, but for my own scruple, I might have been lying in bed at that moment with the most beautiful girl in the city.

How I wished I might turn back and tell Amelia that I had changed my mind! But I must not risk anything that would turn old Colonel Goode against me. The Goode fortune was at stake! I must keep that fact constantly in mind, although my mind insisted that the only thing it wanted to think about right now was Amelia.

I left my hat, coat, and stick in the hall when I came home, and then went into the front parlor, where I found Viola sitting, reading one of her dreadful three-volume novels. She looked up at me, and her eyebrows rose considerably, while her physiognomy contorted into a scowl of disapproval. I caught a glimpse of myself in the mirror above the mantel, and I was a wreck. My collar was detached and all askew; my hair looked as if it had been trying to escape my head; the left lapel of my jacket was turned under. I looked like a man who had been with a lover. How delightful it was to see my sister wallowing in indignation! I turned to face her and gave her a knowing smile—and then I winked at her. She slumped lower in her chair and buried her nose in her book.

CHAPTER XVII.

The question now becomes one of priority.

FAR INTO THE night I labored, writing and re-writing my speech to old Colonel Goode. You may believe that it is absurd to write a speech for such an occasion, but I was unwilling to leave anything to chance. I must make a persuasive argument that I, humble though my origins might be, was the best possible husband for his beloved daughter. I must exercise all the powers of rhetoric to prove that Amelia could be in no safer hands than mine. I was, after all, asking him for his whole treasure—not just his daughter, but also the millions she would inherit. Certainly I would not mention the millions, but they must be present to his mind all the same. Could he safely deposit his daughter and his fortune in my hands? That was the question he had to be able to answer affirmatively. It was true that Amelia might be persuaded to defy her father even if he should withhold his consent; but, much as I lusted after Amelia's beauty, my rational mind recognized that her beauty was transitory, whereas the Goode millions were of permanent value.

My first attempt cost me half an hour of staring at a blank sheet, until at last I was able to bring myself to write something:

"Sir: It behooves every young man to consider carefully how——"

That was as far as I got before I tossed the sheet aside. What a perfectly ridiculous way to begin! I made it sound as though I were applying for a position in his firm. And what sort of word was "behooves" anyway? Could it possibly even be English? The more I turned it over in my mind, the more absurd it sounded. Behooves, behooves, behooves, behooves, behooves. Horses and cattle are among the behooved animals. Obviously I was very tired, but I would not rest until the thing was done. I began afresh:

"Sir: Since I first made the acquaintance of your daughter in the course of rescuing her from a fate worse than death——"

No, I must not boast. He certainly remembered the circumstances under which he met me the first time; that worked in my favor, but to

remind him of it specifically would be distasteful.
I began once more:

"Sir: Unworthy though I am to ask for——"

No—why should I put the notion that I was
unworthy into his mind? My aim was to show
him that I *was* worthy. I must not begin by con-
fusing the argument. That sheet joined the rest in
the waste-basket. So did the next one, which
touched on the Christian duty of marriage, and
the one after that, which began, "I am reminded
of the story of the Irishman and his sister."

At last, as the clock was striking two, I finished an oration that I thought would be wonderfully persuasive. I spent another half-hour com-
mitting it to memory, and then at last settled in
bed to dream of my beautiful Amelia.

The next day, my brother-in-law Bradley was
quite surprised to learn that his wages had risen
to two dollars a day. I told him that he had
proved himself and deserved the additional half-
dollar; I did not tell him that Amelia disap-
proved of low wages, since no one else but Viola
knew that I had anything to do with Amelia. You
may note that I made this decision without consulting my father. I informed him of it later (and
he expressed his approval), but I had decided to
regard the responsibility as mine. My father had
already been made wealthy beyond his poor
imagination by my management of the business,

so he wisely refrained from questioning me in most of these affairs.

Immediately after supper I excused myself, left the house, and walked briskly to the Goode mansion. I was not looking forward to what I had to do, but I had some confidence in my persuasive abilities. Besides, there was Amelia. Any effort would be worth my while for such a prize. I recalled the soft warmth of her lips on mine, the tender caresses that turned my lapel under, and her eagerness to offer still greater liberties—Oh! what a delicious thought! It carried me all the way through the dark and chilly evening until I reached the front door of the Goode mansion and pulled the bell.

The same young man who had been my messenger on Sunday answered the door, and without waiting for me to present my card, told me, "Miss Goode has been expecting you, sir."

I was about to say that I had come to call on her father, but then it occurred to me that Amelia might have some good reason for intercepting me. It would be wise (as well as pleasant) to see her before confronting her father. I followed the boy into the ballroom and through the double doors into the back parlor, where I found Amelia sitting—and her father in the chair opposite her.

The time had come—and suddenly I had forgotten every word of the speech I had so carefully composed. In a single moment, I went through a thousand agonies; my face flushed; I swallowed; and, at last, forgetting even a polite greeting, I began to stammer out the only words that came to me:

"Sir:—It behooves every young——"

"My son!" The old man fairly leaped out of his chair with his right hand extended. "No need to make a fool of yourself with some silly speech—my little girl has told me everything, and I'm delighted, my boy, delighted! I couldn't hope for anything better." He grasped my hand, and at the same time clapped me on the shoulder—which was something of a reach for him, since I was taller by a head.

"Well," I replied,—and at the moment I could think of nothing else to say.

"Darling," Amelia said from behind him, "I hope you won't be angry with me, but you see I've anticipated you."

"She told me that you were going to ask for her hand, and that I was to say yes," the Colonel said with what I suppose was his heartiest laugh —a sort of contralto piping that seemed to emanate from somewhere behind his nose. "She's made her mind up. She does that, my boy—you'll find that out soon enough. But I was more than happy to oblige her—more than happy. Why, a fine young man like you is exactly what I had been hoping for. She won't have me forever, you know."

"Well, of course——" I started out rather uncertainly, but I soon found my footing again. "Of course I shall always take care of her as—as my greatest treasure."

"I know you will, my boy. A man who would risk life and limb for a stranger would certainly take good care of a wife, wouldn't he? —And you have a head for business as well, which is more necessary than most people think. Marriage is a business partnership: two persons combine their assets in hopes of making a profitable venture, just as——"

"Now, Father, don't start talking business with him already," Amelia said with a bright smile; then to me, "If you let him get started you'll never hear the end of it." This provoked another round of piping from the Colonel.

So our conversation turned to other matters: Amelia's dear mother, carried off by a fever when the poor girl was but an infant—my own mother, whose memory my father professed to revere, although I doubt whether he really thought about her very much at all—and my father, to whom Colonel Goode had taken an inexplicable liking. I was told at last that I should consider myself already part of the family; and then Colonel Goode left us, saying, "Now I'm sure you young folks have things to talk about

that you don't need me to hear," and telling
Amelia she could show me out when she was
through with me.

For a few moments after he was gone, we
were both silent;—then Amelia threw herself
into my arms and pressed her lips to mine. Then
she drew back just enough to talk to me.

"Galahad, my valiant knight, tell me—are you
happy that you have achieved your quest?"

"I don't think there's a happier man in Pennsylvania," I replied, and I certainly meant it.

"I knew my father would like you right away.
He's seen so many fortune-hunters and besotted
old widowers try their luck with me that an honest, brave, loyal young man like my Galahad was
bound to please him."

Well, I was not about to correct her impression of me. "I'll always try to live up to his ex-
pectations."

She smiled. "You'd do better to think of living
up to mine, darling. I'm going to expect quite a
lot from you as soon as I have a right to expect
it." She kissed me again.

Our conversation was more physical than verbal for some time after that; but at last we began
to speak of the wedding itself.

"It must be as soon as it can be done
decently," Amelia insisted, and I was certainly
not about to disagree with her. "April, perhaps
—when the daffodils are blooming. I'll speak to

Father about the date, but I think the first Sunday after Easter might do."

"The sooner the better," I agreed.

"It will be the social event of the season, of course," she continued. "It can't be helped: Father's position will make it so. In the mean time, there's so much to do! Father will want to give a ball to announce our engagement, and I'm sure your father will want to have us for dinner, and we must decide on our living arrangements after the wedding—not to mention the wedding itself. It will be splendid, but—darling—I almost wish it did not have to be done, that we could be united to-night and never parted again!"

"Believe me, dearest, I wish it could be so. The wait will be difficult,—but patience will have its reward."

"I know it will," Amelia said with a soft smile. "But, in the mean time, you are now my acknowledged husband to be. I think that position permits you a few pardonable liberties beyond what you might have considered proper before."

Since I could find no flaw in her reasoning, I agreed; and when I parted from her that evening, I was a considerably more educated man. I walked briskly back through the dark and quiet streets feeling as though nothing could possibly be wrong anywhere in the world. I also felt a positive need to proclaim my triumph, though the only possible audience for my proclamation would be my father and my sister. They would have to be told sometime, at any rate, and it might just as well happen immediately.

I entered the hall, left my hat and stick in the rack, and carefully hung my coat in the closet—reflecting, as I did so, that I should soon have servants to take care of those inconsequential tasks. Entering the front parlor, I found my sister sitting straight in a side chair reading one of her appalling novels, and my father slumped in an armchair with a book of sentimental poetry open on his face.

"I'm glad I found you both together," I began with no other greeting. "I have something important to tell you both."

My father awoke with a start and brushed the book off his face; I saw Viola's expression darken a little, and she said without looking up at me, "If you've sold your Graded Stationery to some department store in the Indian Territory, we can hear all about it in the morning,—or never, if that's more convenient." Viola liked to profess a violent distaste for hearing me talk about the firm at all, though she was very happy to spend the money I provided for her.

"Nothing to do with the firm," I replied. "It's a more personal kind of business. I'm going to marry Amelia Goode."

At this Viola did look up, with her jaw gaping in a most unattractive fashion. My father, on the other hand, leaped out of his chair.

"You mean Hiram Goode's daughter?" he asked—quite unnecessarily, since there cannot have been great numbers of Amelia Goodes wandering the streets of Allegheny.

"Yes, that Amelia Goode," I answered cheerfully—for I was in such good spirits that I could not bring myself to be annoyed even by my father's thickheadedness. "She has done me the honor of consenting to be my wife, and her father has given us his blessing."

"Oh! this is marvelous, Galahad!" my father exclaimed. "Hiram and I were hoping the two of you might make a match of it—we thought you might have made an impression on the girl—but we never expected it to happen so quickly! Have you set a date yet?"

"Nothing firm," I answered, while my mind was still trying to grasp the implications of what my father had just told me. Did he really say "Hiram and I"? —"Nothing firm," I repeated, since my first attempt had come out as more of a squeak than a statement. "We had talked of a wedding in April, the first Sunday after Easter. We do want it to be soon, for reasons that—well, that I think should be obvious."

"Of course, Galahad!" My father attempted a sly wink, which was really quite hideous. "No need to elaborate on that, my boy. Well, my heartiest congratulations to you both. I think she's ideally suited to you, Galahad, and I know you'll be an ideal husband to her. —Won't they make a perfect pair, Viola?"

My father and I both looked toward the side chair, but there was no Viola in it. Instead, from the hall, we heard the sound of heels stamping noisily upstairs, and then a door ostentatiously slammed.

Viola refused to speak to me all the next day, which in ordinary circumstances would have suited me admirably; but in this case her blank refusal to be impressed by my greatest triumph irked me. My father, however, did unfortunately deign to speak, and during a brief lull at the store he explained the reason for Viola's petulance. "She had planned her own wedding for June, you know. She seems to think that your wedding will detract from hers somehow."

Well, of course it would. What kind of public glory did she expect for marrying the clerk in the lampseller's store? I was marrying the belle of Allegheny. Nevertheless, I tried to think of something more conciliatory to say to my father.

"I should think that, by having her wedding after ours, she would have the last word, so to speak. Hers would be the wedding everyone would remember." This was nothing but a lie, of course, and a clumsy one. I was not yet very far advanced in my pursuit of evil, and I had not yet learned to avoid all but the most necessary lies. It is greatly to one's advantage to have a reputation for veracity; the rational or evil man must in fact be uncommonly truthful.

"Your sister won't see it that way," my father replied, displaying more knowledge of the nature of sisters than I might have expected of him.

"Well, I can't be held responsible for my sister's unreasonable attitude," I said,—knowing at the same time that I *would* be held responsible for it, because Viola would see to it that I was. But at that moment a patron walked through the door, which put an end to our conversation.

I told Amelia about Viola's unabated petulance a few days later. It was an unseasonably warm and sunny day, and Amelia and I were actually strolling in the park. We should ordinarily have taken the carriage, which afforded us more privacy; but Henry, on whose discretion Amelia and I relied, was off that day, and it really was delightful to walk in the warm sun after so much chilly weather. A good number of other young couples had come to the same conclusion, so the park was quite lively that day.

"It's such a pity your sister should be so cross," Amelia responded when I told her how my sister—who in fact still remained mute when I was present—was behaving. "I had hoped we should be great friends."

Was not Amelia the best-natured girl in the
world? Imagine meeting Viola and hoping one
could be great friends with her! "I'm sure you
will be," I assured her, though not really believing anything of the sort. "Viola will forget all
about it shortly." In fact Viola had never forgiven me for being born, so I suppose twenty-
two years might be a good estimate of the length
of one of her grudges.

Amelia was about to reply, but just then a familiar voice hailed me, and I looked up to see
Gertrude Snyder, her brother, and a moustache
behind which lurked that Hoffman fellow. They
were all strolling toward us.

"How do you do, Mr. Bousted?" Gertrude
greeted me.

"Miss Snyder! How delightful to see you. I believe you know Miss Goode."

"How do you do, Miss Goode?"

Amelia replied with a mumbled greeting,
which was very uncharacteristic of her.

"And this," I continued, taking up the burden
of introductions, "is Mr. Magnus Hoffman"—I
indicated the ambulatory moustache on Gertrude's right,—"and Miss Snyder's brother, Mr.
Edward Snyder."

"Mr. Snyder and I are already acquainted,"
Amelia said quietly. She was gripping my arm; I
felt that same unsettling rigidity in her frame
that I had felt that night in the carriage when I

rejected her amorous advances. I reflected that she must often have seen me walking with Gertrude; I should probably have to reveal the extent of my acquaintance with Gertrude when I talked to Amelia later. But I might at least make that conversation easier by emphasizing Gertrude's current attachment to the moustache whose arm she was holding.

"And how have you and Mr. Hoffman been getting on?" I asked with my pleasantest smile.

Gertrude also smiled—one of those very rare bright smiles of hers that indicated genuine happiness. "We're to be married this spring," she answered.

"What wonderful news!" I exclaimed—quite sincerely, since it would certainly persuade Amelia that there was no lingering attachment between Gertrude and me. "Miss Goode and I will also be married this spring."

"Oh, how splendid, Mr. Bousted! I had no idea you and Miss Goode were even acquainted." There was no accusation in her tone; either it did not occur to her to wonder whether I had already had designs on Amelia when I was courting her, or she did not choose to wonder. For my part, I did not answer the implied question.

"And you, Snyder," I said as cheerily as I could,—"you must be happy to see your sister so well matched."

"H'm? Oh, yes indeed," he answered distract-
edly. He did not look happy, which was not at all
surprising when I considered his stated opinion of
the Hoffman fellow.

Clearly we had exhausted the possibilities of
pleasant conversation, if neither Snyder nor
Amelia was ready to be pleasant. "Well, it was
very good to see you," I concluded, "and my
best wishes to the happy pair."

Gertrude returned my compliments, still smiling, and then continued on her way with her
brother and the moustache. Amelia and I also
resumed our walk, but I could still sense that
strange hardness in her arm.

Finally, after a thoroughly uncharacteristic silence, Amelia spoke in a rather quiet monotone.
"Is Mr.—Mr. *Snyder*" (she pronounced it as if it
were a foreign name and she was not quite sure
if she had it right) "a good friend of yours?"

Something in her tone suggested that there
was more to the question than what was conveyed by mere words. She was probably looking
for information about Gertrude, and I decided
that it was time to tell her as much as it suited
me to tell her about my abortive pursuit of Miss
Snyder.

"More of a business acquaintance really," I
told her. "I know the sister a good bit better
than the brother. Gertrude and——"

THE CRIMES OF GALAHAD.

"Galahad, that was the man," she said suddenly.

I stopped in my tracks. "The man?"

Amelia looked around nervously, but there was no one within earshot. "I told you that there was a man who—who took my innocence. That was the man—the man you called Snyder."

CHAPTER XVIII.

The trouble with Snyder.

SHE WAS FACING me, but looking at my chest rather than my face; which I'm sure was just as well, since she would have seen I know not what confused and conflicting thoughts parading across it.

Receiving no response from me, she continued in a low voice, speaking rather to my cravat than to me. "I didn't know him as Snyder—he called himself Elmer Sanders. I was a foolish girl of nineteen; he was a charming man; he made me believe he was—what he was not. I don't know what to say, Galahad; I don't know what to think. I never thought I should see him again at all, and now to find him among your friends! What will you think of me?"

"What I have always thought," I said softly. "I think you have the purest and noblest heart in the world, and I——"

"But I hate him!" she sobbed, and she buried her face in my chest. Another strolling couple glanced at us, but looked away again promptly. I held Amelia against me, feeling quite helpless and conspicuous, and not a little confused. What did Amelia want from me? Did she want simple reassurance that I still loved her? Did she want me to share her hatred of Snyder?

I gave her some time to sob quietly while I composed my reply. It was necessary to tread carefully, while at the same time appearing to speak from the heart.

"Darling," I began after a minute or two, "I must confess to feeling a little bit the same way. A man who could hurt you, even in the slightest degree, for the sake of his own selfish pleasure—he must be something less than human. It's his confounded drinking! Miss Snyder has told me how the liquor changes her brother—how he becomes almost a different man under its influence. Sober, he seems a model of the decent gentleman; but drunk, he is a terror to his own sister. I own frankly that I don't know what I ought to do now."

"I don't know either," Amelia said, calmer now. "There was a time when men would fight duels over such things."

"Fortunately those days are long past," I put in hastily; and then, wondering whether I might have said the wrong thing, I added just as hastily, "though you know, my love, that I'd gladly fight for you and die for you if——"

"Oh no! I know you are far too good and pure to give or accept a challenge, and I'd never let you do it for the world."

That was certainly a relief. If it became necessary to kill Snyder, I had much rather it were accomplished by simple assassination than by the absurd farce of another duel.

"I shouldn't have said anything," she continued. "There is nothing you can do—nothing you ought to do. Only—only it was such a shock to find that you knew him."

She had absolved me, so to speak, of any duty to do anything about that despicable cad Snyder. Yet I could tell that I was not really absolved. What she had said was what reason had told her to say, but in her heart she wanted me to do something—I'm sure she knew not what. I could still feel that hardness in her arm; and when she kissed me, it was a perfunctory kiss such as a sister might give her brother—at least a sister who was moderately fond of her brother, for rumor says that such things do exist in the world. Thus we parted, with none of those delightful intimacies she had permitted me since she had accepted my proposal. Damn that Snyder! He really did deserve to die,—not for taking Amelia's virtue, which after all any man with the same opportunity would have done, but for depriving me of a single moment's pleasure with Amelia.

That evening I was once again alone after supper, my father having once again taken Viola to Camellia's house to speak of weddings. There was no need for me to go, since (as my father informed me) Camellia now refused to speak to me as well, the two sisters having resolved to form a perfect wall of silence against me. I could sit in silence more comfortably at home; so I took a chair in the front parlor and read a magazine of some sort. And, just as had happened the last time, there was the most appalling pounding at the door.

It must be Snyder, drunk again, and come to invite me to another duel. I stood up, imagining all the ways I might dispatch him more efficiently than by following him to the warehouse district. At least if he happened to be carrying a small case, I should be careful to relieve him of it at once. More annoyed than afraid, I yanked open the door—and found Gertrude waiting behind it.

She and her brother must have learned the art of thunderous knocking at the same school. In every other respect they could hardly have been more different—Snyder a rake and drunkard and his sister sober and virtuous. For the moment, however, she was more agitated than I had ever seen her. She stepped through the door without waiting for me to speak.

"Newman, I—I need you," she said. She was out of breath, as if she had been walking very briskly, or even running.

"Why, Miss Snyder, what is the matter?" I asked with my best tone of surprise and concern.

"It's Edward," she replied; then she seemed to search for words. "He's—tried to kill himself."

Tried—but evidently not succeeded. For a moment I cursed my ill fortune. How many difficulties would have been resolved if only Snyder could have succeeded in his endeavor! But no— apparently the man was such a rotten shot that he could not hit his own head, to say nothing of mine. What was done, however, could not be undone: he had been prevented from killing himself, and now he was not dead. It remained merely to see what could be made of this new development. What would Baucher do in like circumstances? Surely he would contrive to turn this unexpected interruption to his advantage. I must follow this affair to its conclusion, and see what comes of it. Perhaps, if nothing else, it could give me an opportunity to assassinate Snyder privately.

"Is he badly hurt?" I asked, my voice greasy with concern.

"No—I wrested the pistol out of his hand. He was very drunk. But he had prepared this note, and—if it means what I think—oh! Newman, I'm so very sorry!"

I took the paper she handed me—a sheet of Bousted's Grade 6, I noted without thinking about it. The appalling scrawl was almost illegible, but I could make out enough to tell that it was seeing Amelia and me that had put him in mind to extinguish his own life. He wrote that he had dishonored and betrayed the truest friend he ever had, and included enough detail to make it clear, to anyone who knew me, both that I was the friend and that Amelia's honor was the loss I had suffered. He was not only a cad but also a fool: surely any moderately intelligent man would see that, while virginity can be lost in se- cret, honor can be lost only by public exposure, such as—for example—the discovery of a de- tailed confession in a suicide note.

Gertrude gave me some time to read, but not very much, before she began speaking again.

"Edward has behaved very badly—worse than I thought him capable of—and I can only imag- ine what you must think of him. But I've come here to ask for what I've no right to ask—that you should forgive him, and that you should tell him so. Otherwise,—oh! Newman, he might try again! And who knows whether I'd be able to stop him the next time? You must wish him dead

—but I've come to beg for his life, because I really do believe that his life hangs on your word at this moment."

"My dear Miss Snyder," I replied in a soft and soothing tone, "I have already forgiven your brother."

This statement seemed to mollify or perhaps even stun her. My mind was working very hard to discover the course that would be truly evil, which is to say advantageous. Killing Snyder was quite obviously out of the question: if he were to die in otherwise unexplained circumstances, suspicion would naturally light on me, and Amelia's reputation would be ruined, which would ruin my own even if I were not convicted of murder. There remained, however, the possibility of removing once and for all the cloud that hung over Amelia, and at the same time placing the Snyders, brother and sister, forever in my debt, which could not but be useful to me in the long run. I may interpolate here a short observation: it has been my invariable experience that keeping one's acquaintances in one's debt will always prove advantageous in the end. Indeed, I may say that it is one of the things that distinguish the truly scientific evildoer from the mere bounder, who takes what he desires at the present moment without a thought to his own future advantage.—But enough digression. As Gertrude was silent for more than the usual time, I began again.

"I have already forgiven your brother, and his confession is no new thing to me. Amelia, who is as truthful as she is good-hearted, told me all before she consented to become my wife."

"Oh—oh, Newman, could you tell him that? If he hears it from your lips, it may be that he will feel—"

"Of course, Gertrude. We must go to him at once." And immediately I reached for my overcoat.

The walk to the Snyders' house gave me a little time to think. Gertrude talked most of the way, generally repeating expressions of regret for her brother's conduct, and returning often to the subject of his drinking, which I agreed was the root of all his troubles. It was also the root of more than one of mine. If he had not been drinking, I should never have risked my life in a duel; if he had not been drinking, either he would not have attempted to take his own life or he would not have failed so miserably in the attempt; and in either case I should not have been roused from my comfortable arm-chair by Gertrude's violent pounding on the door. Clearly it would be to my advantage if he could be induced to stop drinking. It was also what Gertrude desired most, and even her brother might desire it as well in his sober moments.

I found Snyder prostrate on the divan in the little parlor in his house. He did not see me at first, since his head was buried in the cushions.

"Edward," his sister called quietly, but he did not stir. "Edward!" she repeated, this time with the tone and volume of a drill sergeant—something I had never heard from her before, but doubtless a tone that belongs to sisters by virtue of their office.

"What?" he demanded, or rather not so much demanded as groaned.

"Mr. Bousted is here to see you," Gertrude answered in her ordinary melodious voice.

Snyder slowly lifted his head and turned his gaze on me. It seemed to take his eyes some time to resolve what they were seeing; then, slowly, he opened his mouth and spoke, quietly but distinctly.

"If you've come to kill me, maybe you'll have better luck than I had."

"Don't be absurd, Snyder," I replied. "I have no intention of killing you."

"Why not?" he demanded with sudden force. "Gertrude's told you everything—I know she has. But how was I to know, Bousted? Of all the girls in the world, how was I to know you'd—I mean, Bousted, how was I to know?"

"Snyder," I replied, "you've been a cad, but you know it, and I'm sure that's half the battle. I didn't learn about what you did from your sister;

I learned it from Amelia, weeks ago, and I've had time to forgive you."

"You mean you've had time to grow indifferent," Snyder said. "I know I can't be forgiven." He lay back on the divan in a despondent attitude: it seems that one common effect of alcoholic spirits is to make the drinker susceptible to fits of stage melodrama.

I turned to his sister. "Gertrude, could you please leave us for a little while? I think your brother could speak a little more freely to me alone."

Gertrude nodded and silently left the room. I waited until she had pulled the door shut and presumably walked away before continuing along the line of attack I had laid out for myself on the walk over.

"Look here, Snyder, are you a Christian?"

He looked at me as if he thought I might have meant something else. "What a question! Of course I'm a Christian."

"I don't believe you are," I responded. "A Christian wouldn't put himself in such a ridiculous position. If you really did believe in a just Judge, would you consider the appalling crime of suicide even for a moment? Would you leave your sister unprotected, to be a witness against you on the last day?"

"But I am a Christian," Snyder objected feebly. "It's just that—it's just that I behaved so badly, and it was you..."

"Yes, of course you've behaved badly, and that's the point. You have sinned, as every man does. Perhaps you've sinned more than most. Well, what of it? Would you deny yourself time for repentance? Would you go now to the absolute certainty of eternal damnation? Or would you not rather repent and live, and look forward to the equal certainty of heaven?—Yes, I say equal certainty, for heaven is promised to sinners, not to the perfect. No man is perfect. St. Paul was a murderer; St. Peter denied Christ three times. You know all these things, Snyder, but you forget them when you drink."

"I suppose that's true," he agreed in a thin voice.

"It's the confounded drinking that makes you act such a fool," I continued. "You are not a drunkard. You can live for days without a drop of liquor. There are men—God have mercy on them—who can't pass a day without resorting to spirits, but you're not one of them. Then why do you indulge? It brings you no joy, but only unbounded misery—a misery that involves your sister, whom I know you love, in its web, and your friends as well. Can it be long before it begins to affect your work?"

Here I was silent to give him a chance to reply, and myself a chance to think of a few more specious arguments to hurl at him. Snyder was silent, too, with his hands over his eyes. When he did speak at last, it was in a very weak voice, so full of despair that, had he not already caused me so many inconveniences, I might almost have been inclined to pity him. "But I don't know what to do, Bousted. I just don't know."

I did not know what to do, either; but I had at least enough imagination to invent something that a temperance preacher might have told him. "Well, first you must pray—pray for strength and courage. Without God's help, you can do nothing; but with God's help, there is nothing you cannot do." Was that not a pretty sentence? I might well have made a good temperance preacher myself. After terrifying Snyder with visions of an imaginary hell, and promising him the bliss of an equally imaginary heaven, I had invested my words with something like God's own authority over his superstitious little mind. Then I arrived at my real goal, which was this: "Then you must go to Amelia and beg her forgiveness."

This at least made him look up at me. "I can't do that, Bousted—she'd never forgive me, and I can't face her."

"Her forgiveness will not be easy to obtain," I agreed, "but you can earn it if you can show that you have struck at the root of all your sins—that you have pledged not to drink any more, and that you have taken effective steps to hold yourself to that pledge."

It was a marvel to watch the hope spreading across his face. The despair was melting, or at least it was thawing a little. "Yes," he said. —"You're right, Bousted. I don't have to drink. There's no reason for it. It doesn't bring me happiness. Only misery. Well, sir, from now on, no more misery for mine. I'll take the pledge. I'll be a new man. I'll do it right now. Bring Gertrude in here. I want her to hear this."

And that was how I cured Snyder of his drinking. He swore in front of Gertrude and me that he would never touch liquor again. He wrote it on a sheet of Bousted's Grade 6 and signed his name at the bottom. And then he announced, quite sensibly in his condition, that he was going to bed.

"Newman," Gertrude said when he had gone upstairs, "you are a marvel. I've tried for so many years to accomplish what you've done in one evening. How did you do it? What did you say to him?"

"Only a few things about his Christian duty," I replied with a great show of modesty. "Your brother is a good man, and a good Christian, and he needs only to be reminded once in a while of the truths of the Christian religion." This was all true as far as it went: it was apparently quite an easy thing to terrify the man with the myths of hell he had imbibed in childhood. I might have had equal success by telling him that a hideous green bogeyman would tear him to pieces if he did not abjure spirits.

"Well," Gertrude replied, "I don't know whether he will abide by his oath, but to bring him to swear it was more than I could ever do. You are a good and kind man, and—and Miss Goode is very fortunate that you have a forgiving nature."

She spoke Amelia's name with just a shade of involuntary contempt. Evidently her knowledge of Amelia's indiscretion had evaporated her former admiration and envy. I was confident that Gertrude could never be guilty of such an indiscretion. She had not Amelia's passionate nature. For the same reason, I was certain that Gertrude could never kiss me the way Amelia did. I much preferred the sinner to the saint; I found it wonderfully easy to dispense with Amelia's purity.

"You must remind your brother that he has yet one more obligation," I told her. "My forgiveness he has—it is my duty as a Christian— but he has promised to ask Amelia's, and I know his conscience will burden him until he has done so."

"You are a marvel, Newman," she repeated with one of her enigmatic smiles.

I have described the farcical events of this evening in some detail because it was in the course of confronting Snyder that I discovered an important principle in the pursuit of evil—a discovery that pleased me all the more because I had made it myself, without the explicit assistance of Baucher. Briefly stated, it is this: The appearance of piety can be of great use in promoting an evil scheme. In this case, I was able to make use of Snyder's superstitious attachment to Christian mythology to bring about the result I desired, but I should not have been able to do so had I not appeared to be subject to an equal or greater superstition. By some mere instinct I had already possessed some dim awareness of this truth: I had continued to attend my father's church, with every appearance of devotion, long after I had discovered the absurdity of the Christian religion, knowing that my reputation as a churchgoer elevated my reputation as a stationer. Now, however, the thing appeared to me for the first time in the clear light of day as a definite proposition.

Some delicate diplomacy was required in order to bring Amelia and Snyder together for the little drama I wished to arrange. Amelia was not at all eager to see the man who had defiled her; she recognized that I had done a very good thing for Snyder and his sister, and she insisted that she understood the necessity, as I had explained

it, of his expressing his remorse in a personal interview;—"but it's hard, Galahad," she said on
more than one occasion. "He will ask for my forgiveness, and I don't know whether I can give it.
I have not your virtue, darling. Perhaps I am
positively wicked."

I always assured her that she was not wicked
in the least, but I was somewhat at a loss as to
how to proceed from there.

In the event, however, it was Amelia who proceeded. "I wish to pay a visit to Mr. Snyder," she
said one evening;—and it was clear that those
few words had cost her a great deal of effort.

"I will arrange it," I said; and there was no
more to be said on that subject. But it did seem
as though a weight had been lifted from her. She
was more affectionate with me than she had
been since her encounter with Snyder. It is a curious fact that deciding to do a thing can have
the same effect on the mind as actually doing the
thing. It is not rational, but men and women are
not commonly rational; the rational man, which
is to say the evil man, observes this fact and
turns it to his advantage.

A few evenings later we paid a call, Amelia
and I, on Mr. Snyder and his sister. After a few
preliminary remarks from me, Snyder abased
himself in a hideously undignified fashion, but
one that pleased Amelia immensely by allowing
her to assume an air of Godlike mercy and for-

bearance. We parted from the Snyders after both brother and sister had expressed their profound gratitude to me for helping Mr. Snyder to see the truth of Christian principles and their application to his drinking, and we mounted Amelia's carriage, with the preternaturally discreet Henry as our pilot.

"Oh, Galahad!" Amelia exclaimed as soon as the door was closed. "You were so right—so wise! I do feel a thousand times better! It's as if the clouds had parted and I saw the sun for the first time in—in ages!"

"I'm very glad," I responded. "I know you've done Mr. Snyder much good—more, perhaps, than he deserves, but our God desires mercy, not justice." Our God is something of an imbecile, I thought to myself.

"Galahad, my darling, you're a good man, but you're more than that: you're the cause of goodness in others. I should never have forgiven Mr. Snyder—and yet how well I feel for having done it! And you have forgiven me as well, even though——"

I hastened to interrupt her. "In you, dearest Amelia, there is nothing to forgive."

She smiled brightly. "And you really do believe that, don't you? Oh, darling, you deserve a saint for a wife, but when I'm your wife I'll try every day to make you glad you married a sinner!"

She embraced me, and we did not find it necessary to speak again until Henry stopped the carriage in front of my house on Beech-street.

We kissed one last time, and then Amelia seemed to be examining me with such concentration that I felt compelled to ask her, "What do you see?"

"I was thinking that you might look better clean-shaven," Amelia answered, "the way I first saw you."

I did not wait until the morning: the moustache was gone within half an hour.

VOLUME V.

CHAPTER XIX.

My wedding, with other matters of interest.

MY FATHER AWOKE the next morning with what he called a little cough, though I would have called it a series of hideous hacking spasms—the result, he said, of a slight chill contracted while walking home with Viola the night before. It did not dampen his usual good cheer at all; it merely made him twice as annoying as usual at breakfast.

"I see you've shaved your moustache," he said almost immediately after I sat down at the table. My father believed it was a dreadful sin against good manners to leave the obvious unstated.

"Amelia thought I might look better without it," I replied.

"Well, I——" and here he was interrupted by another spasm of coughing. "I think you look very fine. What do you think, Viola? Doesn't Galahad look fine?"

"I am happy to see less of his hair," Viola replied, "but I am sorry to see more of his face."

At this remark my father fell into another fit of coughing, which very conveniently spared him the trouble of having to take note of Viola's ill temper.

Viola's behavior toward me did not improve at all over the next few days. For my part, I cared not a whit, not even half a whit, whether my sister spoke a civil word to me or not; but Amelia, whose usual good spirits and affectionate nature had completely revived, persisted in imagining, and (what is far more absurd) hoping, that Viola could somehow be made her friend if only this little spell of petulance could be smoothed out. "We're to be one family, after all," Amelia explained, "and I'd like her to think of me as a sister. Surely there must be some way to show her that we regard her wedding as every bit the equal of ours."

"Why don't we just have a double wedding?" I grumbled with ill-disguised sarcasm. Amelia, however, did not penetrate the disguise.

"Oh, Galahad! What a marvelous suggestion! Do you really think she would agree? It would require such a deal of preparation in such a short time,—but it could be done."

I was about to tell her that I had no intention of sharing my wedding with that human pestilence Viola, but at this point Amelia attacked me with kisses, and the battle was lost without a fight.

"You must ask your sister," she reminded me when we parted; and I agreed that I should do so, since my agreement bought me a few more kisses.

In fact I had no desire to speak with my sister on any subject. It would have to be done, however, before I next saw Amelia. Moreover, the more I gave my mind over to thinking about it, the more it seemed as though I had hit accidentally on a very rational solution to my difficulties. Viola was certainly capable of keeping a grudge going for the rest of her life; and, while if anything it improved my own disposition not to have Viola speaking to me, Amelia would be happier if Viola were well disposed toward her. She seemed to regard it as a failure of her own that she could not secure Viola's friendship. I had learned that Amelia's happiness was linked directly to my own: the happier Amelia was, the more affectionate she was, and Amelia's affection was a drug like opium to me, a necessity for which I was willing to make even the extreme sacrifice—I mean the sacrifice of speaking to my sister. As for the wedding itself, it was nothing to me whether we shared it with Viola and her clerk. I had no opinions on the wedding per se; it was the marriage I cared for. The wedding was useful only in that it would make possible that last degree of intimacy with Amelia that was currently denied to me;—or, rather, that I had denied myself, since there had been no unwillingness on Amelia's part. The truly evil man must learn to curb his immediate desires in favor of that which will redound to his ultimate benefit, and I was willing to defer the complete possession of Amelia if it would assure my continued possession of both her and her father's fortune.— Thus the wedding was but a means to that end; if it could be better accomplished in the presence of Viola, it was all the same to me.

The peace between Viola and Amelia that Amelia desired therefore became my object as well. After supper, I lost no time in seeking out Viola to speak with her alone. I found her in the front parlor reading the second volume of some silly three-volume novel.

"Viola," I said, "I wish to speak to you."

"H'm," she replied without looking up from her book.

It was not the most promising beginning to our interview, but I persevered.

"I know that you have been worried that your wedding might somehow be overshadowed by mine," I began, "and while I do not——"

"If you mean," she interrupted, "that you think I have been disappointed to discover that my brother is the sort of man who cares nothing for the happiness of his family so long as his own is assured, and will gladly run roughshod over his own flesh and blood in his rush to attain his own selfish desires,—you are mistaken. It is no new discovery, and can therefore be no disappointment."

Obviously she had turned over this speech and rehearsed it in her mind for days, if not weeks, while she waited for an opportunity to make use of it. In fact it was quite accurate: I was that sort of man. But it is one thing to be that sort of man, and another thing to appear to be that sort of man. It was meant as an insult, and as such it raised my hackles.

"Look here, Viola, there's no reason for you to be so disagreeable when I'm trying to be conciliatory. I was talking with Amelia, and she thinks we should have our weddings together—a double wedding. She thinks it would bring us all together as a family. Frankly, she's a good deal more interested in your happiness than I am at the moment, but I've agreed to the double wedding, if you can get it into your thick head that I'm trying to do you a good turn."

Viola was actually silent for a moment, which is how I always like her best. When she did speak, all the harshness had gone from her tone.

"Galahad—you would really do that for me?"

"No, but I would do it for myself. This is the price at which I am willing to purchase a bit of peace in the family."

"Galahad!" She leaped out of the chair and actually embraced me, for the first time since she had tried to crush the life out of me when I was a small child. "You are the sweetest and best brother in the world, and I love you with all my heart!"

With that unexpected demonstration out of the way, she ran out of the parlor and clattered noisily up the stairs.

Well, that was done, and it looked as though my success had been complete. I was about to retire early and get a good night's sleep for once when my father found me in the hall.

"Galahad," he said,—and then he began a fit of coughing that occupied him for a quarter-hour or so.

"Galahad," he repeated when he had quite finished, "Viola has told me about the wedding. I know that you have not always been on good terms with your sister" (this was a simply extra-ordinary statement, since up to that moment I should have been prepared to wager a large sum on my father's being entirely oblivious to the state of things between my sister and me), "and I know that your sister has been a little bit unrea-

sonable lately" (this was even more astonishing),
"but Viola has told me what you did for her. I'm
very proud of you, Galahad. I know how difficult
it must have been to persuade your Miss Goode
to share her wedding day—in fact, I'm really
very surprised that you accomplished it. You
must have moved heaven and earth for your sister's happiness, even after the way she treated
you. It shows a rare spirit. You have grown into
a fine Christian gentleman, and that, Galahad, is
the best I could ever have hoped for from you."

He clapped me on the back, and then he went
to bed.

I recall this conversation vividly because I
meditated on it for some considerable time afterward. It seemed to me that I had learned an invaluable secret. I had made a small concession
on a matter that meant nothing to me, and as a
result Amelia thought I was an angel; Viola was
actually pleased with me for the first time in my
memory; and my father was entirely persuaded
that I was the paragon of oafish commercial
virtue he had always hoped for in a son. What a
cheap price bought so many treasures! I understood then the value of consulting the pleasure of
others in small things of no consequence, so that
the things of greater import would not be caught
up in their petty displeasures; and I resolved
thenceforth to adapt my wishes in small things to

those of my family, so that my greater schemes might proceed without let or hindrance.

Oh, the things that had to be done to make two weddings happen on the same day! I am sure I never knew half of them; Viola and Amelia, both lacking the mothers who would ordinarily have been in charge of the arrangements, took everything in hand themselves, and showed every sign, in spite of their vast differences in temperament, of becoming fast friends in the process. I saw much less of Amelia, which was a disappointment; but, on the other hand, I saw much less of Viola, which was some compensation. Amelia insisted that the wedding must be at St. Andrew's, to which Viola assented all the more readily because (as she informed me with insufferable pride) St. Andrews was the church where the *better* classes of weddings were performed. Indeed, through the whole planning of the wedding, Viola was torn between the two poles of giving unbridled expression to her glee at having been accepted into the upper stratum of Allegheny society, and affecting the air of having always belonged there. There were times when she seemed to be almost torn in two by these conflicting impulses. I sincerely enjoyed those occasions.

Amelia and I had some discussion about our living arrangements after the wedding,—though in the minds of Amelia and Viola such matters

were clearly of secondary importance to the
wedding itself. Amelia thought it would be most
sensible if we began our married life in her father's house, which was absurdly large for two
people, and hardly less absurd for three. I did not
need much persuading: the Goodes lived in a
luxury that I had scarcely dreamt of before I met
Amelia, and I could imagine nothing better than
to become part of the Goode household. I was
eagerly anticipating the delight of commanding
an army of domestics instead of old Mrs. Ott,
who used her deafness as a shield against any
commands whatsoever. We also discussed the
delicate topic of religion, but Amelia again easily
persuaded me that it would be best if we both
went to the same church, and of course the obvious choice was St. Andrew's. It was nothing to
me, after all, whether I followed the Methodist or
the Episcopalian branch of Christian delusion.

The vicar at St. Andrew's insisted on interro-
gating me on the subject of my Christian beliefs.
Christian beliefs I had none; but clearly that was
not an obstacle I was willing to place in the way
of my temporal happiness. Here my otherwise
useless education came to my assistance: I was
able to give such a good account of my supposed
beliefs that the man was sure I must have been
raised on the Thirty-Nine Articles.

Thus I changed my religious affiliation on very
practical considerations. There was no advantage

to me in remaining in the little Methodist church my father attended; but there might be every advantage in joining the wealthy congregation at St. Andrew's, where the best elements of Allegheny society gathered every Sunday to put on their pious faces and nod gravely at the commandments which they intended to spend the other six days of the week breaking. When my marriage to Amelia was accomplished, I must take my place among those best elements—indeed, very near their head—and therefore ought to be seen nodding as gravely as the rest of them.

To any young man who aspires to true evil, which is to say complete rationality, my advice is to cultivate a studious devotion to the forms and ceremonies of religion: for a reputation for exceptional piety opens every door. It is also of great utility to be seen performing such small acts of charity as cost little effort and make no difference in one's overall wealth, but create an impression of generosity and Christian sympathy with one's fellow creatures. Indeed, the truly evil man may find it to his advantage to make a display of Christian charity even at the cost of some considerable sacrifice, knowing that the temporary inconvenience will be more than balanced by the enhancement of his reputation and the concomitant enhancement of his prosperity in the long run.

One more thing happened during this interval, which is that Viola's clerk came to work for Bousted & Son. Viola insisted that, if Camellia's husband had a place in the firm, hers must as well. His name (I only now discover, reading back over these pages, that I have not mentioned it yet) was Colebrook; even now I sometimes have difficulty remembering it, because he does not make very much of an impression on me. I quickly discovered that he was much too timid to face patrons like the formidable Mrs. Rockland; but he wrote a very fair hand, and was intelligent enough to take over the correspondence with department stores and canvassing agents.

The time of the wedding finally arrived; but you, dear reader in my imagination, shall hear very little of the ceremony, for I myself recall very little of it. I remember my father's coughing, and how I wished that he would be done with it;—but of course he never was, and he continued to make the most appalling din throughout. I remember how beautiful Amelia was in white silk, and the powerful scent of the orange blossoms she wore (they had come up from Florida in a special car), and how stiff my new blue coat was, and how long it took—hours, days, weeks—to walk the whole length of the aisle. I remember the sudden realization that struck me at the end of the ceremony, that Amelia now belonged to me entirely without qualification, and the difficulty of restraining myself so that our first kiss as man and wife was chaste enough for the occasion and the audience. Then there was an interminable dinner, during which, in obedience to the inflexible laws of etiquette, I saw so little of Amelia that I began to wonder whether I had only imagined the wedding. And then, after that interminable feast, where Amelia and Viola reigned as queens, and Colebrook (who looked alternately proud and terrified) and I seemed reduced to a page's estate, there was an even more interminable wait.

We returned to the Goode mansion—my home now, I reflected with no little satisfaction—late in the evening, and Amelia's father immediately bid us good-night, saying that he was very tired, and adding, with no apparent irony whatsoever, that Amelia and I must be looking forward to a good night's sleep as well. He shuffled up the stairs, leaving me alone in the front parlor with my wife.

"I can assure you, Galahad," she whispered to me while her father was still ascending the stairway, "that sleep is the very last thing on my mind."

She gave me a light kiss, and then turned to watch until her father had vanished from sight.

"Now, Galahad," she said in a low voice, "I want you to stay right here. Do not stir from this room until I send Elsie for you. It will be worth your while to be patient, I promise you."

"Yes, of course, my love," I replied, though secretly resenting every minute by which my enjoyment of the conjugal rights I had so laboriously earned was delayed.

She kissed me again. "Stay right here until Elsie comes for you," she repeated; then she turned and floated out of the parlor and up the stairs with a soft rustle of silk.

There I was alone in her parlor—my parlor, I told myself, although it seemed only partly true. I looked around me at all the luxurious appointments: the marble, the mahogany, the stained glass, the Louis XIV this and that. I looked at them, and told myself, "This is mine, and this is mine, and this is mine";—but in fact it all belonged to Colonel Goode, and would not really belong to me until he died and left it to his daughter. He was an old man, but in good health; unless some unexpected reverse hastened his demise, it might yet be many years before the Goode fortune was truly mine.

What was taking Amelia so long? It had already been—I looked at the clock on the mantel —at least three minutes. Well, it was some consolation to know that it had not been as long as I thought. My impatience had magnified those three minutes into half an hour. Surely Amelia must be as impatient as I; it was she, after all,

who had been ready to consummate our marriage before the marriage had even been discussed. She could not keep me waiting very long.
I picked up a book that was sitting on the side
table: Carey's *Ancient Near East*. The preface
promised good fun with the Chaldees and the As-
syrians and the Medes and Persians, but I was
not able to read more than the first page and a
half. I believe it took me half an hour to read
that much. My mind was not with the book; it
drifted off into thoughts of the delights I should
soon enjoy—soon? Surely it must be soon, for I
bitterly resented every tick of the clock. At last I
abandoned my futile attempt at reading and simply sat. It had been more than half an hour, and
still no Elsie had come. Had something terrible
happened? Was Amelia even now lying insensible on a couch, struck down by some unknown
and unsuspected ailment? No, of course not;—
doubtless she was merely attending to some unnecessary details of her toilette—unnecessary
because I could easily have ripped the last stitch
of clothing from her in less than half a minute,
and what more than that was necessary? The
thought of doing so entertained me for another
quarter-hour. Then, for a while longer, I simply
watched the clock. It was just possible to perceive the movement of the minute hand against
the dial. I observed it for a while; then I began
to wonder how often the clock ticked. I waited

until the minute hand exactly covered one of the marks on the dial, and then counted one hundred sixty ticks until it covered the next one. One hundred sixty ticks, or eighty full swings of the pendulum, per minute. It became absurdly important to me to ascertain this fact with certainty. I counted three more minutes with the same result. Yes, I had established beyond the possibility of doubt that the clock in the front parlor was regulated by a pendulum swinging eighty times a minute. I ought to take a survey of the other clocks in the house; perhaps I could write all their periods down in a memorandum-book and keep it with me, and then if someone should ask—perhaps one of the servants—"What is the period of the pendulum in this clock?"—why, then I could produce my memorandum-book, and——good God, would Elsie never come?

I had reached such a pitch of desperation by that time that I can hardly say why I did not break my promise and run up the stairs to see what could possibly be the matter with Amelia. Yet I was in that parlor—sitting, standing, pacing, muttering—for yet an hour after that. The thoughts that went through my mind in that time reflect no credit upon me, I am sure. I gave in to despair; I wondered again whether I had not merely imagined the wedding, or indeed my whole life. Was I not born in that parlor, and should I not die there?

——But at last Elsie did come, a wisp of a girl who could not bring herself to look straight at me.

"Miss Goode—that is, Mrs., uhm, Bousted—is ready," she said in a voice so quiet and tremulous that I had to strain my ears to hear her. Then she turned away and took a few steps; and then she looked over her shoulder, and added, "If you could follow me, sir."

So I followed her up the stairs—and it struck me that I had not been upstairs in the Goode house, my house, since I was first brought there after my heroic rescue of Amelia. At the top of the great staircase Elsie turned left into what seemed to me then to be an impossibly long hall, a hall that might have engulfed our entire Beech-street house. She glanced backwards to ascertain that I was still following her; but as soon as her eyes met mine she turned back abruptly and tripped ahead at a faster pace, as if I were some object of supernatural terror. I matched my pace to hers, striding briskly through the hall, past innumerable doors (no more than a dozen, but to my eyes the hall seemed infinite), until at last we reached the end of the hall, with a window before us and doors to the left and right.

For a moment—an interminable moment—
Elsie simply stood facing the window. Then at
last she turned to face me, with the most ghastly
pale countenance I have ever seen on a living
woman. She opened her mouth to speak, but no
words proceeded from her lips; then all at once
she turned deep rose, pointed to the door on the
left hand, and almost pushed me out of the way
as she suddenly dashed off and quite literally ran
back down the hall.

After that performance, I certainly did not
know what to expect behind the door. I knocked
lightly, and then gently turned the knob. The
door opened silently on perfectly oiled hinges.

The far wall was hung with deep red curtains,
and in the middle of the room was a couch
draped profusely in red velvet; and on the couch,
La Belle Anglaise. Every fold of the drapery, every line of the furniture in the painting had been
reproduced as accurately as lay within the power
of feminine industry. And Amelia herself, the
central figure in the composition, recumbent,
her every limb exactly as in the picture—oh!
reader, there are not words in our poor language
to describe the vision that met my eyes.

"Lock the door," she said with an inviting
smile; and I did lock it.

CHAPTER XX.

My inperial anbitions seen to be thwarted by the folly and ignorance of ny elders.

No MAN COULD have been happier than I in the days after my wedding. I had every reason to be happy: my possession of Amelia was at last complete, and my wickedest lusts now found fulfillment with the sanction and approval of Christian convention. What a strange thing it is that a man who, in the eyes of all society, would be condemned as a vicious criminal if he ravished an unmarried woman, can be, by a few words spoken in a church, made into a paragon of virtue, with the uncontested right to ravish the same woman whenever he pleases!—Indeed, in my case, I believe Amelia ravished me at least half the time. It had never occurred to me, when I began to pursue Amelia, that a woman could take as much pleasure in conjugal relations as a man, or perhaps even more. It may be that Amelia is exceptional in that regard. I do not know; I know only that if you, young reader, should find such a woman, you ought to marry her at once, and let no scruples against foolish Christian morality stand between you and a lifetime of pleasure.

My happiness, therefore, was intense,—but it was not unalloyed. After my first few days as a married man, I began to consider that my position, while immeasurably improved, was not yet all I might wish for. The wealth I enjoyed in the Goode household was not mine; I did not control it, and indeed could not really do anything with it. At times it almost maddened me to think of all that money sitting idle (for Colonel Goode had a great personal fortune just sitting in banks) when it could have been building my empire of pens and paper. Then Amelia would call for me, and I would forget to be anything but happy. Only when I was not with Amelia did I perceive any deficiency in my life.

I took an entire week away from the firm after the wedding (though we took no wedding-trip, such things not being the fashion then among Allegheny society as they are now), and by the end of it I had begun to worry about how the store might be faring in my absence. Most of our revenue was coming from sales of paper and pens to department-stores and stationers across the country; but the store was still the capital, so to speak, of my empire, and I was not certain that I trusted my father to run it without me.

When I did come back for the first time, I was appalled to discover that my father, whom I had supposed to be running the place to the best of his ability, had not set foot in the store at all for the previous week, and that the management of the whole store had been left in the hands of Bradley. Even more shocking was that a new hired man was stocking shelves and waiting on patrons as if he knew his business. Bradley explained that my father's health had not permitted him to spend his days in the store; and, as he had not wished to trouble me with business so soon after my wedding, he had permitted Bradley to hire another clerk, who had been working since Wednesday. I was forced to admit a grudging admiration for the man who had persuaded my father to lay out the money to hire another man; and, having observed him for some time, I found the new man to be quite good at what he was doing. Bradley had made an excellent choice. Moreover, a quick glance at the books informed me that the store was thriving under Bradley's management. He took particular care to see to it that he served all the society matrons himself, and his unaccountable skill in dealing with them never failed to make a sale.

It appeared that the store on Wood-street could do without me after all. It was time to broaden the scale of my enterprise,—which doubtless would involve taking a great many risks of which my father would not approve. If only I had the Goode fortune to draw on for capital! But at least I could make the most of what I had.

For that reason, I resolved to pay a visit to my father, hoping that his current indisposition might be turned to my advantage. Leaving the store again in the obviously capable hands of Bradley, I took the horse-car back across the Allegheny (I believe this must have been very nearly the last time I availed myself of the horse-cars) and presented myself at the front door of the house on Beech-street. I was just about to commence the usual thunderous cacophony of ringing and knocking that was necessary to bring Mrs. Ott to the door when the door opened and a well-dressed man nearly ran into me on his way out of the house.

For a moment he registered surprise; then his brow lowered into an expression of hostile doubt.

"Who are you?" he demanded.

I was not accustomed to such a greeting on what had been, until very recently, my own doorstep. "Galahad Newman Bousted," I replied, drawing myself up to my full height, and perhaps a little more.

"Ah—the son." His face opened a little, as if I had been moved from the class of enemies into the class of mere nuisances in his estimation. "Well, I suppose you may go in. But he is not to be agitated. He is to have no other visitors—do you understand, my boy? I want him to have rest. I have every hope if he has rest. And no heavy foods at all. Rest, beef broth and a bit of toast, and above all no agitations of the mind. Do you think you can do that, my boy? Very good." (He had not waited for a reply.) "I must be off now. I shall call to-morrow to see how my instructions have been carried out. Good day." He touched the brim of his hat in the most perfunctory manner possible and slipped past me.

I remember feeling rather peevish at being called "my boy" twice. I, the husband of Amelia Goode Bousted, the son-in-law of Hiram Goode, the prime mover of the Bousted stationery empire—I was surely no "boy"! But it would not be very rational to dwell on some perceived slight from a stranger when my father was busy turning a slight cold into a Verdi opera. I had better go up and see him, make the proper expressions of filial concern, and then proceed with my original purpose of turning his temporary indisposition to my advantage.

I found my father sitting up in bed, with a half-finished bowl of broth on a tray beside him. "Ah! Galahad," he greeted me with his usual oafish good cheer;—and then a protracted fit of coughing overcame him. He was certainly playing the melodrama consumptive well, with every turn and trope executed to perfection. Perhaps his pallor was off by a few shades, but it would answer the purpose.

"Why haven't you told me you were ill?" I asked with what I hoped was just the right mixture of reproach and sympathy.

"Oh, my boy, there's no need to worry yourself. Dr. Gratz says I'll be just fine if I rest. I'd never have sent for him myself, but——" and here another bout of hacking came over him, and I had to wait an eternity to hear the end of a very dull sentence—"but Camellia insisted. She's a good girl, but she will have her way."

"And she's quite right," I told him. Privately I wondered whether Camellia had ever been right about anything in her life, but it suited me that my father's indisposition should be magnified in his eyes. "Would you have been resting now if Dr. Gratz hadn't insisted on it? You must rest, and you must leave everything else to your dutiful children. Viola and Camellia, I'm sure, can take care of your domestic arrangements, and I can take care of the business. I want you to think no more about it at all. Your wise guidance has fortunately placed Bousted & Son in such a position that it no longer needs your direct supervision, and the recovery of your health must be your primary, and indeed your only, consideration." As I look back on those days, I see that I was in the habit of talking like an historian, which I probably thought added to the impression of gravity I desired to leave on those around me.

My father did not respond quite as I had wished. "Ah! Galahad, you really are everything I hoped you would be. But you needn't worry so much about me. I'll be much better in a week or two."

"Nevertheless," I said (with a broad and ingratiating smile), "I want you to turn the operation of Bousted & Son over to me entirely. You've earned a rest from your labors by a lifetime of ceaseless care for your business and your family."

My father laughed merrily, which brought on another spell of coughing. There was nothing to do but wait it out. The time dragged appallingly as my father coughed and coughed; and each time I thought he had finished, and was about to resume our conversation, he started up again. Of all the embarrassing habits he had fallen into throughout his life, this coughing was by far the most annoying. Did he have to draw it out so?

At last he was ready to speak. "Oh, Galahad, you are a devoted son, to be sure," he said with a smile, "but I'm not quite yet the permanent invalid you seem to think I am. I can see I've worried you too much. Dr. Gratz thinks I'll be just fine with some rest, and I'm not ready to give up business just yet. What would I do all day? Please set your mind at ease, and—" (here he was interrupted by another spasm of coughing) "—and don't give me another thought."

This entirely unsatisfactory answer was all I could get from him. I had hoped to seize complete control of the firm, relieving my father of the last vestiges of his authority (and thus his ability to stand in the way of my grander schemes), and I had failed. Imbecile that he was, he was still capable of blocking my imperial ambitions. Really, it was too bad of him. I expressed the expected wishes for his speedy recovery, and I left in a foul mood.

Still, I had half-formed a scheme of action by the time I came back to the Goode mansion that evening. It was true that I saw my course through a glass darkly, but at least I had thought through enough of it to conclude that, if I could not convince my father of his own incapacity, I could at least implant that notion in the minds of the rest of the family. If he were surrounded by people who sincerely advised him to retire from business, he might be more willing to consider the idea; and if it came to open conflict with my father, I ought to have as many allies as I could impress into my service.

"My father's health," I told Amelia that evening, "is very discouraging. He didn't wish to trouble me, but he hasn't been well at all. And he has only old Mrs. Ott to take care of him, which is hardly any help at all."

"Oh, the poor man!" Amelia said with genuine concern,—for she, like the old Colonel, had taken a perfectly unaccountable liking to my father. "Has a doctor seen him?"

"Yes—Camellia sent for a Dr. Gratz. I spoke with him today. He's not very hopeful unless my father will rest—but you know him; you know that he doesn't like to give up his daily business. I told him he ought to turn everything over to me, but he won't hear of it.—And of course Mrs. Ott is of very little use, even if he can make himself heard. I worry about him in that house alone, or as good as alone. What if——"

"He must come here," Amelia announced decisively.

For a moment, I was not certain what I had heard. "You mean—but you see, he is meant to be resting, and——"

"Well, of course, and he can do that so much better here. Our staff is not all deaf"—she smiled —"and you know my father would be delighted to have the company. There's no reason for him

to keep up that whole house when all his children have married, and we have ever so much
more room than we need here."

This was not at all what I had had in mind. I
had only just escaped my father a week ago! But
the notion had entered Amelia's head, and now
there was no getting it out. Her father had
warned me, and he was quite right: once she had
decided on something, Amelia was as unstop-
pable as a Baldwin locomotive. She took it for
granted, of course, that I would be delighted by
her attention to my father, and she set about
making arrangements at once. In two days, the
cavernous halls of the Goode mansion were
echoing to the melodious sound of my father's
incessant hacking. Viola and her husband, meanwhile, took over the house on Beech-street. I did
wonder why, if my father was so dreadfully ill,
Mr. and Mrs. Colebrook could not have moved
into the house while he was still there, to give
him the assistance he needed; but my one hint of
a question to Viola was met with such an indig-
nant glare that I did not ask again. At any rate,
the thing was done: my father was now part of
the household, and the only consolation was in
the size of the house, which was big enough that
it was perfectly possible to lose one's way between one end and the other.

The worst thing about the arrangement was
that everyone else felt so positively jolly about it

that I had to pretend to be jolly as well. The first morning of my father's stay, he insisted on coming down to breakfast, which I am quite sure would have displeased Dr. Gratz. Colonel Goode immediately fell into familiar conversation with him, and soon the two of them were exchanging dull stories and feeble witticisms as if they had known each other all their lives. Sometimes they included Amelia and me in their conversation, but it was clear that our fathers were two kindred souls, knit together by a shared imbecility. How Colonel Goode had managed to amass his great fortune was a thing I could not explain at all: luck must have had a great deal to do with it, or perhaps he was a very different man in his youth.

"Your father is such a charming man," Amelia remarked as I was preparing to go into town for the day.

"What makes you say that?" I asked with my best jolly smile. I was working very hard at being jolly, but I was genuinely puzzled.

"Oh, he's always so happy—even when he's so ill. He laughs so easily, and he always has a good word for everybody."

Privately, I thought that Amelia's description would exactly fit a good number of the idiots at the asylum; but I had to pretend to be pleased. "Yes, he's always been like that. I was fortunate to have such a good example in my youth. Now, don't let him wear you out with tending to his whims. I know your good nature, but you needn't run to him every time he calls for one of the servants. It will make him feel as though he's taking advantage of you." That might or might not have been true, but I had my own private reasons for not wishing Amelia to be worn out when I came home, as I am sure any man who has ever been a new husband can imagine.

It was very different going in to the store since my marriage. For one thing, I began to arrive by carriage instead of by horse-car, which caused no little sensation among the other shopkeepers on the street the first time it happened. There could be no surer indication that I had risen far above them. It was Amelia who thought I was foolish to take the horse-car: "Surely Henry could drive you," she said, "and wouldn't you be much more comfortable that way?" I felt a little foolish myself when I realized that none of the other members of the Allegheny aristocracy were familiar with the horse-cars at all, except as conveyances for their day-laborers and scullery-maids.

Within the store it was very different as well. My father was no longer there to annoy me, and Bradley was perfectly capable of running the place by himself, with the able assistance of the new clerk. (I have forgotten the new man's name; I cannot distinguish him in my memory from the innumerable clerks we have had in the store since then.) I occasionally waited on a lady who seemed particularly likely to place a large order, but I am not sure that I handled the patrons any better than Bradley did. Colebrook was doing a fine job with the correspondence, although there was so much of it that I often lent my assistance there as well. On the whole, though, I had much less to do. Clearly it was time to apply my own efforts to expanding the reach of Bousted & Son, making it the colossus I had intended it to be since I first heard the prophetic message of that can of tooth powder.

The great problem to solve was the problem of money. I desired not merely a national but an international reach, an empire of six continents, with ladies from Norway to New South Wales scrawling their fatuous correspondence on Bousted Stationery, with Bousted pens dipped in Bousted ink, perhaps even sitting at Bousted writing-desks. Such an empire could hardly be built by three or four men working in the little store on Wood-street; we already had more correspondence than Colebrook could handle, and even without any special effort it was clear that I would require five or six Colebrooks in a few months. No, to expand my empire to satisfactory dimensions I should need many men working in many offices in a big building with my name at the top. That would require a prodigious investment,—but one that would reap suitably prodigious returns, if my guess about the market was correct.

These thoughts were revolving in my mind more and more when I heard a bit of business gossip that suddenly accelerated their revolutions. It was said that old Mr. Rohrbaugh had decided to retire from trade, and that he was looking for a buyer for his store. Now, I had no desire to run a department store, but it occurred to me that the building itself was just about the size I had in mind for the expanded Bousted & Son empire. It was ideally located: a larger Bousted & Son store might occupy the ground floor, near enough to the original location that our regular patrons would suffer no inconvenience from the move. —This at least was the reason I gave myself, and it was very true that we did require a larger building for our expanding firm; but I am sure that my true motive was vanity. I had always regarded Mr. Rohrbaugh as the great man of Wood-street; by conquering his establishment, I should become the universally acknowledged great man of Wood-street.

The opportunity must be seized; but it required much more in capital than Bousted & Son possessed. My father-in-law, however, had enough filthy lucre stashed away in various places to buy half the city of Pittsburgh. Surely he could spare the necessary amount.

Such was my reasoning, but I was doomed to disappointment. I presented the idea to him as an opportunity for a sound investment that could be reasonably expected to pay unusually high dividends, but he flatly refused to give me even the paltry sum I required to buy the Rohrbaugh building. In fact, he laughed in my face. It was not an ill-natured laugh; it was oafishly good-natured, which was all the worse. "I think you're a bit young to be making such grand plans for yourself," he said cheerily.

I did try to reason with him. "I only thought it might be a good opportunity for you as well," I said, "one that would make you a substantial profit in time."

"I doubt whether I have that kind of time on this earth," he replied with another oafish laugh. "You'll have it all when I'm gone, anyway, but I intend to stick around for a little while longer."

"Oh, many years, surely, I trust." Of course I had to pretend to be just as pleased as punch by his refusal, telling him that I valued his wisdom and experience more than I could say, and that he should dispose of his money as he saw fit. I put on a smile to cover my bleak mood and walked out into the street to compose my thoughts. But I must confess that they were still in some disarray when I came back home.

Meanwhile, my father affected to be worse and worse. He could no longer come downstairs, but had his meals brought up to him. Colonel Goode spent a great deal of time by his bedside, and of course I, ever the dutiful son, did what I could to make myself look useful. I knew that I had created the proper impression of filial concern when Amelia warned me not to wear myself out too much with worry over my father. "I know how you love him, Galahad, but he has me and the staff to take care of him as well. I don't want you growing old before your time."

"Hardly any danger of that," I assured her. But I did agree to spend less time with my father, which suited me better than she knew.

In the mean time, it was definitely announced that Rohrbaugh's had been sold,—but the firm, not the building. Rosenbaum's had bought up the stock, the name, and whatever else went with the store, and would be operating as "Rosenbaum & Rohrbaugh." (This did not last long, of course; the name of Rohrbaugh disappeared from the signs a few years later.) That left the big store empty and looming ominously over the rest of Wood-street.

I was ruminating, hardly for the first time, on my frustration in being unable to purchase that building when I visited my father for our nightly talk. This particular evening he wanted to talk about me, to which I should have had no objection if he had not been so distastefully maudlin about it.

"You've become everything I hoped you would be," he told me, "and I suppose a great deal more than I'd hoped. I won't be around much longer, but I can see that I have no reason to fear for you after I'm gone." Here he began to cough—not the vigorous, house-shaking coughs to which he had treated us a few weeks earlier, but a softer, altogether more civilized cough.

"I trust you'll be with us a good many more years," I told him; and I really did believe it. How could he leave me and deprive himself of the pleasure of annoying me every day?

"Well," he said, his cough momentarily settling down, "I've lived to see all my children well established and happy, and how could I wish for anything more than that? If I go now, I know I'm going to my reward, and you'll do a first-rate job of managing the firm. You'll keep your sisters in mind, too, won't you, Galahad? They depend on you more than you know."

Well, of course they depended on me; I knew the exact extent of their dependence. One word from me, and their husbands would find themselves without positions. "I'll always make sure they have everything they could possibly need," I promised him, which was an easy promise to make, even if I intended to keep it. How much, after all, could they possibly need? Their desires might be infinite, but their actual needs were few.

"Of course you will. Now, Galahad, if you'll forgive an old man——"; but here he began to cough again, and kept it up for two or three minutes. He liked to keep me waiting for the end of a sentence; it gave his statements a gravity they would not otherwise possess. "Well, Galahad," he was able to say at last, "I don't think you need much advice anymore. But a man likes to feel that he hasn't lived his whole life without learning something. So I'll pass on to you the little I've learned over the past sixty years. The one thing you can't forget, Galahad, is your family. You live with people every day, and you never think how much they mean to you; but a moment, Galahad, a moment can take them away, and then where are you?"

Rather better off, I thought to myself; but I held my tongue.

"Your dear mother," he continued after another coughing spell, "was everything to me, but she was taken away from me long before her time. But she left me the greatest gift in her power—my three children. I know your mother would be proud beyond words to see what you've made of yourself, Galahad. For her sake, remember your sisters, your precious wife, my friend Colonel Goode—all your family. Always put them first, and in everything you do make their happiness your guiding principle. If you do that, your mother will look down from heaven and smile, and—and so will I."

I had to sit through a great deal more of this dime-novel sentimentality, which it pains me to repeat even more than it pains you, dear reader, to hear it; but eventually I left him and retired in the infinitely more satisfactory company of my wife.

I went into town as usual the next day, which was quite dull and rainy; and I had been in the store for about three hours, helping Bradley with the patrons (for we were very busy that day), when Henry suddenly appeared in the doorway.

"Mrs. Bousted needs you at home right away, sir," he told me—more words, I believe, than I had ever heard him speak in one sentence.

"Did she say why?" I asked, looking up from the ugly scrawl in front of me.

"The elder Mr. Bousted is not well," he answered.

Well, that was to be expected, I thought. I tried to tell Henry that I should come as soon as I had finished helping the lady in front of me, but the patron told me that I was not to worry about her, and that my father (whom she remembered, it seemed) was more important than her stationery. Bereft of my only excuse for delay, I glumly followed Henry to the carriage, which was waiting in the rain in front of the store, thinking all the while that here was yet another indignity I should be suffering more and more often. My father was obviously set on a long course of decline. He had made up his mind to play the part of the melodrama consumptive, and every day must bring some new crisis, or the play would lose its excitement for him. Well, somehow a stop must be put to this at once. Before he got accustomed to sending for me whenever the notion entered his head, he must be made to understand that we had servants to take care of his whims, and it simply would not do for him to have Amelia call me away from business every single day on some foolish pretext or other.

I was still ruminating on these things when I stepped into the entry hall at home; but my thoughts were brushed aside when I saw Amelia standing there, waiting for me. I had formed in my mind a certain picture of what she would look like when I arrived: she would look a little apologetic,—cheerful as usual, but understanding that she had allowed me to be inconvenienced, and rather wishing that she had not been put in that position. But that was not the picture that greeted my eyes at all. The Amelia I saw was standing still, with her head tilted a little downward, but her eyes meeting mine. Her cheeks were pale; her eyes were red. She was calm, but it was a calm that had come after a storm.

"Galahad," she said quietly, "your father died a half-hour ago."

I looked at her blankly; I remember I felt as if I ought to say something, and could think of absolutely no words that would suit the occasion.

"Dr. Andick was here, and I sent for you as soon as I could, but—— "

She could think of no more to say after that; and for a moment we stood there in that hall, silently, looking at each other, separated by a distance of about two yards. I remember how sharp and distinct all the sounds around me were in my ears: the ticking of the hall clock, and the rain gently splattering in the puddles outside, and in the distance the rumble of Henry opening the door to the carriage-house, and the creak of a floorboard and the distinctively soft and quick footsteps of Elsie somewhere above me. And all at once I heard a wailing, unearthly sound, like a grief welling up from the chartless caverns of the earth; and it continued, and augmented, and to my astonishment I felt it coming from my own throat, while hot tears burned my eyes, and I could barely breathe; I felt Amelia embracing me, and I felt my head bury itself in her shoulder, while my whole frame shook with great racking sobs that came one after another, each one like a blow from a fist to my chest. Even now I cannot think of it without feeling the same burning in my eyes, the same constriction of my throat;—even now my sight is blurred with tears that come pouring out when I remember that day. Damn him! How can he do this to me, at the distance of so many years? Damn him! I was free at last from all his oafish prattle—free from the hideous embarrassment he caused me every time he opened his ignorant mouth—and all I could do was weep, wailing to the heavens, as if I had lost the one thing I loved most in the world, as if I could see nothing but despair; and even now, I think about that moment, and the tears pour out—— Damn him! Damn him to hell! I do not wish to continue this chapter.

CHAPTER XXI

I dedicate myself anew to the principles of evil, and discover a perfectly rational way of obtaining the capital I desire.

MY FATHER WAS dead and buried, and my life was in every way improved by the loss, but I was uncharacteristically sullen for two weeks after the funeral. In fact I was filled with anger, almost rage. How could I have been so unmanned by grief? I had thought myself enlightened; instead, I was a slave to the same follies as every other man. I had mourned when I ought to have celebrated. I had wept openly again at the funeral; now that I look back from the distance of so many years, I see that it was a good and useful thing for me to do, since it cemented the impression that I had been a loving and dutiful son, but at the time I was very angry at myself for having done it. It did not happen because I had lost anything precious to me by any reasonable accounting; no, it could only be because I was not yet the rational man I thought I was. It seemed to me as if I had been attacked by goodness and virtue at an unexpectedly weak point in my defenses; I was as angry as a general whose sleeping sentries have allowed a breach in his fortifications.

Amelia did her best to console me. "It *will* be better," she assured me. "You *will* be happy. I know it seems hopeless now, but there will be a time when instead of grief you will have happy memories. You'll see."

That was all very well, but she did not understand, and could not understand, the source of my gloomy disposition. I felt as though a great accomplishment had been taken away from me. How could I call myself wicked if I reacted to an ordinary loss in such an extraordinarily undignified manner? Amelia could never understand my turmoil, because I could never tell her the reason for it. She was a perfect angel, and I was rather cold to her; but she never blamed me for it. "I understand," she always told me, though of course she could not understand at all. "You *will* feel better soon."

As if my rage at my own grief were not enough to keep me in a foul temper, old Colonel

Goode started to show signs of illness as well. He had grieved as much as I had at my father's death; my father, I know not why, had become his intimate friend, and the man really had no other intimate friends. He took to his bed with a chill, as he called it, but it rapidly became something worse. Amelia tried her best to keep the household together; but with my ill temper and her father's illness, she found it very difficult to keep up any degree of cheer herself.

Nothing seemed to be going well for me (except that the firm continued to grow, but not at the rate I desired). In my despair I turned to the one source from which I derived all my consolation: the words of Baucher, or rather the few discoveries of his that had been transmitted by the reviewer in the *Gentleman's Cabinet*.

What did Baucher tell me? What was his marvelous discovery? That there was no crime, no matter how monstrous it might be judged by inferior minds, that the enlightened man would not commit if it brought him some advantage. He would let no inferiors stand between him and the thing he desired.

And what stood between me and the thing I desired? Merely the existence of my father-in-law. As soon as he ceased to exist, every penny of his vast fortune would belong to me. —But what was preventing him from ceasing to exist at once? He was old, and he was ill; was it not to be expected that he should terminate his earthly existence rather sooner than later? And would not the truly enlightened man—the one who did not merely understand the principles of evil, but actively put them into practice—find some way of making sure that it happened sooner?

As soon as the thought occurred to me, I understood that I had hit on, not merely a solution to my difficulties, but a redemption from my temporary backsliding. It would be the most audacious crime I had ever contemplated, but surely such a superior mind as mine would discover some way of accomplishing it without undue risk. Did I dare attempt it? The moment the question was put that way, it was answered. I had dared myself to do it: I must murder Colonel Goode. Out of habit, my hand rose toward my lip, but my fingers found no moustache there to twirl.

That evening after supper I spoke to Amelia. "I know that I have been difficult since my father died," I told her, "and I can hardly make any excuse for my cruelty—— "

"Oh, you haven't been cruel," she insisted. "Don't think that of yourself. You have only been—sad, really. How could you not be so? I know how much you loved your father. I loved him almost as much, in the short time I knew him."

"But I have not loved you enough," I said with perhaps the first smile I had given her in more than two weeks. "You have done so much for me, and I have repaid you so badly. And now you're wearing yourself down taking care of your father. You've lifted so many burdens from me; now you must let me lift some of your burdens, my dear."

She smiled as well, obviously happy to see me in better spirits again. "I haven't any burdens too heavy for me to carry."

"But you must still let me take some of the weight," I insisted. "Let me spend some of the evening with your father. I know you've been keeping him in good cheer, but you can't keep up spending so many hours by his bed. I don't ask you to leave him to the servants—I know you wouldn't, and you're quite right. But he's the only father I have now, and for myself as well as for him I can surely spare a few hours here and there."

Amelia looked at me quietly for a moment. "I understand," she said at last. "Yes, it would do him good. He thinks the world of you, you know. And I can see that it will do you good as well."

So that was settled: I should be spending time regularly alone with the Colonel. I walked out into the hall and puffed out a long sigh. It had actually pained me, almost physically, to make Amelia part of my plot that way. She would mourn the loss of her father terribly. How could I do such a thing to her? —But the old man must die soon whether I killed him or not, and she would mourn the same either way. I must not let virtuous impulses creep over me and steal my resolve! My anger at my own failings must sustain me in my enterprise.

Now, it may already have occurred to you, my dear hypothetical reader, that I had a particular motive in relieving Amelia of some of the burden of keeping her father company. I had already decided that, of all the means there were of ridding the world of one superfluous old millionaire, poison was the most suitable to my purposes. A well-chosen poison would not be suspected: if a sick old man died, who would suppose that he died from any other cause than being sick and old? Then his fortune would be mine. It was true that I could not apply it to my own purposes right away: that would look too suspicious. A decent interval must be maintained between his death and my reaping the benefits of it; it was an inconvenience, but it could not be helped. Still, with his death I should be confirmed in the eventual enjoyment of his fortune. And if poison was to be the means, then I must seek the best opportunity for administering it. I must be familiar with his habits, and find some way of getting the poison into him that would excite no suspicion either in him or in anyone else.

"Galahad!" the Colonel greeted me cheerfully when I appeared in his chamber after supper. "I'd been expecting Amelia."

"But you've got me," I replied with a convincing affectation of good cheer. "A poor substitute, I'm sure, but Amelia needs a rest now and then. I insisted."

"Well, that's very good of you, Galahad. Very good indeed."

And so I spent two or three hours with him, talking about nothing of consequence and reading to him from his Bible by the bedside. We were reading from the General Epistle of James; I remember it well, because I recall thinking how well the words applied to my own case. "Ye lust, and have not: ye kill, and desire to have, and cannot obtain: ye fight and war, yet ye have not, because ye ask not." Well, I had asked and been refused. And so the next verse continues: "Ye ask, and receive not, because ye ask amiss, that ye may consume it upon your lusts." See how readily this Christian religion provides a way to keep the inferior man in his place! He is told that he may have anything he asks for, as long as his motivation is not to spend it upon his pleasures. But upon what else would he desire to spend it? Thus the superior man may hoard all the wealth and keep it from the inferior man, and the latter remains convinced that, if his motives were pure—which he knows is not the case, since all men desire pleasure—he would have what the rich man has. It is through the fault of his own impure thoughts that he is poor. But the superior man knows that, when there is any thing he desires, if it is not his, then the only reason is because he has not yet taken it.

Shortly after this passage, we were interrupted by the appearance of Sheridan, who bore a glass containing an amber-colored liquid.

"Here's my tonic," Colonel Goode announced as he took the glass. "The worst part of my day. Dreadful stuff. Brimstone in a glass. But Doctor Andick insists." He looked at the glass for a while as if gathering up his courage, and then downed it all in one draught, after which he made the most appalling faces.

Immediately it occurred to me that this might be an opportunity. The tonic had a flavor strong enough to mask anything I might choose to adulterate it with. Now I had only to find the proper ingredient.

The next evening I intercepted Sheridan on his way to Colonel Goode with the tonic. "I can take it to him," I said. "In fact, from now on, I'll take care of the tonic—that way you won't have to interrupt our devotions."

Sheridan nodded, doubtless content to be relieved of one of his duties, and I took the glass in to the Colonel.

I did not have the resources for an exhaustive study of poisons. Colonel Goode had many books, but his large collection was shockingly lacking in treatises on successful murder; and my friend Mr. Carnegie had not yet begun to litter the continent with libraries. From the limited information at my disposal, however, I concluded that strychnine would be my best choice. This poison was just becoming fashionable in those days; it was not yet the chief ingredient in every sensation novel. Yet it was readily available in several stores downtown. I obtained a small amount of it, along with some rat traps and other similar items that were of no use to me, but would avert suspicion from my purchase.

Night after night I spent by Colonel Goode's bedside, observing everything he did, and everything else that happened in the household at the same time. I desired to leave nothing to chance. When I did strike, it must not even be suspected; there must have been nothing out of the established routine.

At last I determined that the time had come. The Colonel seemed if anything to be getting better; I must strike while he was still frail enough that his death would excite no suspicion. I prepared the tonic as usual, but with a liberal addition of strychnine.

"I've brought your tonic," I said as I entered the chamber. It was my usual greeting. This evening was an unusually warm one, but a cooling breeze was coming through the open window by the chair where I sat next to the Colonel's bed. "You might as well get it down now, and then you'll be done with it," I added, trying not to sound at all impatient.

The Colonel scowled at the glass, but he took it in his hand. This was the moment: the consummation of my career of wickedness. The Colonel had the poisoned cup in his grip; he was about to administer his own destruction.

"I've been thinking, Galahad," he said; and I privately thought to myself that he would not be troubled by thinking much longer.

"Have you?" I asked with feigned interest.

"I may not last very much longer, or I may recover and live for several more years." (Little chance of that, I thought to myself.) "But I remember what it was like to be young. I used to have a little sense of adventure myself, you know. There were times when I did things that might not have seemed wise at the moment. But they worked out well in the end. I'm sure I owe a lot of my wealth to luck. But you have to give luck a chance to operate, don't you?"

"I suppose you do," I agreed, only half attending to the conversation. I wished he would simply drink and be done with it.

"Well, that's what I've been thinking about, Galahad. It was luck that brought you to my

Amelia, but the two of you made the most of that chance, didn't you?"

I had almost said that we made the most of it every night, but I restrained myself.

"You're a young man who knows how to profit from opportunity," the Colonel continued. "There was a time when I had little money, but plenty of opportunity. Now I have plenty of money, and I've forgotten how much I needed opportunity in those days. And here you are, looking at an opportunity, and I'm standing in your way."

Yes, I thought, but not for much longer.

"Well, I ought not to be standing in your way. You need a chance to rise by your own talent. And if you fall—which I still regard as a distinct possibility—you're young, and you'll have time to pick yourself up again. I've become cautious in my old age, Galahad, but youth isn't the time for caution. If I'd been as cautious in my youth as I am now, I'd never have built my first glass works. I see that now. I also see that no one deserves this chance more than you do. In spite of a hundred other things I'm sure you'd rather be doing, you take the time to cheer an old man in his sickbed."

"Now, you know that's not a burden to me," I insisted, looking down at the glass in his hand.

"Which is exactly what you would say no matter how much of a burden it was," the Colonel replied with a bit of a twinkle. "You've made sacrifices for me, Galahad. You've been a dutiful and loving son, as much to me as you were to your own natural father. And I've decided to give you that opportunity I know you've been longing for, even though you've been far too good-natured to complain."

This had me pricking up my ears. I was now completely attentive to the old man's words. "Opportunity?" I asked, as if I had no idea what he was talking about.

"You've been wanting to buy the Rohrbaugh store and make Bousted's into a big concern. I have the money that could do that, and I wouldn't give it to you. Well, now I'm giving it to you. In fact, from this moment, half my fortune is yours. As soon as I can have it done, it will be put in your name—the part that's in banks, at any rate. So you see, I haven't forgotten what it was like to be young—although I doubt whether I was such an admirable young man as you are."

This was such an unexpected victory that the most ridiculously absurd response passed my lips before I could recall it: "Are you certain that is what you wish to do?"

The Colonel laughed weakly. "Don't look a gift horse in the mouth, Galahad. You and Amelia are worth more than my whole fortune to me. You can at least take half of it without complaining."

At that moment, a light burst over my intellect, and I understood where the course of true evil had led me. It was not by the commission of a single spectacular crime that I had accomplished this great conquest: it was by insinuating myself gradually into the Colonel's affections. With no risk at all to myself, with no crime attributable to me, but merely by assiduously attending to the whims of a harmless old man, I had gained everything I wanted.

"Well, then," I said after a moment's silence, "I shall attempt to make the best use of it."

"I'm certain you will. At least you'll make some use of it, where I've been hiding my talent in the ground. At any rate, that is my decision, and we'll have the papers drawn up in the morning. Now I suppose I'd better get this tonic down."

"No!" I nearly shouted; and I seized the glass from his trembling fingers and flung the liquid out the window.

"Why, Galahad, what's the matter?" he asked with more than a touch of surprise.

"Oh, it was——a fly. A perfectly enormous fly. Didn't you see it? Not a very pleasant thing to find in your glass! I'll get you another one right away."

CHAPTER XXII.

Amelia takes me to Paris, where at last I am introduced to the admirable author of The Pursuit of Evil.

I SUPPOSE THE previous chapter might have been as good a place to end my memoir as any. My empire at last was truly begun; as soon as was practicable, I had the necessary papers drawn up and signed by my father-in-law, transferring control of half his kingdom to me. With that capital I was able to expand the empire of Bousted & Son (I have not changed the name, since it was already so well recognized in the trade) at a prodigious rate. All my endeavors, as you doubtless know already, were crowned with success; and to-day it is impossible to walk into a well-stocked stationer's without seeing the Bousted name on every article. Of course the famous Graded Stationery, "Much Imitated but Never Equaled" (as the watermark now states explicitly), still accounts for a large portion of our sales, and our canvassing agents extend the reach of my empire into every dusty hamlet in the trackless wastes of the West.

As for old Colonel Goode, he recovered marvelously over the next few months, and in fact is still with us at the age of ninety-eight. I honestly believe the man is immortal, but I no longer grudge him his immortality. He may outlive me and my daughters and their children for all I care; I have long since passed the time when his death would be of any use to me. I always take care to see that he has everything he could possibly desire; I have learned from my experience with him that a concerted campaign of ostentatious kindness is worth more than the most spectacular crime in promoting my own selfish interests. This, by the by, was one of the last things I had to learn to become a truly wicked man: though great crimes are within his power, the enlightened man seldom finds the trouble of them worth his while, when, at infinitely less risk to himself, he can win the same results with a few simple kindnesses that cost him nothing.

To all appearances, therefore, I am the very picture of prosperous virtue. My reputation for scrupulous honesty in business has served me well, for a man who is trusted will find opportunities that never present themselves to a man who has allowed his temporary desires to cloud his judgment and obscure his long-term advantage. My frequent and generous philanthropy keeps the Bousted name before the public eye, and I am convinced that, merely owing to the reputation my generosity purchases for me, I easily make back in profits the enormous sums I have donated to endow the Bousted Gallery in Allegheny, the Bousted Fund for Injured Workmen, the Bousted Bath-House in Dutchtown, and a dozen other institutions that bear my name.

—So you see we have really come to the end of the story, or at least of the story I promised to tell: the story of how I became perfectly wicked, and of the success that followed my adoption of the enlightened principles of true evil. But I cannot forbear adding one more chapter to these reminiscences of mine; and I believe that, should any readers of the distant future have followed my adventures up to this point, this last chapter will prove an instructive one. It is the story of my meeting with the great Comte de Baucher himself, and of the conclusions I drew from my observations of the man.

Amelia and I had been married nearly a year when she suddenly told me that we ought to go to Paris. "We've had so much trouble this past

year that I think we ought to enjoy ourselves for
a while. And I know you would love Paris, darling. So much beauty, so much music and art!"

"I'm not sure I can take the——"

"Now, don't you dare tell me that you can't
take the time away from the firm," she interrupted with mock severity. "Charles is perfectly
capable of managing the ordinary affairs, and if
anything extraordinary comes up, you can take
care of it by telegram as quickly from Paris as
you could from Pittsburgh. —Or are you just
hoping to make me persuade you?"

I laughed. "Well, of course I always like to be
persuaded," I said; and Amelia laughed, too, and
then persuaded me.

So we went to Paris, which was quite a voyage
for a man who had never been farther from
home than Altoona until he was married. It was
a strange thing being confined to a Cunard liner
without any communication from home: for the
first two days, I ached to know what was happening with the firm, though I had left it in capable enough hands, and I might have gone mad
had Amelia not been by my side. But by the time
we reached Le Havre, it was marvelous how little I cared for business. There were two tele-
grams from Bradley waiting for me; in both of
them he merely sought approval for a sensible
action he had already taken. I wired him back
telling him that he had done well, and that I had

complete confidence in him, which—such is the mellowing effect of an ocean voyage—I actually did have.

What can one say about Paris? It is at once everything an American expects it to be and completely unexpected. I did not expect, for example, to find so many Americans there. At first I thought there must be as many Americans in Paris as in Pittsburgh. For several days, it was perfectly possible for me to get along without a word of the French I had so laboriously reviewed in preparation for our voyage, and for an hour or two every day on the steamer. Amelia knew Ambassador Noyes and his family well, and through him the best of the American society in the city; so our first few days were a whirlwind of galleries and operas and dinner parties, in all of which I was surrounded by a cloud of chattering Americans. Even the hotel staff, with whom I attempted to communicate in my imperfect French, brushed aside my attempts and spoke to me in nearly perfect English.

After a few days in Paris, however, Amelia began to find things to do without me during the day. She would disappear from the middle of the morning until just before supper; I once asked her where she was going, but she just told me, "A wife has to have *some* secrets from her husband, or she'll be a bore." Occasionally she would return followed by a train of bundles, so I assumed she must be off improving her ward-robe. How, after all, could she resist the oppor-tunity of appearing in the latest Paris fashions a year before the other Pittsburgh belles could get their hands on them?

Since Amelia was off by herself, I spent my days wandering around the city, and for the first time saw Paris without my protective shell of American expatriates. My French was abysmal in the beginning, but rapidly improved with use; and the many hours I spent in the Louvre and other shrines of art soon persuaded me that I had a real love for pictures by the great masters of the past. I began to haunt Parisian galleries, buy-ing about a picture a day—the foundation of my now considerable collection. "I can't tell you how pleased I am to see that you like pictures so well," Amelia told me as the crates of pictures took up more and more of the drawing-room. "It will give you and Father so much to talk about when we go back home." And indeed it has been a blessing to have at least one thing in common with the old Colonel, since I still see him every day whether I like it or not. But I did find out later that Amelia had another reason for being pleased.

In the mean time, at one of those dinners filled with Americans, where a few notable French-men were invited to delight the guests with their wit, or at least their reputation for wit, I heard something that suddenly attracted my lagging attention.

"You certainly have brought together some singular characters," one of the Americans—a Chicago meat-packer who reeked of cigar-smoke —was saying to the hostess.

"Oh, Paris abounds in singular characters," the hostess agreed. (I cannot remember her name; she was the wife of some banker or some such thing.) "I only wish the Comte de Baucher could have been here. We expected him, but his health is not good, and he was unable to leave his apartments tonight."

"Baucher?" I asked, betraying as little of my sudden excitement as I could. "You mean the author?"

"Yes," our hostess answered, "the very scandalous author. You've heard of him?"

"Only from—I believe it was an article in a magazine. Was it Harper's? Or Scribner's? Boli's, perhaps?" I knew very well which magazine it was, of course.

"Well, I'm very sorry you didn't have a chance to meet him. He is the most positively wicked man in Paris, of course, but he is old and harmless, and rather charming in conversation."

With that began a rather tedious colloquy by which, without seeming to be more than half-interested in the subject, I extracted enough information from the woman to be able to locate the

Comte. The following morning, I wrote to him, expressing my desire to make his acquaintance, as I had been much taken with what I had heard of his writings. I am sure I was very flattering in my letter; at any rate, it provoked the desired response, and the day after that, while Amelia was off on her usual all-day excursion, I was invited to pay a visit to the Comte de Baucher.

The Comte, it turned out, lived in a few neat but small rooms over a bakery in one of the less fashionable neighborhoods of Paris. Merely from the location, it was clear that he did not possess much wealth.

I was greeted at the door by a girl who could hardly have been more than seventeen. She told me that the Comte was expecting me and led me up the stairs to his little parlor, where she presented me to a very old man wrapped in a mauve silk robe and half-recumbent on a chaise. He was frail-looking, with a few wisps of pure white hair not quite covering his head. His face had doubtless once been well-made, but it was more than a little distorted by disease. As he slowly rose to a sitting position, I noted an uncontrollable tremor in his limbs.

In response to a whispered instruction from the Comte, the girl left the room, and the Comte began the conversation.

"Mister Bousted," he greeted me,—cheerfully, but with a weak voice that obviously cost him some effort to produce.

"Monsieur le comte," I returned, and I bowed as he offered me his withered and shaking hand.

"Your letter was such a delight," he continued, "and I was desolated that I could not come to see you, but at present I am confined to these rooms."

"I understand," I responded, and I was about to tell him that I did not wish to give him any more trouble than his health could support, but he went on:

"Ah! You know what it is to have debts. If I show my face in the street, they are upon me, like the jackals. It should be sufficient for them to have the patronage of a Comte, but they are very unreasonable about the silver."

"That is a pity," I agreed, not knowing what else to say.

"And of course the debts of gambling, they are much worse. I should avoid them, but what can one say? When one is drunk, one feels invincible."

Here the girl returned with two glasses filled with a liquid that smelled strongly of patent medicine, but which the Comte assured me was absinthe. "It is one of my little indulgences," he said as the girl set the glasses on the table between us.

As the pretty maid turned to leave, the old Comte reached out toward her with obviously

lewd intent; but he was so slow, like a clockwork
toy whose mainspring is almost wound down,
that she easily slipped out of his reach with a little sideways shuffle, a familiar movement so
much practiced that she appeared to do it without thinking.

The Comte laughed in soft little wheezes.
"You see, even at my age, I still have an eye for
the young beauties. I still pursue the little ones."
He wheezed a few more times before adding,
"Years ago, of course, I used to catch them."

I nodded, not really sure what else to say, and
picked up one of the glasses of foul-looking green
fluid the girl had left. But I could not bring myself to drink it.

I could report the rest of our conversation, but
it is better left unrecorded. What can I say? The
man was a complete imbecile. He had seen the
way to true greatness, but instead he had squandered his endowments on petty pleasures and appetites of the moment. I do not believe he ever
denied himself anything that he took it into his
head to desire. He had no thought for the future;
and even now, wasted away by self-inflicted disease and intemperance, he could think of nothing but the next little indulgence.

What a strange and bitter lesson for every
evildoer! It is not enough to understand the principles of evil, as the Comte had done; they must
be acted upon. Every waking moment of the

wicked man's life must be devoted to the pursuit
of evil: he must not allow a temporary enjoyment to distract him from his true advantage. He
must forgo pleasures now that will have ill consequences later, and exercise manly self-restraint
at all times. Without such dedication, a mere
knowledge of the principles of evil is useless.

I returned from my interview with the Comte
to find Amelia waiting for me. She greeted me
with even more than her usual affection, and
then told me to sit in the arm-chair in the drawing-room. "I have a gift for you," she said, "and
you must tell me that you love it, or—or I don't
know what I'll do." She was flushed a beautiful
shade of rose as she walked over to the corner of
the room where my latest pictures were waiting
to be crated. There was one exceptionally large
one, covered with a blanket, that I did not remember having bought.

"Now you'll know what I was doing all day
these past two weeks," she told me. "And if you
were any other sort of husband, darling, I'd
never have done it. But I know you trust me as
completely as I trust you, and I thought—well, I
thought that this might please you."

She took hold of the blanket and hesitated for
a moment, as if gathering her courage. Then,
with a flourish of her right arm, she unveiled a
picture that left me utterly speechless.

Amelia also stood silent for a few moments, letting me admire her gift. "It's not Boucher," she said at last, "but I went to the only artist I know in Paris today who can compare to him in —this sort of subject."

"It's the most beautiful thing I've ever seen," I said quietly. "I mean, except the model herself, of course."

Amelia smiled brightly. "I was sure you would like it. If you were any other sort of man, I'd never have dared, but you're so full of goodness and love that I knew you could never be angry with me."

She came to me and sat on the arm of the chair, bending down for a kiss.

"I don't quite know where you'll put it," she continued. "It's not the sort of thing my father should see."

"Not if his heart is as weak as Dr. Andick says it is," I agreed with a smile.

"Do you really love it, Galahad? I wanted so much to give you something no one else could give you."

"I really love it, Amelia," I answered with absolute conviction.

"The artist has written the title on the back of the canvas," she said. "He calls it 'La Belle Americaine.'"

Let this picture, dear reader,—which is before me right now, on the wall of my inner office, where I have written this manuscript,—let it serve, I say, as an emblem of everything that can be gained by pure wickedness: wealth, reputation, beauty,—yea, even love, properly understood as the satisfaction of a man's desires without danger or inconvenience. Let every enlightened young man take his example from me: let him avoid the fatal follies of men like Baucher, who understood the principles of evil in the abstract, but was not able to rein in his appetites. Let him gain a reputation for scrupulous honesty in every branch of affairs; let him be remarked for his humble piety and conspicuous in charity; let him devote himself with assiduous care to the happiness of those around him, that they may be found useful in promoting his own happiness. Let him deviate neither to the left nor to the right, but keep to the straight and narrow path of truly enlightened self-interest. Then, if he has been faithful to these principles, he cannot fail of enjoying the many rewards of true wickedness.

THE END.

47679508R00226

Made in the USA
San Bernardino, CA
05 April 2017